MURDER IN THE HOMETOWN

THE PRIVATE INVESTIGATOR ANNIE HUDSON REAL ESTATE MYSTERY SERIES

BOOK 6

VALERIE BRANDY

Published by: Emerald Lion Press, LLC.

23901 Calabasas Rd., Ste 2088,

Calabasas, CA 91302.

info@emeraldlionpressbooks.com

This is a work of fiction. Names, characters, businesses, events, and incidents either are the products of the author's imagination or are used fictitiously. Any resemblance to actual persons, living or dead, businesses, companies, events, or locales is entirely coincidental.

ISBN: 978-1-964161-96-9

Editing provided by Sharon Lennon-Mehlschau.

To request permission to use passages from this book in any context other than a review, please contact the publisher at info@emeraldlionpress-books.com.

Visit the author's website at: www.valeriebrandy.com

Formatted with Vellum

CONTENTS

CHAPTER ONE

"*MEGAN*?" Ethan said. Her name sounded strange in his mouth. He hadn't said it in years— hadn't *allowed* himself to say it.

Annie watched as Ethan stepped toward his sister— a ghost made flesh after so many years of wondering, of searching. His mouth opened and closed twice, but no words came out. Around him, the desert seemed to close in on them, mountains stretching tall toward the sky, their tops convex and looming. Whether the desert was cradling or suffocating them, Annie couldn't say.

A gentle breeze kicked sand into the air, swirling around the entrance to abandoned mines. The mines were waiting to swallow them whole, but Megan stood in front of the open maw, blocking their passage. Her lifted cheekbones and skeptical eyes stood out beneath short, asymmetrical hair. She looked, to Annie, like a Sphinx awaiting payment— if they could only answer Megan's riddle, they might be allowed to proceed.

"This isn't possible," Ethan said, shaking his head. "This *can't* be possible."

"You just learned UFOs are real," Harlan added helpfully, his voice echoing out from over Annie's shoulder. Annie turned, taking in the group that had accompanied them from the nearby town of Rachel, Nevada— where they'd just solved a murder. Sheriff Giselle in her uniform. Her mother, Maria. Harlan, a conspiracy theorist who just happened to be right this time. Bianca, the YouTuber and alien hunter. They were all still there— witnessing the biggest moment of Ethan's life. "Why can't this be real?" Harlan concluded. "I told you all I saw a woman driving around, up to no good, if only you'd believed me—"

Annie wished she could give Ethan a moment of privacy, but there was nowhere to hide in the desert.

Megan stepped forward, the desert breeze catching her hair. Her eyes—the same shade of blue as Ethan's, Annie noticed—never left her brother's face.

"I don't have much time," she said, her voice quiet but firm. "We need to get to Russel's compound. It's through the mines. I can get us there but—"

"You know about Russel's compound?" Ethan sputtered, his mouth dropping open. He looked at Annie, betrayed. "You two haven't been— you didn't— *talk*—"

Annie threw her hands in the air, proclaiming her innocence, hurt that he'd think her possible of such a betrayal. "Ethan, no! This is the first time I'm seeing Megan, too."

"But you *knew*?" Ethan asked, his eyes pained. "You knew she was alive..."

"No," Annie pleaded. "I *suspected*—"

"Oh, cut the bullshit, Annie! You should have told me as soon as you even thought there was a chance—"

"I didn't know for sure!" Annie gasped, shocked to find that Ethan was mad at her. It was rare for Ethan to find it in him to be angry at her for anything. Ethan's reaction was so unlike him, Annie wasn't sure what to do with it. It was like her favorite dog had bitten her. "As things played out in Rachel I just wondered if it *could* be her, but it seemed so unlikely. I was worried I only thought it was Megan because I *wanted* to be right so badly…" Her eyes filled with tears as she thought about her own brother, who had been buried in the ground, with no hope of return. "I wanted it to be her so at least one of us could get some closure—"

"Closure!" Ethan shouted, letting out a laugh with a sharp edge to it. "This isn't closure, Annie. This is betrayal. This is—"

Megan cleared her throat, interrupting. Ethan stopped speaking at once, turning back to the ghost of his sister. Megan moved toward him, but stopped short of touching him when he flinched at her approach. "I'll explain everything, I promise." She pushed her short hair to one side, pulling her leather jacket tighter around her shoulders. "But right now, we need to move."

The urgency in her tone was unmistakable, but Annie sensed something else beneath it— fear, perhaps, or desperation. Neither was reassuring. Annie turned to the group behind her. "You need to leave. All of you. Now"

Harlan's voice cut through the silence, his long beard quivering with indignation. "Now hold on just a minute. We've been helping investigate this whole time, and suddenly we're not invited to the grand finale?" He crossed his arms, looking between the three of them with narrowed eyes. "Seems mighty suspicious."

"He's right," Bianca chimed in, pink hair practically glowing in the sunset light. Her phone was out, recording as always. "This is, like, literally the biggest development in this case. I need to document this for my channel."

Giselle stepped forward, her sheriff's uniform dusty from the day's activities. "As the law enforcement officer here, I can't allow civilians to wander into potentially dangerous situations without proper backup." Her tone was professional, but Annie caught the flicker of hurt in her eyes at being excluded. Giselle glanced at her. "But I could make an exception, if Annie would allow it?"

Maria moved to stand beside her daughter, her weathered hands clasped in front of her. "¿Por qué no podemos ir?" *We've come too far to stop now.*

Annie felt the weight of their expectation, their desire to see this mystery through to its end. They had helped her, welcomed her into their strange little desert town, shared their secrets and their strengths. They deserved answers.

And yet.

She met Megan's eyes and saw something there— a warning, perhaps, or a plea. Annie made her decision.

"I think," she began carefully, measuring each word, "where we're going now, you can't follow." She held up a hand as Harlan began to protest. "Not because we don't want you there, but because there are things at stake here that go beyond Rachel, beyond this case."

"What things?" Giselle demanded, her hand drifting unconsciously toward her service weapon.

Annie shook her head. "I don't know yet. But I have a feeling we're about to find out." She looked at each of them in turn, memorizing their faces. "You've all been incredible. I came here looking for answers about Russel, and I found so much more."

The silence stretched between them, taut and uncomfortable. Annie continued, her voice softer now.

"This town— this strange, tiny place in the middle of nowhere— you've shown me something I didn't expect to find. How a group of different people can pull together to protect their own," She smiled, though it felt bittersweet on her lips. She turned to Bianca, holding out her hand. "Bianca?"

Bianca sighed, passing Annie the phone. Annie swiped

through the device, deleting all videos and photographs of Ethan, Megan, and herself. She passed the phone back to Bianca, who nodded somberly.

"This is goodbye, then," Bianca said.

"Just for now," Annie assured her, though she wasn't certain that was true.

Harlan huffed, clearly displeased but recognizing the finality in Annie's tone. "Well, if you find any evidence of government black ops down there, you better come tell me first."

"And you'll keep your mouth shut about it if she does," Giselle said, though there was a hint of fondness in her exasperation.

Bianca gave Annie a quick hug. "This is totally going to blow up my channel when I can finally post about it," she said with forced brightness. "Just... be careful, okay?"

Annie nodded, touched by the genuine concern beneath the young woman's flippant words.

Maria stepped forward and embraced Annie, her small frame surprisingly strong. Then, she stepped back toward her daughter, Giselle, who offered Annie a stiff handshake. She placed a hand firmly on Annie's shoulder, her expression grave. "Remember what I told you," she said, her voice low enough that only Annie could hear. "Don't trust anyone. Not even *her*." She jerked her chin toward Megan, who stood silently beside Ethan.

Annie covered Giselle's hand with her own. "I won't forget."

The sheriff gave a curt nod, then turned to shepherd the others toward her cruiser. They went reluctantly, looking back over their shoulders until they piled into the vehicle. The engine started with a rumble that seemed unnaturally loud in the quiet desert. As the car pulled away, dust billowing behind it, Annie felt a curious emptiness, as if she'd left something unfinished.

She turned back to find Ethan and Megan regarding each other with identical wary expressions.

"You're really here," Ethan finally said, his voice rough. "All these years. All this time thinking you were—" He broke off, swallowing hard. "Where the hell have you been, Meg?"

Megan's face tightened. "We can't do this now, Ethan. I wish we could, but there isn't time. They're coming for us—"

"There's never time, is there?" The bitterness in his voice surprised Annie. In all their cases together, she'd never heard that tone from him before. "Not when you disappeared. Not when I spent years searching for you. And not now."

"That's not fair," Megan said quietly.

"Fair?" Ethan laughed, a harsh sound with no humor in it. "You don't get to talk to me about fair."

Annie stepped closer, sensing the need to intervene before this reunion derailed completely. "Maybe we should head inside? If time is as limited as Megan says, we should make use of it."

Ethan looked at her, his expression softening slightly. He turned back to his sister, keeping his distance. "Lead the way."

Megan hesitated, then nodded, turning toward the dark opening in the rock face. Annie noticed she moved with a fighter's grace— smooth, controlled movements that spoke of extensive training. The woman Annie had known as a teenager wasn't the same person in front of her. Megan— as Annie had known her— was a shy, frail young adult just starting out in a career that called for blazers and collared shirts. This new version of her was something different— more deadly, lethal.

How time can change a person, Annie thought, wondering if Megan felt the same way looking at her and Ethan.

The mine entrance was narrower than it had appeared from a distance. Megan produced a flashlight from her pocket, its beam cutting through the darkness ahead.

"Stay close," she advised, her voice echoing slightly. "The path branches a few times, and it's easy to get lost."

"We know," Annie admitted, thinking about the cave-in they'd experienced in these very same mines just hours ago—the one that had almost killed them.

Annie fell into step behind Megan, with Ethan bringing up the rear. The temperature dropped as they moved deeper into the earth, the desert heat giving way to cool dampness. Their footsteps echoed against stone walls, creating an eerie percussion that set Annie's nerves on edge.

"How did you know about Russel's compound?" Annie asked, partly out of curiosity and partly to break the oppressive silence.

"I didn't," Megan replied without turning. "The Collective did. They've been tracking Russel for years. I only knew because I have access to their systems."

"Access? To their systems?" Ethan repeated flatly, nearly stumbling over a rock. "But you couldn't unless... You're not — you're not *one* of them. The Collective?"

"Define *one of them*," Megan said, her shoulder tense. "Aren't we all operating around blurred lines here?"

Ethan stared at Annie, deep concern in his eyes. Megan caught the glance.

"I'm deep undercover," she said. "Alphabet agency. I'll explain. No time, remember?"

Annie glanced back at Ethan, whose face was a mask of controlled anger in the dim light. She could only imagine what he was feeling— relief at finding his sister alive, warring with hurt at her deliberate absence, all compounded by the revelations about her involvement with a criminal organization, even as an undercover agent.

The tunnel sloped downward, rock giving way to metal supports and eventually concrete floors. They passed several branch tunnels, but Megan moved confidently, never hesitating at intersections.

"Make a right," Annie said when they reached a fork in the tunnels. "Ethan and I made a left earlier and it didn't work out well for us." Visions of the cave-in flashed before Annie's eyes.

"Great tip, thanks," Megan agreed.

Annie moved up to walk beside Megan, studying her profile in the flashlight's glow. The resemblance to Ethan was striking— same determined set of the jaw, same analytical gaze that missed nothing.

"So glad you two are getting along!" Ethan cried, throwing his hands up in the air. "My sister isn't just alive, she's a criminal, and Annie seems *perfectly fine* with that information—"

Megan stopped so suddenly that Annie nearly collided with her. She turned to face her brother, the flashlight beam creating sharp shadows across her face.

"I know you're angry," she said, her voice tight with controlled emotion. "You have every right to be. But I need you to trust me right now— both of you. What we're about to find in Russel's compound might be the key—"

"The key to what?" Ethan asked. "Why does any of it matter anymore? You're alive. You've been lying to me. You could have found me at any point—"

"The key to making sure this never happens to anyone again," Megan said, her voice breaking. "What happened to us when you were a kid? The night I was taken? We can stop someone else from feeling that pain. But only… if you shut the fuck up and keep walking." She patted Ethan's shoulder gently and turned, her cold words snapping him back into reality. He looked like she'd hit him, but still— Ethan fell into step behind her. His jaw clenched tightly into a hard line. Annie wished she could ease his pain, but there was work to be done.

They continued in silence, the tunnel eventually opening into a larger chamber. Megan directed her flashlight toward a metal door at the far end, reinforced and fitted with a keypad lock.

Megan turned to Annie. "I've been trying to find a way in for weeks. I'm hoping this is where you come in. Russel seemed to believe you were quite the codebreaker?"

Annie glanced at Ethan, then lifted Russel's keycard out of her pocket. "I think we can help you out with that."

CHAPTER TWO

ANNIE STEPPED FORWARD with Russel's keycard clutched between her fingers. The metal door loomed before them, cold and impersonal in the beam of Megan's flashlight. She ran her thumb over the worn plastic surface of the card, feeling its scratches like tiny hieroglyphs of a life she barely understood. Russel had entrusted them with this key— this passage into whatever secrets lay beyond. With a steadying breath, she pressed it against the scanner and watched as the small light flickered from red to green.

"Did Russel give it to you?" Megan asked, her voice tight with surprise. The flashlight beam wavered slightly, illuminating Annie's face before returning to the door.

Annie tucked a strand of hair behind her ear, acutely aware of Ethan's presence at her back. "Not exactly," she said simply. "He more… left it to us in his will, you could say." Then, seeing Megan's skeptical expression, she elaborated. "We found him hiding out at a commune called Serenity Peaks in the Sierra Nevadas. He'd been there for years, living under an assumed name. He was dead by the time we got there, but he left us some puzzles to solve and they led us to the key— among other things."

"You actually found Russel," Megan breathed, something like admiration coloring her voice. "The Collective has been searching for years. He was a man who could disappear better than anyone."

"He found us, really," Annie corrected, remembering the lengths Russel had gone to in order to force their arrival in Serenity Peaks. "He left us this keycard along with directions to find this place."

Ethan scoffed behind her, the sound bouncing off the stone walls around them. "I'd hardly call it directions. He let us search the desert for days. Nearly got us killed in a cave-in."

The bitterness in his voice was palpable, and Annie wondered how much of it was truly directed at Russel versus the sister who now stood before them, flesh and blood after so many years of silence.

The scanner on the door suddenly emitted a soft beep, and a small screen lit up, displaying a blinking cursor.

PASSWORD REQUIRED.

"Of course," Megan muttered, stepping closer. "Nothing's ever easy."

The three of them stared at the digital display, its blue glow casting their faces in eerie light. Annie noted the keypad beneath—standard alphanumeric keys arranged in four rows.

"Did he mention anything about a password?" Megan asked, glancing between them. "Any hints at all?"

Ethan shook his head, crossing his arms over his chest and rolling his eyes. "No. Guess he was too busy being *dead* to say anything helpful."

Annie leaned forward, examining the keypad more closely. Surrounding it was a decorative metal border, etched with an intricate pattern. In the corner, a small swirl resembling a flower caught her eye. She traced it with her fingertip, feeling the cool metal beneath her skin.

"Wait," she murmured, a memory surfacing. Images of

Russel's best-kept secret played in her mind: his daughter, Fleur. She imagined Fleur sitting at her sketchpad, her blonde hair draped over one shoulder like a curtain.

"Of course," Ethan nodded beside Annie, reading her mind. "Nobody knew about his daughter."

"Except us," Annie said. She met Ethan's eyes, a silent communication passing between them— the kind that had sustained their relationship through so many cases. She turned back to the keypad and typed five letters.

F-L-E-U-R

For a moment, nothing happened. Then a deep mechanical groan echoed through the tunnel, followed by a series of clicks as locking mechanisms disengaged. The green light on the scanner pulsed once, twice, and then stayed steady. Slowly, with the sound of stone grinding against stone, a section of the wall beside the metal door slid away, revealing a hidden entrance.

"Russel had a daughter?" Megan asked, her voice strained as she stared at the opening.

Annie shrugged, feeling oddly protective of the insight. "One of many puzzles the man presented us with."

A gust of cool, processed air rushed out from the compound, carrying with it the faint hum of machinery. Unlike the raw earthiness of the tunnel, this air tasted filtered, almost sterile. Annie felt the hairs on her arms rise, whether from the temperature change or anticipation, she couldn't tell.

Megan gave Annie a quizzical look, her eyes narrowing slightly.

"I'll explain later," Annie said, deflecting. Now wasn't the time to unpack what they'd discovered about the man who might hold the key to both their pasts.

Ethan cleared his throat, breaking the tension between the women. "Shall we?" he asked, gesturing toward the opening with mock formality that didn't quite hide his unease.

Annie nodded and stepped through first, leaving the

rough-hewn tunnel behind and entering a world of artificial light and humming technology. Megan followed closely, her movements fluid and alert, eyes scanning for threats. Ethan came last, his footsteps hesitant but determined.

As the door slid shut behind them with a definitive click, Annie couldn't shake the feeling that they had just crossed a threshold from which there would be no return. Whatever lay ahead in Russel's secret compound would change everything. And, for the first time, Annie wondered if living in darkness might be better than knowing the truth.

———

The interior of Russel's compound hit Annie like a scene from a science fiction film. Clinical white light bathed a space lined with computer banks and monitors, their screens aglow with scrolling data and pulsing diagrams. Thick bundles of wires snaked across the floor and up the walls, disappearing into steel conduits overhead. The contrast between the primitive mine tunnel and this sophisticated command center was jarring— like stepping from the past into the future.

"We don't have much time," Megan said, her voice tight as she moved swiftly toward the central workstation. Her hands skimmed across the sleek surface of the desk, muscle memory guiding her movements with practiced efficiency. "The Collective has been tracking this area for weeks. They'll be on our tails."

"How would they know we're here?" Ethan asked, following his sister with cautious steps.

Megan's eyes never left the screens. "They have eyes everywhere. I wouldn't be surprised if they've hidden remote cameras in the desert. And they've been watching both of you ever since you started looking for Russel. When you started digging into the past, you flagged their systems."

Annie absorbed this information with a cold shiver,

remembering all the times she'd felt watched during their investigation. She'd dismissed it as paranoia— a side effect of chasing ghosts and conspiracies. Now she wondered how many shadows had hidden actual observers.

"Come on," Megan urged, gesturing them forward. "Whatever we need to find, we need to find it *now*."

They hurried to the main console where multiple screens created a semicircle around a single chair. Megan slid into it and began typing, her fingers flying across the keyboard with practiced speed. The largest monitor flickered and displayed a world map dotted with glowing red pins.

"What is all this?" Annie asked, leaning closer.

"Russel's life work," Megan murmured, her face illuminated by the screen's glow as she deciphered what was in front of her. "Each pin represents a Collective operation or stronghold." She zoomed out, and Annie gasped at the sheer number of markers scattered across continents, countries, cities— thousands of them, pulsing like tiny heartbeats.

"They're everywhere," Ethan whispered, the magnitude of what they were seeing reflected in his voice.

"All of it," Megan said, her eyes wide. "Russel knew everything. This top level stuff. *No one* in The Collective gets this level of access, not me, not anyone lower down. Just the top brass. But Russel— he really did it."

Megan reached into her jacket pocket and produced a small external hard drive, which she plugged into the console. A progress bar appeared on a side screen, indicating the beginning of a data transfer.

"I'm copying everything," she explained, fingers still typing. Megan was breathless as she worked, and Annie could help but note her excitement. It was clear— Megan had been waiting for this moment for years. "Names, locations, operational details—everything Russel gathered about them. With this, we might finally be able to dismantle their network."

Annie watched the progress bar inch forward, each percentage point representing data that might bring down the organization that had haunted them for years. But her focus narrowed to one specific question.

"Megan," she said, "all of this is important, but right now, we only care about one place."

Their eyes met, and understanding passed between them — two women connected by parallel losses, by the same unseen enemy.

"Cedarsburg," Megan nodded, already typing the name.

"Home," Ethan said softly.

The map zoomed in, centering on a small pin in Indiana. Megan clicked it, and the screen filled with files—newspaper clippings, photographs, chat logs.

"My God," Ethan breathed as the headline appeared: "REAL ESTATE RIPPER CLAIMS FOURTH VICTIM." Below it was a picture Annie knew all too well— the house where her brother was killed, surrounded by police tape. She felt her chest tighten as memories surfaced: the bloodstain the cleaning crews could never quite scrub from the hardwood, the funeral where she stood in shock, unable to process what had happened.

"Russel was tracking it," Annie said, her voice hollow.

Megan scrolled through more files, revealing a chat window with a username that stood out: LittleBug2000.

"An informant," Megan explained, clicking on the chat history. "Someone feeding Russel information about The Collective's operations, specifically in Cedarsburg."

Annie leaned in, enthralled by the idea of a direct informant in her hometown. "Open the chat."

"It could be nothing," Megan cautioned as she clicked to open the window. "Informants are only one part of the puzzle, and sometimes they're cold leads."

The messages scrolled by, cryptic exchanges about meeting places and dead drops. The most recent message, dated just three days ago, read simply: "Where are you? Hello?"

Megan scrolled through the chat, revealing multiple similar attempts at contact.

"They don't know he's dead," Annie realized.

Megan nodded, already typing a response: "Russel compromised. We're on his team. Meet with us?"

The three of them stared at the screen, waiting. Above them, a distant thud reverberated through the compound. Dust sifted down from the ceiling.

"That's not good," Ethan said, looking up.

A second, louder thud followed, and this time the floor trembled beneath their feet. One of the smaller monitors flickered and went dark.

"Definitely not good," Megan said, her voice unnervingly calm. She glanced at the hard drive, still downloading. "We need to go. Now."

A third impact rocked the compound— this one unmistakably an explosion. "They found us!" Megan shouted. The lights flickered, plunging them into momentary darkness before emergency power kicked in, bathing everything in pulsing red.

"We're running out of time! Get out!" Megan shouted over the sudden blare of alarms. She yanked the hard drive free, tucking it securely into her jacket. "We have to go! Annie— leave the chat— we already have the hard-drive!"

Annie remained transfixed by the screen, where the cursor still blinked, awaiting a response from LittleBug2000. "Not until they answer," she insisted, her voice steady despite the chaos erupting around them.

The ceiling groaned, and a section of metal paneling crashed to the floor mere feet away. Sparks showered from exposed wiring, and smoke began to fill the room.

"Annie, please!" Ethan begged, grabbing her arm. "This place is coming down!"

She shook him off, eyes never leaving the screen. "This could be our only chance to find out who was behind it all— what happened to my brother.

"Annie, it's probably all here, on the drive! Surely the informant already told Russel—" Megan shouted.

"They didn't," Annie said, shaking her head. "I want to meet with them. I have to know who they are— I'm not leaving until they write back—"

The mine rumbled again and Megan grabbed her brother's arm, steadying herself on his strong form. "Ethan, get her out of here!" she shouted.

"Working on it!" Ethan called back, leaning against a bank of monitors to stay upright.

Megan braced herself and added, "Damnit, Annie! I didn't make it this far just to die while waiting for some unconfirmed informant with a screen name as lame as *Littlebug!*"

Another explosion rocked the compound, closer this time. Annie felt the heat of it against her face, heard the scream of twisting metal as the structure began to fail.

Ethan lunged for her, wrapping his arms around her waist to physically drag her away. "Annie, we won't get answers if we're dead!"

As he pulled her backward, the chat window suddenly filled with a new message. Annie twisted in Ethan's grip, straining to see the screen through the thickening smoke.

"Wait! Look!" she cried, pointing.

Through the haze, three lines of text appeared:

"Cedarsburg. At the water tower.

Friday.

Midnight."

The message burned into Annie's memory as Ethan dragged her away from the console. The main support beam overhead gave way with a thunderous crack, bringing down a cascade of debris that obliterated the workstation they'd just abandoned.

"Run!" Megan shouted from the doorway, beckoning them frantically.

Annie sprinted toward the exit, Ethan close behind her. The ground shuddered beneath their feet, and the air grew thick with dust and smoke. Behind them, Russel's life work—years of surveillance and investigation—disappeared under tons of rock and twisted metal.

But Annie carried something more valuable than hard drives or data files. She had a meeting place. A time. A chance to finally face the truth they'd been chasing for so long.

As they fled through the collapsing tunnel, dodging falling rocks and sparking electrical lines, Annie repeated the three lines to herself like a chant: *At the water tower. Friday. Midnight.* Annie had a perfect memory. But she'd never been more afraid of forgetting anything like she was those three lines— except, maybe, long ago, when she'd worried about forgetting her brother's face, or the sound of his voice.

At the water tower. Friday. Midnight.

They had three days to prepare for whatever—or whoever—awaited them there.

It was finally time. They were going home.

CHAPTER THREE

THE TUNNEL GROANED around them like a dying beast, rock and metal shrieking as another explosion rocked the earth above. Annie stumbled forward, lungs burning with each ragged breath of dust-filled air. Megan led their desperate charge toward daylight, her silhouette flickering in and out of view as emergency lights failed in sequence behind them. The information they'd just uncovered pulsed in Annie's mind with each footfall. If they could just make it out alive, they might finally learn the truth about her brother's murder. A truth worth dying for, perhaps—but Annie much preferred the option where they all survived to find it.

"Move!" Ethan shouted from behind her, his hand firmly pressed against the small of her back as another blast shook the tunnel. This one was different— closer, more deliberate. A targeted strike. Annie could feel the tunnel failing— a beast on its last breath.

Annie caught Megan glancing back, her expression shifting from determination to cold calculation. "They're throwing explosives down the shaft," she called over her shoulder. "They're trying to bury us."

"Not very friendly of them," Annie joked, ducking as a chunk of ceiling crashed beside her.

Megan's laugh held no humor as she vaulted over a fallen support beam. "I'll forward The Collective your complaint."

They rounded a bend in the tunnel, and Annie's heart leapt at the sight of daylight streaming in from the mine entrance ahead. Fifty feet. Just fifty more feet and they'd be out. The desert air never looked so inviting.

A deafening crack split overhead as the wooden supports near the entrance splintered under the force of another explosion. Debris cascaded down, partially blocking their exit.

"We're gonna get sealed in!" Ethan yelled, pulling his gun from its holster.

Megan didn't slow. "Keep moving!" she ordered, lowering her shoulder as she charged toward the narrowing gap of light. The tunnel behind them was collapsing in earnest now, a chain reaction of failing supports and falling rock.

Annie felt Ethan's hand grab hers, pulling her forward as her feet stumbled over the uneven ground. The roar of destruction chased them, a wave of dust and stone threatening to swallow them whole.

Megan reached the entrance first, scrambling through the gap and turning immediately to help Annie through. Daylight blinded her momentarily as Ethan gave her one final push from behind. She tumbled forward onto the hard-packed desert soil, Ethan diving through the opening seconds before it disappeared in a final, thunderous collapse.

For a precious moment, they lay there, gulping fresh air as dust billowed out from what had been their escape route. Annie's ears rang with the echo of falling rock, her body trembling with spent adrenaline.

The harsh crack of gunfire shattered their reprieve.

"Down!" Megan shouted, tackling Annie back to the ground as dirt kicked up inches from where they'd been lying.

Annie's face pressed into the hot sand as more shots rang out. Through the settling dust, she made out an unmarked black van parked fifty yards away, its side door open. Men in tactical gear leaned out, faces hidden behind black masks, rifles aimed squarely at them.

"My SUV," Megan hissed, nodding toward a dark green vehicle parked behind a small outcropping of rocks. "It's our only chance."

Ethan had rolled to his knees, his service weapon already drawn. "Cover fire?"

Megan nodded, pulling her own gun from a holster Annie hadn't noticed before. "On three. Annie, you run straight for the passenger side. Don't stop, don't look back."

Annie nodded, her throat too dry for words. *At the water tower. Friday. Midnight.* The words replayed in her mind, a chant that promised a better future. They couldn't die here, not when they were so close to answers.

Ethan grabbed Annie's arm, a strange urgency flashing across his face. "You're 'gonna make it Annie," he said, clutching her arm tight. "Whatever happens to me, make sure you stay safe."

"One," Megan counted, interrupting the moment. She checked her weapon with practiced efficiency.

"Two," Ethan continued, his eyes meeting Megan's for the briefest of moments. Annie noticed the glance— the moment between siblings. She saw in Ethan's eyes something beyond fear—determination, but also a question. Could he trust the woman who had been dead to them for so many years?

"Three!"

Megan and Ethan rose in unison, their guns spitting fire as Annie sprinted toward the SUV. The desert stretched endlessly around her, offering no cover beyond the distant rocks where Megan's vehicle waited. Annie's lungs burned, legs pumping as bullets kicked up dust in her wake.

Behind her, she heard Megan shouting something, her voice

almost lost in the exchange of gunfire. Annie risked a glance back to see one of the masked men fall, clutching his shoulder. Another leaned further out of the van, taking more careful aim.

"Keep going!" Ethan yelled as Annie slowed, struck by the urge to run back to him. He squeezed off two more shots as he backed toward her, keeping his body between Annie and the shooters.

Annie reached the SUV, yanking at the passenger door. Locked. Of course it was locked.

"Keys!" she screamed, ducking behind the vehicle as a bullet pinged off its metal frame.

Megan was sprinting toward them now, one hand firing back at their attackers while the other dug into her pocket. She slid the last few feet like a baseball player stealing home, coming to rest beside Annie behind the relative safety of the SUV's engine block. A small remote beeped in her hand, and the doors unlocked with an incongruously cheerful chirp.

"Get in!" Megan ordered, already moving toward the driver's side.

Ethan dove into the backseat as Annie scrambled into the front passenger seat. A bullet shattered the rear window just as Megan jammed the key into the ignition. The engine roared to life, and she slammed her foot on the accelerator before the doors were fully closed.

The SUV lurched forward, tires spinning in the loose desert soil before finding purchase. A spray of sand and rocks showered behind them as they shot forward, bullets pinging off the frame.

"They saw me," Megan said, her voice oddly calm as she wrenched the steering wheel hard to the left, taking them away from the main road. "My face wasn't covered. My cover's blown."

Annie gripped the dashboard as the SUV bounced over a ridge, momentarily airborne before crashing back to earth.

Through the side mirror, she saw the black van in pursuit, dust billowing behind it.

"Oh gee, what a shame," Ethan snarled from the backseat, reloading his weapon with practiced hands. "What exactly was your cover, Meg? Just how deep are you in with these people?"

Megan's laugh was sharp as she navigated the SUV through a series of punishing turns, the desert landscape blurring outside the windows. "Well, Ethan, I'd love to tell you my sweet little story about human trafficking, but I'm a little busy at the moment *trying not to die.*"

A bullet punched through the remaining back window, embedding itself in the dashboard inches from Annie's hand. Annie jerked back with a startled cry, relieved to find her hand was still intact.

"Cover now, explanations later," Annie agreed, ducking lower in her seat.

Ethan leaned out his window, returning fire at their pursuers. "They're gaining!" he shouted, ducking back inside as a volley of bullets answered his attack.

Megan cursed, slamming the SUV into a higher gear. The vehicle shuddered beneath them, engine screaming in protest as she pushed it to its limits. The desert floor opened up ahead, a vast expanse of nothing that offered both escape and exposure.

"How many?" Megan asked, eyes flicking to the rearview mirror.

"Two vans," Annie reported, twisting in her seat to look back. "Six shooters that I can see."

"Great odds," Megan muttered, her mouth quirking into an unexpected smile. "I was getting bored anyway. Wouldn't want to make it too easy!"

Ethan fired again, then dropped back into his seat to reload. His face was a mask of tightly controlled fury. "Is this funny to you?" he demanded. "Being hunted by killers? Letting me think you were dead for over a decade?"

"No," Megan admitted, voice softening for just a moment before she yanked the wheel again, sending them skidding sideways to avoid a rocky outcropping. "But finding the humor in terrible situations kept me alive undercover."

"Undercover," Ethan repeated, the word bitter on his tongue. "With The Collective. The same people who—" He broke off as another barrage of gunfire peppered the SUV.

"CIA," Megan countered, wincing as a bullet grazed the side mirror, sending shards of glass across the hood. "Deep cover for eight years. And yes, the same people who—" She jerked the wheel again, cutting herself off. "Look, I want to explain everything, but right now I'm trying to make sure we don't end up as tumbleweeds! I didn't survive the biggest crime ring in the world just to die in the middle of nowhere more than an hour drive away from the nearest Sephora."

Annie's mind raced as fast as the landscape blurring past her window. All these years, Megan had been alive, working undercover, while Ethan mourned her. While they both searched for answers about that night in their hometown.

The SUV crested a small hill and for a brief, stomach-dropping moment, they were airborne. Annie's head nearly hit the roof before they crashed back to earth, the impact jarring her teeth.

"Sorry about that," Megan said, not sounding sorry at all. "I forgot you should always change gears before a dune. I'm out of practice when it comes to car chases."

"Forgot?" Ethan shouted. "You've been in a car chase before?"

"Yes," Megan replied, her eyes constantly scanning the terrain ahead. "Though usually I'm not the one being chased. I have to be honest... this kind of sucks from the other side."

A bullet zinged past Annie's ear, so close she felt the air displacement. "They're faster than us," Annie said calmly, almost cheerfully, as if the news were nothing important at all. "We're not going to win if we keep trying to outrun them."

Megan nodded grimly, pressing the accelerator harder. The SUV's engine whined in protest. "Good thinking, Hudson. We need an advantage." Megan jerked the steering wheel to the left just in time to avoid another bullet, which exploded the passenger-side mirror. "I'm very open to ideas at this time, if anyone would like to volunteer?"

Annie peered through the windshield, searching the landscape for anything that might help. In the distance, a narrow canyon cut through the desert floor, and spanning it—

"There!" she pointed. "Head for the bridge."

Megan followed her gaze to where a wooden footbridge stretched across the canyon. It was old, weathered by years of desert sun and wind, clearly designed for hikers rather than vehicles.

"It's for pedestrians," Megan said, though she was already adjusting their course toward it. "It won't hold us!"

"It will," Annie insisted.

"And you know this because…" Megan whined.

"Always trust Annie," Ethan said, impatient. "When she knows, she *knows*—"

"The support structure is stronger than it looks," Annie added. "The wood is Western red cedar. It resists rot. Very rare. It might look old, but the joints are reinforced. It's built to withstand flash floods."

"Your girlfriend is a woodworking expert?" Megan glanced at Ethan, trying to decide if she should believe Annie.

"She's a genius," Ethan said simply. "An expert in everything."

Megan shot Annie an appraising look. "Fine. Let's hope you're right, because Plan B is 'die in a hail of bullets.'"

The vans were closing in, one on either side now as they

tried to flank the SUV. Ethan fired out the left window, forcing one van to swerve away momentarily.

"If we make it across," Annie continued, her mind racing ahead, "there's a weak point in the central support. One well-placed shot could bring the bridge down behind us."

Megan's grin was fierce as she accelerated toward the bridge. "I like the way you think, Annie Hudson."

They approached the canyon at breakneck speed, the wooden bridge growing larger in the windshield. It looked even narrower up close, barely wide enough for their vehicle, with simple wooden railings that would offer little protection from the sheer drop on either side.

"Brace yourselves," Megan warned, slowing just enough to line up their approach.

The first impact came as their tires hit the wooden planks. The bridge shuddered beneath them, boards creaking in protest at the unaccustomed weight. Annie held her breath, counting the seconds as they crawled across, the canyon yawning beneath them.

A bullet splintered one of the railings inches from them. In the rearview mirror, Annie saw the lead van slowing as it approached the bridge, its driver clearly hesitant to follow them onto the fragile structure.

"That's right," Annie whispered at the van behind them. "One at a time."

The SUV reached the midpoint of the bridge, and Annie felt the structure sag slightly beneath them. Please hold, she silently begged, her fingers digging into the seat cushion.

"We're almost there," Megan said, her voice tight with concentration as she guided them forward inch by careful inch.

Ethan kept his gun trained on the pursuing vehicles, which had stopped at the edge of the canyon. "They're waiting to see if we make it across," he reported.

The front tires touched solid ground on the far side, and

Annie allowed herself a small breath of relief. Just a few more feet...

With a final groan of protest, the bridge released them onto solid ground. Megan immediately accelerated away from the edge, putting distance between them and the fragile crossing.

"Now, Ethan!" Annie called, pointing back at the bridge. "The central support— where the cables connect to the main beam!"

Ethan leaned out the window, taking careful aim as the lead van cautiously began to edge onto the bridge. He squeezed the trigger once, twice, three times in rapid succession.

The bullets found their mark. For a moment, nothing happened. Then, with a sound like a giant's sigh, the central support splintered. The cables groaned, tension releasing as the bridge began to twist upon itself.

The driver of the lead van realized too late what was happening. The vehicle reversed frantically, tires spinning on wooden planks that were already tilting precariously. Annie watched, heart in her throat, as the bridge gave way completely, collapsing into the canyon in a spectacular tangle of wood and metal. The van managed to back up just in time, its front wheels teetering at the newly formed edge before it retreated to safety.

Megan slowed the SUV to a stop, all three of them turning to watch as their pursuers gathered at the edge of the canyon, separated from them by an unbridgeable gap.

"Well," Megan said after a moment of stunned silence, "there goes my cover." She turned to look at them, her face surprisingly serene for someone who had just blown a multi-year undercover operation. "Nice work on the bridge Hudson. Good instincts." She turned back, raising a hand to protect her eyes from the sun.

The three of them sat in the SUV for a moment, staring out

the windshield at the remainder of the SUVs across the deep sliver of canyon they'd just crossed. The vehicles stood in place, and then, a man emerged, his face covered by black piece of cloth he'd pulled from neck to mouth.

No one spoke. Instead, they gazed at the man, considering him as they would any other desert feature.

Then, Megan broke the silence:

"Are you guys hungry?" she asked casually. "Because I'm starving."

The question was so incongruous, so utterly disconnected from the life-and-death situation they'd just survived, that Annie couldn't help the startled laugh that escaped her.

"I could always use a cheeseburger," she replied, feeling the tension drain from her shoulders as the adrenaline began to subside.

Ethan stared at them both like they'd lost their minds. Then, slowly, the corner of his mouth twitched upward—not quite a smile, but something close to it.

"A cheeseburger," he repeated, shaking his head as he holstered his weapon. "Sure, why not? Nothing says 'we just escaped death' like processed meat and American cheese. It's a Hudson favorite."

Megan laughed, starting the SUV again and pulling away from the canyon edge. "Sounds good," she said, revving the engine. "We'll drive for an hour and then we'll check out our options. Something tells me we'll find a spot."

As they drove away, Annie watched the men from The Collective grow smaller in the side mirror, until they disappeared altogether, as if they had never existed in the first place.

CHAPTER FOUR

THE DINER they chose was a hole in the wall, and Annie liked it that way. It sat at the crossroads of three states—Nevada melting into Arizona and Utah—a perfect metaphor for their current situation, Annie thought. Neither here nor there, caught between the past and the future, truth and lies. The neon OPEN sign buzzed and flickered against the desert sky as they pulled into the gravel lot, the SUV's engine ticking as it cooled. Megan had driven for exactly one hour as promised, but then one hour turned into two, and no one spoke. The buzz of surviving a shoot-out had been replaced by the uneasy realization that The Collective would be hunting them, now. They spent the rest of the drive glancing at the back window to see if they were being followed. Now, they were finally stopping for food, hoping they'd put enough distance between themselves and their pursuers.

"Mesquite Diner," Megan announced unnecessarily, killing the engine. She checked a collection of Yelp reviews on her phone. "Cash only, which helps us out. No credit card records." She leaned forward, surveying the diner's exterior. "No cameras. Doesn't look like they could afford them if they wanted to."

"Practical," Annie murmured.

"Better safe," Megan replied with a half-smile that didn't reach her eyes.

They entered the diner single file—Megan first, then Annie, with Ethan bringing up the rear. The bell above the door jingled. Inside, the air smelled of grease and coffee and artificial lemon cleaner. A waitress with tired eyes and a name tag that read "Darlene" guided them to a booth by the window, slapping down three laminated menus before walking away.

Megan slid into one side of the booth, her back to the wall, eyes tracking the entrance. Annie recognized the posture— someone who never sat with their back to a door. She'd seen it in Ethan countless times. The siblings, despite fifteen years apart, moved with the same cautious awareness of their surroundings. Some things, it seemed, ran in the blood. Or, maybe, were the result of being exposed to the dangers the world posed too young— too early.

Annie sat opposite Megan, leaving Ethan to choose. After a moment's hesitation, he lowered himself beside Annie, maintaining the physical distance from his sister that he seemed to need.

"So," Megan said, her fingers drumming a nervous pattern on the tabletop. "Cheeseburgers?"

"With extra pickles," Annie replied, grateful for the mundane conversation starter. "And a chocolate milkshake."

"Some things never change," Megan said with a genuine smile this time. "You always did have a sweet tooth, Annie."

Annie blinked, surprised that Megan remembered such a detail about her from so long ago. Before she could respond, Ethan spoke, his voice flat.

"You know what else never changes? Corpses. They stay dead." His hands were clasped tightly on the table. "At least, that's what I thought. Turns out I was wrong." He paused looking up at the ceiling, then added. "But I'm glad I was wrong." He turned his gaze back to Megan. "I'm so thankful you're here."

Megan's smile faltered. She reached for a paper napkin from the dispenser, folding it into smaller and smaller squares. "Me, too," she said quietly.

The waitress returned, pencil poised over her order pad. They each ordered cheeseburgers—Annie with her milkshake, Ethan with black coffee, Megan with water—and fell back into uneasy silence when she left.

"Perhaps, now that there's food involved," Annie said cheerfully, "we should get to the story portion of the evening?"

Megan visibly flinched at Annie's odd way of addressing the elephant in the room.

"Annie's right," Ethan said, unmoved by her strange, upbeat way of tackling the worst moments. Ethan was used to Annie's quirks. They comforted him now. "Megan, I need to know what happened."

Megan looked down at the napkin she'd folded into a tight square, then up at him again. "I don't even know where to start."

Annie watched the siblings, feeling like an intruder in their moment of reconnection, yet knowing her presence was somehow steadying for both of them. She remained quiet, a witness to their pain.

"What happened that day?" Ethan asked, the question hanging between them like an unexploded bomb. "The real story. Were you— were you always working at The Collective and we just didn't know? Did you fake your disappearance?"

Annie's heart pounded in her chest. As much as she hated to admit it, she'd been wondering the same thing.

Megan's mouth dropped open, shocked at the accusation. She looked at Ethan like he'd slapped her. "You don't really think I'd—."

"I don't know what to think," Ethan said, his jaw tightening. He'd seen too much of the world to take anything for granted.

Megan took a deep breath, her shoulders rising and falling with the effort. "I had just saved up enough money to buy my first little condo, just on the edge of town. I was so excited, so proud. Mom and Dad threw that little party, remember? Dad made those terrible meatballs he was so proud of."

A ghost of a smile crossed Ethan's face. "They were like hockey pucks."

"But we ate them anyway," Megan continued, her voice warming with the memory. "Because he was so proud of me. Saving up to buy a home— even a cheap one in a place like Cedarsburg— it was my first adult accomplishment." She looked at Annie, her expression pained. "I was excited to sign the papers with your brother. I don't know if you know this, Annie, but he was in my graduating class in high school, always encouraging me."

Annie nodded, her throat suddenly tight. She remembered her brother's enthusiasm about looking at houses, his dreams of owning one someday. Dreams that died with him.

"The house was normal when we went in," Megan continued, her voice growing strained. "Joshua gave me a final tour and I was so excited I looked in every closet, opened every cabinet. I swear I did, Annie. Everything was fine. Every room, every closet. I wasn't even looking for a person because things like that just didn't happen in Cedarsburg. I was just excited about my first home because it looked nice—."

The waitress arrived with their drinks, momentarily halting Megan's story. Annie wrapped her hands around the cold milkshake glass, grateful for something to hold onto.

"Someone must have already been in the house," Megan continued after the waitress left. "I've thought about it every day since, wondering how they could've gotten inside, and the only thing that makes sense is that they were already there when we arrived. They were inside, waiting. I've replayed it in my mind a million times and I just can't figure out where they might have been— if only I'd heard— I could've run— I could've gotten help..." Megan's hands began to shake, and suddenly Annie saw the girl she had once known. The tough, competent tiger that had just participated in a shoot-out was gone, replaced by the real Megan.

"There's nothing you could have done," Annie said warmly. "Nothing."

Megan nodded, and Ethan reached across the table, putting a hand over Megan's. He curled his fingers around his sister's, his touch easing the tremor.

Megan took a deep breath, pulled her hand away before continuing."They knocked me out. I saw black. All I remember is—" She paused, swallowing hard. "The smell of mint. And the sound of your brother shouting, Annie."

Annie's hand tightened around her glass. Mint. Hardly the case-busting clue she'd been hoping for.

"I'm so sorry, Annie," Megan said, her eyes filling with tears. "I'm so sorry I couldn't stop it. If I'd been the woman I am today back then, maybe I could have helped him. Maybe I could have fought back. But I wasn't. I couldn't do anything."

"It wasn't your fault," Annie said automatically, though part of her had spent years looking for someone to blame. "You were a victim too."

"What happened after?" Ethan asked, his voice softer now. "Where did you go?"

Megan took a sip of water, her hand trembling slightly. "I can't— it's hard to explain—."

"They trafficked you?" Annie said, filling in the blanks to spare Megan from reliving the experience.

"Different houses. Always drugged. New locations. It was a blur and I thought I'd never feel alive again until… until I met *him*."

"Who?" Annie asked, even she already knew the answer.

"Russel," Megan said. "He turned me from a trafficking

victim into an accomplice, which, trust me, is a merciful place to be. I only knew him for a short time, and then never saw him again. But in those few weeks… he rescued me."

"Probably because he had a daughter," Annie suggested, thinking of Fleur. "He was trying to help—."

Megan's eyebrows rose in surprise. "He never told me anything personal." She shook her head slightly. "But he always had this... sadness about him."

Their food arrived, plates clattering on the table. Annie stared at her burger, suddenly not hungry despite their earlier joking. Megan picked at her fries, continuing her story between small bites.

"Russel vouched for me to a boss, helped keep me safe. Linked me up with a job within the group moving drugs." She gave a humorless laugh. "From one cage to another, but at least I wasn't being..." She trailed off, shaking her head.

"You could have left then!" Ethan exclaimed, throwing his hands in the air. "You could have found a way to call me, to call the police…"

"Ethan…" Annie cautioned, but Megan spoke before she could say more.

"You think that didn't cross my mind?" Megan said, slamming her hands on the table. "You really don't get it, do you Ethan? Once they have their claws in you, you're in for life. This is bigger than the cartels you deal with. This is an international criminal organization that spans the globe! They have eyes everywhere. Police. Politicians. Access to cameras. Bank accounts. Personal records." She leaned in, her eyes manic. "Even if I left The Collective, they would have found me. Because no one *ever* gets to leave. Not really."

"How did you end up with the CIA?" Annie asked, concerned.

Megan leaned back in her seat, looking out the window with a painful stare. "Luck, maybe fate. The CIA busted one of our locations. They took everyone."

"And you?," Ethan asked, his coffee untouched before him.

"They gave me a choice when they learned about how I'd ended up in The Collective," Megan said, meeting his gaze directly. "They could tell I hated the organization, but my life had just been so messed up at that point, I felt like I had no other choice. I knew too much, and The Collective would always find me. Even prison wasn't safe. The CIA said I could keep working with The Collective and report back to them as a mole. They would make it look like I escaped during the raid. And that's exactly what we did. They dropped me in front of a safe house looking like I'd just run from the processing center, and I told my boss at The Collective the whole story about the bust, at the CIA's request. Even gave him some names of agents to make it look legit. He bought it. So I've been working with them for years, acting as an undercover agent. We left burner phones at shared locations as a back channel communication and I've been feeding them everything I can—."

Ethan groaned, putting his head in his hands. "Megan, that's not being an agent! That's being a tool! They're just using you and the second they don't need you anymore they'll leave you out there like you never existed—."

"You think you would have had better ideas?!" Megan almost shouted, leaning forward in the booth with a rage that turned her cheeks red. "You try living my life and see how you do! I'm a survivor. They tried to destroy me and I'm still here, secretly chipping away at them every day—."

"We're getting some unwanted attention," Annie cleared her throat with a smile, gesturing at a pair of diners across the room, who were staring at their table with a disturbed glance. "Maybe we take it down a notch."

Megan regained her composure and sat back down, unfolding her napkin on her lap.

"I could have helped you," Ethan said, his voice cracking.

"After you disappeared I dedicated my life to law enforcement. I'm with the FBI."

"I know," Megan said simply. "I looked you up in The Collective's system. Turns out I'm pretty good at being a criminal, and over time I climbed the ranks. Got partial access to their network. I found you, and I knew you were with the FBI."

Ethan sat back in the booth, reeling. The pain that crossed his face made Annie want to hug him, but she thought better of it.

"Why didn't you get a message to me?" Ethan asked, shattered. "Some sign that you were alive? Mom and Dad died not knowing, Meg. The grief of losing you probably killed them. I had to do it all alone—."

Megan's face crumpled for an instant before she schooled it back to composure. "All I wanted was to contact you, but I couldn't. I didn't want to drag you into all this. You had a successful career, you had Annie—" she glanced across the table. "I just didn't want to put a target on your back. When someone betrays The Collective, they take their families, Ethan." Tears fell down Megan's face. "I was trying to protect you."

Annie watched Ethan struggle with his emotions, his face cycling through anger, grief, and confusion. She knew him well enough to see that he wanted to believe his sister, but fifteen years of loss wasn't easily erased.

"Ethan never gave up on you, Megan," Annie said quietly. "We've been working together to try to find the Real Estate Ripper. We've been trying to figure out what happened to you all this time."

"How did you end up in Rachel?" Ethan asked, still trying to figure out what magic had brought them all together.

"Twelve months ago, something happened," Megan said, her voice dropping to ensure only they could hear. "Russel Grey secretly reached out to me again. I hadn't heard from him in years, but he sent me a message. A puzzle to solve. He told me he'd found a way to leave and that he was out—which is incredible, because *nobody* leaves. I almost didn't believe him."

"He was telling the truth," Annie said, remembering the peaceful commune where they'd found him.

"He was in hiding, planning to take them down," Megan said, nodding. "I had no idea he had also involved my own brother and Annie until I spotted you in Rachel, looking for the same compound as me."

"You wonder if Russel arranged it that way?" Annie asked, though she already knew the answer. Russel had been playing chess while the rest of them struggled with checkers.

"He must have," Megan agreed, looking concerned. "But I never wanted this. I wanted you to be safe, Ethan."

"A little late for that," Ethan said. But his eyes softened. He reached across the table again and took Megan's hand in his. "I'm so glad you're alive. And I'm not losing you again."

"But you will lose her," Annie said darkly, surprising everyone. "Unless we finish this. We can't run. Not forever."

Ethan nodded, understanding. "What's the move? We go to our hometown and find the Real Estate Ripper? Meet this informant?"

"Yes," Megan said, leaning forward eagerly. "We can work together to take down The Collective. I've been doing this all alone—well, apart from Russel's help—but now that I have you two, we can finally work as a team. We can bring down the whole organization."

Annie noted the way Megan's eyes lit up, her passion evident. This was a woman who had found purpose in her trauma, who had channeled her pain into a mission.

"The Collective spans the globe," Megan continued, her voice intense. "They're behind so much evil in the world: human trafficking, drug deals, even higher-up stuff in politics and geopolitical world order. It's bigger than you can imagine. And you can come with me, both of you. We can fight them together."

Ethan was already shaking his head before she finished speaking. "Megan, three people can't take down the whole thing. And Annie and I— we're going to have a quiet life. All I wanted was to find out what happened to you, and now that I know, I just want... peace. You can have that, too. We can find someplace for all of us to go—."

The hope in Megan's eyes dimmed. She looked at Annie, clearly seeking backup, but Annie remained silent, caught in her own thoughts.

"Ethan, you may have peace," Annie finally said, her voice soft. "But I still don't."

Ethan put a hand over Annie's, his eyes softening. "Hudson, of course I'm going to help you find out who was behind your brother's murder," he said. "And I won't stop until that's done. But it doesn't mean I have to commit to spanning the globe trying to play whack-a-mole with an unbeatable criminal organization even the combined powers of multiple alphabet agencies haven't been able to stop."

He turned back to Megan, his voice firm but gentle. "I just want to help Annie find out who the Real Estate Ripper is, what their connection to The Collective is, and then go live a peaceful, quiet life somewhere. That's it."

Megan looked from Ethan to Annie, her expression a mixture of disappointment and understanding. "What about you, Annie?" she asked. "What do *you* want?"

Annie stared down at her half-eaten burger, considering the question. What did she want? Revenge? Justice? Peace? The truth? All of these things seemed both vital and insufficient.

"I don't know," she admitted, looking up at both of them. "I won't know until I solve the mystery of my brother's murder." The admission felt painful, like confessing a weakness.

Ethan squeezed her hand, understanding in his eyes. He'd never pressured her to move on, to let go of her quest for answers. It was one of the things she loved most about him.

"We can't make you any promises right now," he said to Megan, his voice gentle but firm.

Megan took another bite of her burger, chewing thoughtfully. "You'll change your mind," she said with quiet certainty. "Once you figure out who the Real Estate Ripper is. You'll see that this is so much bigger than just one person."

"Don't bet on it," Ethan replied, though there was less hostility in his voice now. He finally took a bite of his own burger, as if the act of eating might bring some normalcy to this surreal reunion.

Annie watched them, these two siblings connected by blood and separated by circumstance.

The neon lights of the diner cast colored shadows across their faces as they ate in relative silence. Outside, the desert darkness deepened, stars appearing one by one in the vast sky that stretched over three states. Annie wondered which direction was home—the place they'd all left behind so long ago, the place that now called them back with promises of answers and threats of more pain.

"Let's go home," Annie said. And to that, at least, the group could agree.

CHAPTER FIVE

ANNIE WATCHED the digital clock on the dashboard flip to 12:15 am. It was past midnight. They were already fifteen minutes late to meet their informant. They'd been driving for three days, trading places at the wheeling, pulling over to sleep and eat only when absolutely necessary. Annie glanced at Ethan beside her, his knuckles white against the steering wheel as they drove through the silent streets of Cedarsburg. He had switched places with Megan hours ago, giving her a break from driving so she could sleep in the backseat. But now, Megan was awake. She'd opened her eyes as soon as they'd crossed city lines, almost as if she could sense they'd arrived in their hometown.

"Make a left here," Megan said from the backseat, her voice unnaturally loud in the quiet car. "It'll be faster."

Ethan obeyed without comment, turning down Maple Street. Annie took in the apocalyptic sight before here. There was no denying it: Cedarsburg had changed. The town she remembered had been alive, and brimming with promise. Maybe memories were rosier, but Annie recalled a place ripe with the fruit of Americana dreams. Flags had flown on holidays. Kids had picnicked in the park. Small businesses had crowned the town square— all of them unique, and a testament to the independent spirit that made America great.

But now, Cedarsburg was different. Planks of wood blocked off the windows of vacant businesses. Trash sat on the street, left to blow in the wind until some good samaritan had their way with it. Only the occasional big-brand store emerged: a Walmart on the corner. A Chevron in the distance. The chain outlets were sterile and clinical, uniform in their appearance, lacking the charm individual shops had once offered. Family restaurants Annie had known as a child had closed, replaced by fast-food emporiums.

Cedarsburg felt empty. Clinical in its uniformity.

"Not the same, is it?" Ethan said, clearly noticing the decay.

"No," Annie agreed, a little shaken. "The form is there but not the function. It's the outline of the place we once knew— but now—" Annie paused looking for the words to describe what she was seeing.

"It's hollow," Megan offered softly from the backseat, finishing Annie's thought for her. Megan leaned against the window, watching as the empty streets rolled past. "It used to be so charming. Now, it's like it's trying to look like everywhere else, but failing."

"'The old world is dying and the new world is not yet born,'" Annie said, offering up a quote. "'Now is the time of monsters.'"

"Who's that?" Ethan asked, recognizing that the words were not Annie's own. Annie remembered everything she read, word-for-word. It made her an interesting dinner guest.

"Gramsci. He wrote during the Fascist takeover of Italy."

"Still applies," Megan nodded. She pointed out the window at a cinderblock building, looming under the moonlight. "Look, it's still there— our high school." Annie turned to take in the familiar space, her chest tightening at the building's shadow. A sign outside read: "CEDARSBURG HIGH:

Home of the Panthers." A grass lawn circled the school's entrance.

"At least one thing hasn't changed," Annie answered.

The three of them fell silent as they passed the building that had housed so many of their formative moments. Annie could almost see her younger self walking those front steps, laughing with friends who had long since scattered to the winds. She was a different person before her brother died. Now, she was like her hometown— gutted, and angry.

"I've driven through Indiana eight times since I joined the FBI," Ethan finally said, breaking the silence. "Never once took the exit for Cedarsburg. Even if it took an extra hour. I've avoided it."

Megan leaned forward, her face appearing between them in the rearview mirror. "I couldn't come back even if I wanted to. The Collective was watching." She paused, her expression darkening. "But I thought about it every day."

Annie understood all too well. This town held nothing but memories for them now.

"We've all ignored this place for fifteen years on purpose," Annie mused. "And now here we are, together."

"It changed as much as we have," Ethan said without humor. He pointed up a long street to the facade of an enormous manufacturing plant, its doors shuttered, parking lot empty. "The auto parts plant closed. Dad told me a few years ago when he got laid off. Thankfully he was close to retirement, but everyone else—"

"That plant employed half the town," Annie said, her heart aching for the loss. The plant had not made the cars themselves, but the pieces that had gone inside: transmissions, brakes, and safety equipment. People who worked there had felt they were doing something important. Annie remembered her high school's career day being filled with parents employed by the plant.

"Probably sent the jobs overseas," Megan said, shaking

her head. "The Collective tracks places like this, did you know that?" She whispered, leaning closer to the front seats. "They look for ways to own what's coming up for sale. They prey on people and places in vulnerable states—"

"Megan," Ethan said, swallowing hard. "Can you let me take in one piece of bad news at a time?"

"I'm only saying—"

"Let me process the collapse of my hometown before you start going on about an international shadow organization attacking America one location at a time—"

"Hey," Megan said, an edge to her tone. "It's not *my* fault if you can't handle the truth about life—"

"Oh, the truth? You think I can't handle the truth when I've been living it, every day—"

"So have *I!*"

"Guys!" Annie shouted, breaking up the impending fight. She had a feeling she'd be doing that a lot, now that the siblings were reunited. "Look. Over there, on the corner. They're watching us." Annie pointed to a group of young men standing on a street corner despite the late hour, smoking and watching their car pass with suspicious eyes. There was nothing for them here – no jobs, no future. Just the night, and whatever it offered.

The SUV turned a corner and entered a neighborhood, passing a row of houses Annie remembered as being well-kept, the pride of middle-class families. Now their paint peeled and porches sagged. One had a blue tarp stretched across a section of roof, a temporary fix that looked to have been in place for years.

"It's like someone forgot to tell the town it's supposed to keep living," Annie said, her voice soft with unexpected sadness.

Ethan nodded, his expression grim. "Americana, where are you?" He paused, noticing a sign in someone's front yard. It read: "I'm Voting for Bellows." Ethan let out a snort. "Looks like we came during election season. Can't believe Bellows is still the mayor. Is the guy ever going to leave?"

Their headlights swept across the town square, illuminating the gazebo where summer concerts had once been held. Annie remembered sitting on picnic blankets, watching local bands play while fireflies danced above the crowd. The memory felt both sharp and distant, like looking at an old photograph of strangers who happened to share your face. She noticed a banner hanging from the town square that read: "Vote Prim Rosington for Mayor. She Knows what You Need."

"Looks like Mayor Bellows does have some competition," Annie nodded at the banner. So much had changed, and yet—stayed the same.

"Even though I left home," Annie said suddenly, her eyes fixed on the passing landmarks of her youth, "it feels like it never really left *me*. Does that make sense?"

Her fingers brushed Ethan's, and they felt a spark – static from the dry air, but it jolted them nonetheless. Annie's words hung in the air, simple yet profound.

Ethan's face softened. "I know exactly what you mean, Hudson." He gestured at the town around them. "All these years, telling myself I was moving forward, but some part of me never left this place. Cedarsburg became the negative space around everything I built."

Megan leaned back, her face disappearing into the shadows of the backseat. "For me, it was the opposite. I was taken from here against my will, but I carried this town with me everywhere. It became a shrine I built in my mind – the last place I was truly free. I think I was afraid to come back because *I'm* not the same. But now I see: it's not either." Megan's voice broke with grief. All the time, she'd been dreaming of a place that didn't exist anymore.

Annie turned to look at her, struck by the poignancy of her words. Despite everything that had happened to them, despite all the years and distance, Cedarsburg still lived in them.

"We're late," Annie said, checking the clock again. "I hope LittleBug2000 is still there."

"Such a dumb screenname," Ethan said, shaking his head. But he accelerated slightly, the car humming beneath them as they left the residential area behind. In the distance, the water tower rose against the night sky, its silhouette familiar and ominous. Annie felt her heart rate increasing as they approached, adrenaline beginning to course through her veins.

This was it – the moment they might finally get answers about her brother's murder, about the Real Estate Ripper, about the organization that had stolen Megan's life and cast a shadow over their hometown. The water tower grew larger in the windshield, its metal legs splayed like a giant insect against the starry sky.

Annie found herself holding her breath as Ethan pulled onto the access road. Whatever awaited them at the top of that tower, she knew with absolute certainty that Cedarsburg would never again be just a place she used to live. It would become the setting for the next chapter of their story – one that had begun fifteen years ago and refused to end.

The water tower loomed before them, its metal structure gleaming dully in the moonlight. Annie checked her watch again – 12:25 AM. Their informant was late, or perhaps had already come and gone. *Maybe we missed them,* Annie thought but didn't say aloud. The gravel crunched beneath their feet as they circled the base of the tower, searching for any sign of LittleBug2000. A circle of tall hedges encompassed the water tower, their prickly, exposed branches discouraging trespassers. The wind whispered through the structure's supports, a lonesome sound that raised the hair on Annie's arms.

"No sign of anyone," Ethan said, his hand resting instinctively on his holster as he scanned the darkness surrounding them.

Megan stood with her back straight, alert and vigilant. "We should check the top. They might be waiting up there."

Annie nodded, her eyes already tracing the metal ladder that ran up the side of the tower. It had been years since she'd climbed it. When Annie was young, the water tower had been a popular gathering spot for teenagers looking to escape parental supervision, to drink cheap beer and carve their initials into the weathered metal railing. She wondered fleetingly if her own teenage markings remained somewhere up there, fossilized remnants of a different life.

"I'll go first," Megan said, already moving toward the ladder. She tested the lowest rung with her weight before beginning her ascent.

Ethan gestured for Annie to follow, positioning himself to come last. He hoisted her up with a hand placed a little too high on her leg. "Just like old times, Hudson," he said, his voice tight with tension despite the attempt at lightness.

Annie grasped the cold metal and began to climb, the familiar motions returning to her muscles as if she'd last done this weeks rather than years ago. The rungs felt smaller now, the distance between them shorter. The climb was easier physically but weighted with a dread she'd never felt as a carefree teenager.

The wind grew stronger as they ascended, whipping Annie's hair around her face. She kept her eyes focused upward, watching Megan's steady progress. The night spread out around them, Cedarsburg's dim lights scattered like fallen stars below. From this height, the town almost looked whole again, its decay hidden by darkness and distance.

When they reached the top, Annie pulled herself onto the

narrow walkway that circled the water tank. Megan was already moving around the perimeter, checking every shadow.

"No one's here," Megan called, her voice carried away by the wind.

Annie joined her at the railing, peering into the darkness beyond the tower. Their informant should have been here – this was the meeting place agreed upon in Russel's compound. Something had gone wrong. She felt it in the hollow pit forming in her stomach, in the way the night seemed to hold its breath around them.

Ethan completed his circuit of the platform, shaking his head. "Maybe they got spooked. Saw us coming and left."

Annie leaned further over the railing, searching the ground below for any sign of movement. The moonlight cast long shadows across the field surrounding the water tower, creating patterns that shifted and changed with the passing clouds.

That's when she saw it– a shape on the ground that didn't shift with the wind, a darkness too dense to be a shadow. A human form, splayed unnaturally on the earth below. It was tangled in a mess of bushes— hidden from view on the ground, but visible from overhead.

"No!" Annie pointed, her voice barely audible. "There! Someone's down there."

Megan and Ethan rushed to her side, following her gaze. For one frozen moment, they stood in silence, processing what they were seeing.

"They're not moving," Ethan said, the blood draining from his face. "Why didn't we see the body from the ground?"

"The body's too tangled in the brush," Annie said, swallowing hard.

Megan was already halfway to the ladder. "We need to get back down there. Now."

They descended in a rush, hands sliding against metal,

feet missing rungs in their haste. Annie's heart hammered in her chest, each beat counting down precious seconds. As soon as her feet touched the ground, she was running, following Megan toward the motionless figure.

The body lay face down, blonde hair spread over the hedges like pale seaweed on dark sand. It was a girl, small in stature, wearing jeans and a leather jacket. Even before they reached her, Annie could tell from the unnatural angle of her limbs that the fall had been devastating.

Megan reached her first, kneeling beside the still form and gently turning her over. The girl's face came into view – young, impossibly young, with a small silver ring in her nose that caught the moonlight. Annie felt the world tilt beneath her.

"Ethan," she whispered, her voice breaking. "She's a teenager. She's no older than we were when—"

"I know," Ethan nodded, his face grim with understanding.

Megan was already checking for a pulse, her fingers pressed against the girl's neck with desperate hope. Annie knew it was futile – the broken angles of the girl's body told the story clearly enough. No one survived a fall from that height. But watching Megan try anyway, her movements precise and determined, Annie felt a surge of affection for this woman who had survived so much yet still fought to save others.

"No pulse," Megan announced, immediately shifting to begin chest compressions. "Ethan, call it in. Now."

Ethan pulled out his phone, stepping away to report the death to local authorities, his FBI credentials ready to smooth the way. Annie heard his voice, steady and professional, providing coordinates and details with the controlled calm he'd perfected over years of similar calls.

Annie knelt on the girl's other side, her investigator's eye cataloging details even as her heart ached for this young life cut short. The victim's clothes were rumpled but good quality. She had chipped blue nail polish on her fingers. And there, visible now in the moonlight – bruises around her wrists, fresh marks that hadn't had time to darken.

"These bruises," Annie said, pointing. "There was a struggle before she fell."

Megan paused her futile CPR, following Annie's gaze. "You're right. Someone held her down." She traced the pattern of marks with her finger, hovering just above the skin. "Strong grip. Deliberate."

"Not suicide," Annie concluded quietly. "Murder." Annie sat back on her heels, devastated. "If I'd known our informant was a teenager I would have never—"

Ethan put a hand on Annie's shoulder. "You couldn't have known."

"Littlebug," Annie whispered, remembering the girl's screenname. "Of *course* I should have known. I was so rattled by coming home. I wanted answers— I overlooked the obvious—"

"Annie," Ethan said, gripping her by the shoulders and looking her straight in the eye. "There's only one way you can help her now. You're the only one who can bring her justice."

His words snapped Annie back into the present. She nodded and stood. Seeing that his work was done, Ethan took out his phone and called in the murder. As Megan resumed compressions, Annie began a careful examination of the girl's clothing, searching for any clue to her identity. The leather jacket had several pockets, and Annie methodically checked each one. In an inside pocket, her fingers closed around a folded piece of paper.

She withdrew it carefully, unfolding it under the beam of her phone's flashlight. Three words stared back at her, written in a hasty, angular scrawl:

"Welcome home, Annie."

The night air suddenly felt colder, wrapping around her

like a shroud. Annie's hands trembled slightly as she passed the note to Ethan, who had just finished his call.

"It's addressed to me," she said, her voice steadier than she felt. "This confirms she's our informant. He killed her for it."

Ethan read the note, his jaw tightening. "They knew we were coming."

Megan sat back on her heels, finally accepting that her revival efforts were useless. She took the note from Ethan, her expression darkening as she read it.

"The Real Estate Ripper," she said, the title like poison on her tongue. "Still here, all these years later."

Annie stared at the girl's face, committing every detail to memory. This was the person who might have held all the answers they sought— and she was just a kid. No older than fifteen. Now she was another victim, another body added to the tally of the killer who had taken Annie's brother.

"They killed her to send us a message," Annie said, tucking a strand of the girl's blonde hair back from her face with gentle fingers. "To taunt us."

In the distance, sirens began to wail – Ethan's call bringing the local authorities to the scene. Soon this quiet spot would be crawling with police, the girl's body taken away, evidence collected. But the real evidence, Annie knew, was the killer's message to her. This was personal.

She looked up at the water tower, then back down at the girl who had been dropped from it like a discarded doll. Over a decade ago, Annie had fled this town, trying to outrun the horror of her brother's murder. But now, she had come home.

"We'll find him," Annie said. And with that— her investigation began.

CHAPTER SIX

THE SHERIFF

SHERIFF HOMESTADDER GLANCED up at the wall clock, its steady ticking a counterpoint to the quiet hum of the station. His coffee had gone cold an hour ago, but he sipped it anyway, grimacing at the bitter taste. Fifty-eight years had taught him not to waste things, even bad coffee. The night shift was always quiet in Cedarsburg— most nights, anyway. He rubbed his eyes with the heels of his hands, feeling every minute of the day's twenty hours weighing on his shoulders. The brown uniform still fit well enough, though the belt cinched a bit tighter these days.

He stood, stretching his back until something popped, and walked to the window. Cedarsburg at night was a collection of scattered lights, most businesses long closed, most citizens long asleep. His town. His responsibility. He'd been Sheriff for over twenty years now, watched children grow up and leave, watched businesses close and open and close again. Watched the slow decay that had eaten away at the town's edges like rust on an old car. And he was in charge of it all— the mess that lay before him.

"Sheriff?"

The voice came from behind him, soft and wavering. He

turned to see Marjorie, the night dispatcher, standing in his office doorway. Her face was pale, her eyes rimmed with red. His stomach tightened— he knew that look. Bad news.

"What is it, Marjorie?" he asked, already reaching for his jacket.

"Call just came in. There's been—" her voice caught, and she swallowed hard. "There's been a death at the water tower. It's Brenda Welsh."

The name hit like a physical blow. Brenda Welsh. Fifteen years old. Blonde hair, small, with that little silver nose ring her father hated. The computer whiz who'd helped set up the station's new filing system last summer. He'd seen her just yesterday, walking home from school, backpack slung over one shoulder.

"What happened?" he asked, keeping his voice steady even as his mind raced.

"They're saying she fell," Marjorie said, a tear tracking down her lined face. "But the FBI is already there. And some others. Strangers in town, asking questions."

Homestadder's hands stilled on his jacket. *FBI.* That was new. They'd never cared much before about what happened in his little domain.

"FBI?" he repeated, careful to keep his tone merely curious, professional. "Did they identify themselves properly?"

"Yes, sir. Agent Ethan Beckett. Said he happened to be first on the scene. There was a woman with him. Private investigator, according to the officer who called it in. And another woman they didn't get a name for."

Three strangers at the water tower. Three strangers finding Brenda's body.

"Should I call the Mayor?" Marjorie asked, her eyes wide. "I think he'd want to know, don't you?"

Sheriff Homestadder bristled at the question. Although the Mayor was technically in charge of Cedarsburg, the Sheriff liked to consider himself the real protector of the town.

This place was *his* house, as far as he was concerned. It was *his* job, as Sheriff, to protect, serve, and administer justice. Still, it was necessary to play nice, sometimes.

"Give him a call," the Sheriff relented. "I'll head out there now," he said, slipping his arms into his jacket. The familiar weight settled across his shoulders, a uniform within a uniform. Authority upon authority.

"Such a shame," Marjorie said, wiping her eyes. "Her poor parents. First that trouble with her brother running off to the city last year, and now this."

"Life isn't fair, Marjorie," Homestadder said, his voice softening. He reached into his desk drawer, fingers finding the pack of cigarettes he kept there. "Not in this town, not anywhere."

He tapped one cigarette out and placed it between his lips. The ritual of it calmed him— the weight of the filter, the faint taste of tobacco. He flicked his lighter, the small flame illuminating his office in a brief, golden glow.

"Sheriff, you know you're not supposed to smoke in here," Marjorie said, but the rebuke was halfhearted. She'd been telling him the same thing for years.

Homestadder took a long drag, feeling the smoke fill his lungs. The first cigarette of the crisis— a habit he'd developed over decades of bad nights. He'd tried to quit once, but only made it three weeks before a particularly horrific domestic assault sent him right back to the corner store for a fresh pack.

"Who can resist their vices, in a world like this?" he said, exhaling a plume of smoke toward the ceiling. He considered the world as he saw: a place where power was all that mattered, and people were guided by their worst impulses. "A man's gotta cope somehow."

Marjorie sighed, a sound of familiar resignation. "I'll let them know you're on your way," she said, turning back toward the dispatch desk.

Alone again, Homestadder moved to his filing cabinet,

opening the bottom drawer where he kept his service weapon for night shifts. The gun felt heavy in his hands— heavier than usual, somehow. He checked it methodically, muscle memory guiding his fingers, before holstering it at his hip.

FBI. Strangers. A dead girl at the water tower.

The edges of something larger were taking shape, a darkness gathering at the periphery of his carefully ordered world. He'd seen it coming for weeks now— little signs, small disruptions. The anonymous tips about drug activity that led nowhere. The unusual number of out-of-state license plates passing through town. The increased chatter on channels that should have been quiet.

And now Brenda Welsh was dead.

Homestadder took another drag from his cigarette, holding the smoke in his lungs until it burned.

He gathered his keys and wallet, checking that his badge was properly displayed on his uniform.

The station was quiet as he walked through, just the soft hum of computers and the distant sound of a radio from the break room. Night shift was always skeletal— Marjorie at dispatch, a deputy on patrol, and himself. Small town budgets didn't allow for much more.

"I've notified Deputy Carnes," Marjorie said as he passed her desk. "He's heading to the scene from the south side of town."

"Good," Homestadder nodded. "Let the coroner know we'll need him too."

"Already done," she said. Her efficiency was one of the reasons he'd kept her on long past when most would have retired. That, and her uncomplicated loyalty. "Be careful out there, Sheriff."

"Always am," he replied, offering her what he knew was a reassuring smile. The mask of concern and competence slipping into place as easily as breathing.

The night air was cool against his face as he stepped

outside, a welcome change from the station's stale heat. His cigarette glowed orange in the darkness as he took a final drag before flicking it away, watching the ember arc through the air and disappear. He climbed into his patrol car, the leather seat creaking beneath him. As he started the engine, a sense of calm settled over him—the calm that always came with purpose, with having a clear objective. Whatever storm was brewing, he'd weather it as he had all the others. He'd protect the town. Protect the order of things. Protect the secrets buried beneath Cedarsburg's quiet streets.

He pulled away from the station, lights flashing but siren silent. No need to wake the town just yet. They'd all know soon enough what had happened at the water tower. News traveled fast in Cedarsburg, carried on whispers and worried looks, spreading from house to house like fire through dry grass.

And fire, Homestadder knew, could be controlled if you knew where to set the backburns.

CHAPTER SEVEN

THE MAYOR

MAYOR BELLOWS SAT in the leather chair that had belonged to three mayors before him, staring at the portrait of Cedarsburg's founder that hung above the fireplace. The old bastard looked stern in his painted form, like he was judging every decision made in this study for the past hundred years. Bellows wondered what the founder would think of the town now—the shuttered businesses, the young people leaving in droves, the slow decay that no amount of ribbon-cutting ceremonies could hide. He'd kept this town alive, hadn't he? That had to count for something.

The study smelled of old wood and leather polish, scents that were supposed to convey authority and tradition. Bellows had learned early in his political career that appearances mattered more than substance, that people wanted to believe their leaders worked in rooms that looked like this— dignified, serious, important. The reality was messier. The reality was compromise after compromise, each one a little easier to justify than the last.

He was sixty-two now, his silver hair carefully styled to look distinguished rather than old. He wore his usual white button-down shirt even at this late hour, tucked into his slacks, though he'd removed his tie hours ago. The baseball cap from the high school team sat on the desk beside him— he'd worn it to the game last Friday, making sure to shake hands with every player afterward. One of the people, that was his brand. Self-made businessman who never forgot where he came from.

The desk phone rang, shattering the quiet of the study. Bellows glanced at the clock on the mantel—nearly one in the morning. Nothing good came from phone calls at this hour. He picked up the receiver, already steeling himself for whatever crisis was about to unfold.

"Mayor Bellows," he said, keeping his voice steady and professional.

"Mayor, it's Marjorie from the Sheriff's office." Her voice was tight with distress. "I'm sorry to call so late, but there's been an incident. A death."

Bellows's stomach dropped, though his expression remained carefully neutral. Years of practice had taught him to control his face even when no one was watching. "Who?" he asked simply.

"Brenda Welsh," Marjorie said, and he heard her voice catch on the name. "The Sheriff is on his way to the scene now. They found her at the water tower."

Brenda Welsh. Fifteen years old. He'd seen her at the town hall meeting last month, sitting in the back with her laptop, taking notes. Smart kid. Too smart, maybe. His mind immediately began cataloging the implications— her family, the community reaction, the press coverage. And then the bigger concern, the one that made his chest tighten: what had she been doing at the water tower at midnight?

"What happened?" he asked, reaching for the pen on his desk. Old habit—take notes, stay organized, maintain control.

"She fell from the tower— or was pushed—" Marjorie replied. "But Mayor, there's more. There are strangers in town.

FBI, for one— and a private investigator, a woman. They were the ones who found the body."

The pen stilled in Bellows's hand. FBI. Private investigator. Strangers asking questions. This was worse than a simple tragedy. This was the beginning of something he'd feared for years, ever since that night when the Real Estate Ripper had killed Joshua Hudson and taken Megan Beckett. Ever since he'd made the deal that had secured his first election and bound him to The Collective.

"I see," he said, his voice carefully measured. "And the Sheriff is handling it?"

"Yes, sir. He's on his way to the scene now. I just thought you should know, given—" she paused, choosing her words carefully. "Given the election and all."

Election season. Of course. Bellows allowed himself a small, bitter smile that Marjorie couldn't see. A girl was dead and the first concern was political optics. But that was the world they lived in, wasn't it? The world he'd helped create, where everything was about maintaining appearances while the rot spread underneath.

"You did the right thing calling me," he said, already standing, already moving toward the closet where he kept a jacket. "I'll need to go see the family tomorrow. First thing. They'll need to know the town is here for them."

"Of course, Mayor." Marjorie's relief was audible. She wanted someone else to take charge, to tell her this would all work out. "Should I notify anyone else? I mean, should we tell—"

She didn't finish the sentence, but Bellows knew exactly who she meant. Prim Rosington. His opponent in the upcoming election. The Yale-educated activist who thought she could save Cedarsburg with economic theory and democratic socialism. The woman who had no idea what it actually took to keep a town running when the jobs had left and the money had dried up and the only people offering help came with strings attached.

Bellows gritted his teeth, feeling the familiar surge of frustration that came whenever he thought about Prim. She was young—early thirties—and full of idealistic nonsense about working people and resistance. She had no idea what she was walking into, what forces she'd be up against if she somehow managed to win. But it was no matter. Mayor Bellows was going to win again, just like he did every election cycle.

Because he had a secret weapon. One that no one could discover.

Still, appearances mattered. Protocol mattered. And if he didn't suggest notifying his opponent, someone would notice and wonder why.

"Of course she should know," he said, forcing warmth into his voice even as he wanted to throw the phone across the room. "Prim should be informed. This affects the whole community, not just one side or the other."

"I'll call her office first thing in the morning," Marjorie said.

"Actually," Bellows said, an idea forming even as he spoke, "I'll be heading out to the scene myself right now. To comfort the family, of course. And also to talk to the press, if they show up." He paused, letting the implication hang in the air. "Someone needs to be there to represent the town's leadership. To show that we care, that we're taking this seriously."

He could practically hear Marjorie nodding on the other end of the line. "That's very good of you, Mayor. I'm sure the family will appreciate it."

"It's what we do," Bellows said, the words automatic after years of practice. "We take care of our own. I'll head out now. Thank you for calling, Marjorie."

He hung up before she could respond, already shrugging into his jacket. The baseball cap went on his head— folksy, approachable Mayor Bellows, the man who never put on airs.

He checked his reflection in the window, adjusting the cap to the right angle. Concerned but composed. Accessible but authoritative.

But his mind was racing beneath the carefully constructed exterior. FBI meant federal involvement. Private investigator meant someone was digging into things that should stay buried. And Brenda Welsh dead at the water tower meant someone had sent a message, or silenced a voice, or both.

He thought about the girl he'd seen at the town hall meeting, her fingers flying over her laptop keyboard. What had she been researching? What had she found?

Certainly not his secret. She couldn't have.

He'd run on a platform of safety, of law and order, of bringing stability back to Cedarsburg. And he'd won. And he'd kept winning. And the town had stayed safe, hadn't it? No more murders. No more terror. Just the slow, manageable decline of economic forces beyond anyone's control.

That was the story he'd told himself for years, That he'd chosen the lesser evil. That someone else would have made worse choices. That he'd protected his town the only way he could.

But standing in his study at one in the morning, with a dead girl at the water tower and FBI agents asking questions, the story felt thinner than usual. The justifications rang hollow in his own ears.

Bellows moved to the bookshelf and pressed the hidden latch he'd had installed five years ago. A section swung open, revealing a small safe. His fingers worked the combination automatically—his wedding anniversary, though Mary had been dead for three years now.

If she knew what he was up to, she'd die all over again, he thought.

He pulled out the phone, holding it in his palm like it might bite him. This was the phone he used to contact *them.*

The people who'd ensured his political survival and demanded certain concessions in return.

Small prices to pay, he'd thought. Manageable compromises. And in return, Cedarsburg had stayed functional. The schools stayed open. The hospital kept running. The police force stayed funded. He'd kept the town alive when it should have died along with the auto parts plant.

Bellows stared at the burner phone, his thumb hovering over the power button. If he made this call, he was admitting the situation had escalated beyond his control. If he made this call, he was acknowledging that the careful balance he'd maintained throughout his tenure was about to collapse.

But if he didn't make the call—

He powered on the phone and dialed the number he'd memorized years ago. It rang once, twice, three times. He almost hoped no one would answer, that he could tell himself he'd tried and failed to make contact. But on the fourth ring, someone picked up.

"Yes?" The voice was neutral, giving nothing away. It was never the same voice twice, never the same person.

"It's Bellows," he said, his voice low even though he was alone in the study. "We have a situation in Cedarsburg."

"We're aware," the voice replied. "Can you handle it?"

The question stung, implying that he might not be. That after so many years of faithful service, they still doubted his ability to manage his own town.

"Well, there *are* federal agents here," Bellows said, unable to keep the edge from his voice. "FBI. And a private investigator. They're going to meddle, I'm certain. There's the death of a young girl to consider—"

Silence on the other end. Bellows could hear his own heartbeat in the quiet, feel the sweat starting to form on his palms despite the cool air of the study.

"Make sure they think it was an accident," the voice on the other end of the line told him.

Then, the line went dead.

Bellows powered off the burner phone and returned it to the safe, closing the bookshelf panel behind it. The study looked the same as it had before the phone call—dignified wood paneling, stern founder staring down from his portrait, leather chair that had belonged to better men.

As he headed for the door, one thought echoed in his mind, the words he'd use later when this all came crashing down, when the FBI agents and the private investigator uncovered what he'd been hiding from the day he was sworn in as Mayor:

It's all about to come crashing down. Everything.

But for now, he had a role to play. The mayor who cared. The leader who showed up in times of crisis. The man who'd kept Cedarsburg alive, no matter the cost.

Bellows walked out of the study and into the night, toward the water tower where a dead girl waited to be mourned by a town that had no idea how deep the rot really went.

CHAPTER EIGHT

THE ACTIVIST

PRIM ROSINGTON SWIRLED the amber whiskey in her glass, watching it catch the light from her desk lamp as she stared at the campaign poster propped against the wall. It wasn't quite right—the font too stern, the colors too muted—but it would have to do. Prim had spent thirty-three years preparing for this moment, many of those years away from Cedarsburg, acquiring the education and connections needed to return and save this town from itself. The whiskey burned pleasantly as she took another sip. Prim liked drinking whiskey because of the irony in the selection— whiskey had been the drink of choice for powerful men for generations. Now, Prim liked to think she was going to become a powerful man. Her eyes drifted to the Yale diploma hanging in its heavy frame, the credentials that separated her from every other mayoral candidate in the town's history. Credentials that, to her constant frustration, impressed some townsfolk and alienated others.

Prim was living with her parents. Their living room had become her campaign headquarters over the past three months. It wasn't glamorous. The space had all the charm of an empty warehouse. Stacks of flyers promising "Real Change for Working Families" occupied one corner, next to boxes of buttons sporting her deliberately simple slogan: "Prim for Progress." She had agonized over that slogan for weeks, wanting something that conveyed both strength and accessibility. Something that wouldn't make the old-timers bristle at words like "socialist" while still signaling to younger voters that she understood their struggles. Prim felt disdain at the fact she had to use her childhood home to launch her campaign— she worried that working out of her parents' house made her look like a novice. Still, she reminded herself, Jeff Bezos had started Amazon in his father's garage. Prim was no different— entitled to no less benefit of the doubt.

A framed photograph of Prim shaking hands with the head of the local steelworkers union sat prominently on the mantel, positioned directly across from the couch where her army of interns would circle up for meetings. Next to it, a candid shot of her serving meals at the community kitchen, her sleeves rolled up, her expression serious but engaged. She remembered the photographer asking her to smile more. She had refused. Hunger wasn't a photo opportunity.

"Staged authenticity," she murmured to herself, the irony not lost on her as she adjusted the photograph's angle slightly. Everything featured in Prim's campaign had been carefully curated to tell a story: local girl makes good, comes home to fight for the forgotten. It wasn't untrue, exactly. But like any good narrative, it emphasized certain elements and minimized others.

Prim's stockinged feet sank into the plush carpet as she moved to the window, parting the curtains to look out at the neighborhood street. Colonial facades blinked back at her, unkempt lawns and chain-link fences marring classic architecture. The houses needed work. This neighborhood had been so nice when Prim was a child: how things had changed.

Her phone rang, startling her from her thoughts. The display showed "Marcus" with a small star next to it— her campaign adviser, the star indicating priority. She set down her whiskey and answered.

"It's nearly midnight, Marcus," she said, her voice carrying the slight professional crispness she had developed during her years in corporate consulting. A tone she now worked to modulate when speaking to constituents.

"I know, and I'm sorry," Marcus replied, the edge in his voice immediately setting her on alert. "But you need to turn on Channel 7 right now. There's been an incident at the water tower."

Prim reached for the remote, keeping the phone pressed to her ear. "What kind of incident?" She hit the power button, the television flickering to life with the low hum she found increasingly irritating these days. She lowered the volume preemptively.

"They're calling it an accident, but there's already FBI on scene," Marcus said. "A local girl. Teenager."

The screen filled with the familiar image of Cedarsburg's water tower, now surrounded by police vehicles, their lights painting the night in rhythmic flashes of red and blue. A reporter stood in the foreground, her expression appropriately solemn as she delivered the breaking news.

"I'm at the scene where just hours ago, the body of fifteen-year-old Brenda Welsh was discovered at the base of Cedarsburg's water tower," the reporter was saying. "Authorities have not yet determined whether this was an accident or if foul play was involved."

Prim felt her mouth go dry. Brenda Welsh. The computer science prodigy from the high school who'd helped set up Prim's campaign website. Quiet, serious girl with a silver nose ring and a talent for finding information that wasn't readily available. Information about Cedarsburg's budget discrepancies, about Mayor Bellows' questionable allocation of federal infrastructure funds. Information that had proved invaluable to Prim's campaign.

"Wow," she whispered, not sounding at all surprised, momentarily forgetting Marcus was still on the line.

"Yeah," Marcus replied. "You won't believe it but Mayor Bellow's told the Sheriff's office to let us know. Surprising, isn't it?"

"How kind of him," Prim said sardonically.

The camera panned across the scene, showing Sheriff Homestadder speaking with a man whose stance and bearing screamed federal agent. Behind them, crime scene technicians moved with deliberate care around the area where the body had been found.

"This is going to dominate local news for days," Marcus continued. "We need to decide how to respond—"

Prim barely heard him. Her attention had fixed on the screen where the camera had briefly zoomed in on a particular patch of ground near the water tower's base. Muddy footprints, being photographed by a technician. The recent rain had turned the area around the tower into a tableau of evidence, footprints preserved in the soft earth like fossils.

Something cold and heavy settled in Prim's stomach, a sensation entirely separate from the whiskey.

"Prim? Are you still there?" Marcus asked, his voice faint against the sudden rushing in her ears.

"Yes," she said automatically. "I'm here. Listen, I need to call you back. I'll consider our response options and touch base in the morning."

"But we should really—"

"In the morning, Marcus," she said firmly, ending the call before he could protest further.

Prim muted the television but left the images playing as she walked to her front door, a sudden urgency driving her movements.

Her heels sat on the mat by the door where she had kicked them off earlier— expensive leather pumps she had worn to a community forum that afternoon. The right heel was entirely clean, but the left... Prim stared at it, her breath catching.

The back of the left heel was caked in mud, now dried to a dark brown crust that flaked slightly at the edges.

Mud that matched exactly what she was seeing on her television screen.

"No, no, no," she whispered, grabbing the shoe and examining it more closely.

Just hours ago, Prim had been at the water-tower. And now, what she had done there was about to cost her a future she'd been working toward for years.

There was only one solution, Prim decided. Footprints could be explained in the aftermath. She needed to return to the scene of the crime. She needed to go back— wearing these shoes— and she needed *everyone* to see her.

She slid on the heels and grabbed her purse, slipping her keys out of the front pocket. She was careful not to make too much noise— she didn't want to wake up her parents, who were asleep in the other room, proud of their daughter and blissfully unaware of what she had done.

As she opened the door, her cell phone buzzed on the counter—a text message. With shaking hands, she picked it up.

A message from a blocked number read, simply:

You passed your first test.

A chill ran down Prim's spine. She glanced back at her campaign poster—"Prim for Progress"—and let out a hollow laugh that echoed in the empty apartment. Progress. What a clean, simple word for the dirty, complicated truth.

CHAPTER NINE

THE PASTOR

PASTOR TIM ERICKSON slept fitfully in the rectory adjacent to his amphitheater church, the sheets tangled around his legs like sins he couldn't escape. His dreams were fragmented— faces from his congregation looking up at him with adoration, the Mayor's firm handshake after his endorsement speech, the blueprints for the new expansion spread across his desk. He was planning an expansion of the church that would help so many people find their way to a better life. The Pastor was obsessed with the renovations, and found himself tossing and turning at night, thinking about how long the construction would take, and what it would mean for the community. That's the kind of person Pastor Erickson was: passionate, to a fault.

The buzzing of his phone on the nightstand sliced through his troubled sleep, illuminating the darkness with its cold blue glow. The Pastor didn't mind. He'd only been half-asleep, as it was.

Tim's eyes snapped open. The buzzing continued, insistent and demanding. He glanced at the digital clock— 2:17 AM. Nothing good ever came from calls at this hour. Beside him, his wife stirred, her breathing changing rhythm as she hovered at the edge of wakefulness.

"Shhh, it's okay," he whispered, gently placing a hand on her shoulder. "Go back to sleep."

Lisa murmured something unintelligible and turned away, pulling the covers up around her neck. Tim watched her for a moment in the dim light. She'd been up since five with the kids, making breakfast, handling school drop-offs, running the church's community outreach program, then dinner and bedtime routines. She deserved her rest.

The phone buzzed again. Tim slipped from the bed with practiced quiet, the hardwood floor cool beneath his bare feet. He grabbed the phone and his robe, padding silently into the hallway before answering. The hallway was dark save for a small nightlight near the children's rooms— a soft, golden cross that cast elongated shadows along the wall. Tim opened a pocket door and stepped into his office.

"Hello?" he whispered. He paused, waiting for the voice on the other end. The voice asked him for a favor. One he didn't want to do.

"I can't," he said simply, shaking his head. "I mean— I *won't*. Not anymore."

There was a long pause on the other line. Then, Tim's breath caught in his throat as the person he was speaking to delivered terrible news. News that changed everything.

"Brenda?" Tim asked, horrified. He could picture her clearly— quiet, serious, always taking notes during his sermons. Her parents sat in the third row every Sunday, her father's hand always first in the air when the collection plate came around. "Her parents are patrons."

The Welshes had been among the first to pledge to the building fund. They believed in his vision for Renewed Hope, believed that the amphitheater would revitalize their dying town, bring people back to both God and Cedarsburg. They trusted him.

Tim's free hand clenched into a fist, nails digging crescents into his palm. He had entered the ministry to help people, to guide them toward light and hope.

"I'll head out there right now," the Pastor said, already exiting the office. He hung up the phone, sliding it into his pocket as he emerged into the quiet hallway. He moved back through the bedroom, pausing at Lisa's side of the bed. She slept peacefully, one hand tucked beneath her pillow, the other outstretched toward where he should be. He leaned down and pressed a gentle kiss to her forehead. She stirred slightly but didn't wake.

"I'm sorry," he whispered, hoping the apology would cover a number of unspoken things— all of them a greater offense than leaving in the middle of the night.

He grabbed his coat from the hook by the bedroom door, the leather cool against his skin. The weight of his keys in the pocket felt heavier than usual.

Outside the rectory, the night air was crisp and clear, the stars spread across the sky like witnesses to his shame. The amphitheater church rose before him, its modern lines cutting a sharp silhouette against the darkness. The construction was nearly complete—a monument to faith, he'd called it in his sermons. The construction of the amphitheatre meant everything to the Pastor— and he intended to see it through, no matter the cost.

Tim slipped into his car, the engine roaring to life in the quiet night.

The road stretched out before him, dark and uncertain. *Life is like that*, Tim reminded himself. A long, narrow road that one must walk by faith, not by sight.

CHAPTER TEN

THE REALTOR

ANOTHER LISTING. Another day with no leads.

Zara Kane prided herself on being both the best and the *worst* realtor in Cedarsburg. She laughed to herself as clicked through yet another listing that wasn't selling, uploading new photographs in the hopes some digital staging would make a difference. Zara was worse simply because the marketplace in this area had tanked— single family homes weren't moving, and if you hired her to sell your house, you'd probably be disappointed. But she was the best because she tried hard, no matter what. She hired the best photographers, ran a strong mailing list, and even came into the office late on nights like tonight. Knowing she was doing all she could Zara peace, and she held the local record for commercial property sales— an area in which she'd had some success. Of course, Zara had also had more *help* being the best than she liked to admit. But Zara tried very hard not to think about that.

Zara Kane was about to check one of those commercial listings when the television murmured something that made her fingers freeze above the keyboard. She had the TV on for company more than anything else—the office felt too empty this late at night, the silence pressing in from the dark windows like an unwelcome visitor. The local news played at a volume just loud enough to remind her she wasn't completely alone, but she rarely paid attention to the anchor's droning voice or the rotating carousel of small-town tragedies. Tonight, though, one word cut through her concentration like a knife: "teenager."

Her eyes flicked to the screen mounted on the wall opposite her desk. The blue glow reflected in the dark window behind it, creating a ghost image of the broadcast. A reporter stood in front of Cedarsburg's water tower, her face professionally somber in the portable lights that had been set up around the scene.

"—found at the base of the water tower just after midnight," the reporter was saying. "Police have not yet determined whether this was an accident or if foul play was involved."

Zara's hand moved to the remote, fingers fumbling for the volume button. The reporter's voice grew louder, filling the small office.

"The victim has been identified as fifteen-year-old Brenda Welsh, a sophomore at Cedarsburg High School—"

The remote slipped from Zara's fingers, clattering against the desk. Her other hand flew to her mouth, pressing hard against her lips as if she could physically push back the gasp that escaped anyway. When something like this happened in Cedarsburg, Zara paid attention.

The camera panned across the scene, and Zara leaned forward, her dark eyes narrowing as she studied every detail. Police vehicles. Crime scene tape. Sheriff Homestadder's familiar silhouette. And there—her breath caught again—two people she hadn't seen in over a decade but would have recognized anywhere.

Annie Hudson stood near the water tower's base, her posture rigid, speaking with the Sheriff. Even from this distance, even through the grainy news footage, Zara could see the intensity in her stance. Beside Annie stood a man—tall, FBI written all over him in the cut of his suit and the way he held himself. Zara squinted at the screen. The resemblance was unmistakable. Ethan Beckett. It had to be.

"Jesus," Zara whispered, pulling her hand away from her mouth. Her fingers were shaking. She pressed them flat against the desk, trying to still the tremor, but it only spread up her arms and into her shoulders.

She and Annie had gone to the same high school, though they'd never been close because Zara was older than Annie and in a different grade. Annie had been the quiet, brilliant one—always reading, always knowing the answers, always a little separate from everyone else. Zara had been more social, more concerned with fitting in, with being liked. They'd existed in different orbits, intersecting only in the mandatory ways that small-town high school enforced.

But Zara had known Annie's brother. In fact, she'd had a huge crush on him. The kind of childhood coming-of-age crush that movies were made about.

Joshua Hudson had been in Zara's graduating class, a few years ahead of Annie. He'd been kind to everyone, the sort of person who remembered your name and asked about your day and actually seemed to care about the answer. When Zara had nervously announced her plans to go into real estate during their senior year career presentations, Joshua had been one of the few who'd offered genuine encouragement instead of the usual small-town skepticism about big dreams. He'd been planning the same path and, if Zara was being honest, she'd only started showing an interest in the field because she hoped she'd run into Joshua. Over time, she'd grown a genuine love for the business. But it had all started because of him.

The memory of his murder hit her like a physical blow.

Zara pushed back from her desk, the wheels of her chair squeaking against the linoleum floor. She stood abruptly, then sat back down just as quickly, her legs suddenly unreliable. The television continued its report, but she barely heard it now. Her mind was fifteen years in the past, remembering the fear that had gripped Cedarsburg like a vise.

The Real Estate Ripper. That's what the media had called him. Four murders across the Midwest, all connected to real estate transactions. Victims found in empty houses, open houses, properties for sale. Joshua had been showing a house. Just doing his job. Just trying to help someone find a home. And then—

Zara's stomach churned. She had been twenty-two years old, fresh out of her real estate certification program, when Joshua Hudson was murdered. The news had spread through town like wildfire. She remembered sitting in this very office— though it had belonged to her mentor then, not to her—and seriously considering throwing away her newly minted license. Finding a different career. Anything that didn't involve walking into empty houses alone, didn't involve trusting strangers, didn't involve the constant low-level terror that maybe, just maybe, you'd be next. She would never see Joshua's smile again. Never have an excuse to call him about a listing. It was a simple childhood crush that made her get into real estate, and — even though she'd realized by now nothing would come of her wanting— the death of her love made her want to leave.

But she hadn't quit. The Real Estate Ripper had moved on. Or stopped. Or been caught—the stories varied, and Zara had been too afraid to dig deeper. She'd stayed in real estate because it was the only thing she'd ever been good at, the only future she'd ever imagined for herself. She had no other degree— what else was she going to do? Work at the five and dime? She'd learned to compartmentalize the fear, to push it down into a dark corner of her mind where it couldn't interfere with her work.

And now Brenda Welsh was dead at the water tower, and

Annie Hudson was back in Cedarsburg, and Zara's hands wouldn't stop shaking.

She forced herself to look back at the television. The reporter had moved on to interviewing a neighbor, but Zara's attention remained fixed on the background, where she could still see movement near the crime scene. Annie and Ethan were talking to another woman now—dark hair, leather jacket, someone Zara didn't recognize.

Zara's eyes drifted to her computer screen, where the Henderson listing still waited for her updates. The cursor blinked in the description field, patient and accusatory. She minimized that window and opened her email instead, her fingers moving almost without conscious thought.

She knew what she needed to do. What she was supposed to do.

With mechanical precision, she navigated to her MLS database and pulled up the search parameters. Location: near the water tower. Status: active listings. Her results populated immediately—she'd been watching this area for months now, ever since the instructions had come through.

There it was. A parcel of undeveloped land, three acres, zoned commercial. Prime real estate, if you didn't know that a teenage girl had just been found dead within sight of its borders. The listing photos showed scrubby grass and a rusted chain-link fence. Nothing remarkable. Nothing worth killing for.

But Zara had learned that worth was relative. That value existed in dimensions she couldn't see, in networks she didn't understand, in purposes that were deliberately kept hidden from people like her.

Her hand trembled as she clicked to open the full listing. The details loaded slowly, each piece of information appearing line by line as if the computer itself was reluctant to reveal them. Owner: LLC registered out of state. Price:

deliberately set just high enough to discourage casual buyers. Days on market: 47.

Zara had been instructed to forward all new listings in certain areas to a specific email address before they went public. This listing was different—it had been public for weeks—but the instructions had been clear about anomalies. About situations that might require... attention.

A dead girl at the water tower definitely qualified as an anomaly.

She clicked the forward button, her breath coming shallow and quick. The ghost email address auto-populated in the "To" field—she'd used it so many times it was saved in her contacts now, though she'd never received a single reply from it. The address was generic, forgettable: . Could have been anything. Could have been nobody.

Zara knew better.

In the subject line, she typed: "a problem?"

Her finger hovered over the send button.

She'd only been trying to make a living. To survive in a dying town where opportunities were scarce and competition was fierce. When the offers had started coming—forward listings to this email, nothing more, easy money for simple work—she'd been grateful. Suspicious, yes, but grateful enough to override the suspicion.

Now a girl was dead, and Zara's gratitude had curdled into something that tasted like bile in the back of her throat.

She hit send.

The email whooshed away into the digital void, and Zara immediately pulled up her inbox, refreshing it compulsively. Nothing. She refreshed again. Still nothing. The cursor blinked at her from the empty inbox, mocking her expectation of a response.

On the television, the news had moved on to the weather.

Five minutes passed. Then ten. Her leg bounced under the desk, a nervous habit she'd never been able to break. She picked up a pen, put it down, picked it up again. Clicked refresh.

Nothing.

She pulled out her phone, checking the email there instead, as if the message might arrive on one device but not the other. The same empty inbox stared back at her. She refreshed. Nothing.

The office suddenly felt too small, the walls pressing in. Zara stood, paced to the window, looked out at the dark street. Cedarsburg at night was a collection of amber street-lights and closed storefronts. Dead space. Empty space. The kind of town people left and never came back to.

Except Annie Hudson had come back. And Ethan Beckett. And now a girl was dead, and nobody was answering Zara's email, and the silence felt more threatening than any response could have been.

Zara grabbed her purse, slinging it over her shoulder with sudden decision. She needed to see for herself that the ghosts of her past had really come home. With that, she headed for the elevator, which would deliver her to the nearly-empty parking lot where her car lay waiting. It was a short drive to the water tower: Zara could get to either side of town in five minutes or less. She left her office abandoned— lights still on — the TV blaring in the background like an urgent alarm, shouting over and over— *this one, Zara, you cannot outrun.*

CHAPTER ELEVEN

THE WATER TOWER looked different under crime scene lights— harsher, somehow, its white paint too bright against the black sky. Annie stood at the edge of the police tape, watching technicians photograph muddy footprints that led nowhere useful. The air smelled of wet earth and the particular chemical tang of portable floodlights burning too hot. Somewhere behind her, Ethan was speaking quietly into his phone, his FBI credentials already displayed to the deputy who'd tried to turn them away.

Annie's eyes tracked across the scene with methodical precision. The body had been removed, but the impression remained—a dark shape in the hedges where Brenda Welsh had landed. Around the tower's base, evidence markers dotted the ground like yellow flowers, each one flagging something the investigators deemed important.

The wind picked up, carrying voices from the growing crowd of onlookers beyond the outer perimeter. News traveled fast in small towns. Death traveled faster.

"Annie," Ethan said, appearing at her elbow. He'd finished his call. "Sheriff's on his way over. Looks thrilled to see us."

Annie turned to follow his gaze. Sheriff Homestadder was

indeed approaching, his brown uniform crisp despite the late hour, his expression carefully neutral in that way that meant he was working very hard not to show what he was actually thinking. He was a ghost to Annie. He had assisted with the investigation of her brother's death fifteen years ago, and had come up short. She would have found it in herself to hate him, except that she noticed how much he had aged in the last decade. Time had not been kind to the Sheriff. Still, she recognized his walk— measured, deliberate, the gait of someone who'd spent decades establishing authority.

Megan stood a few feet away, her leather jacket zipped to her throat, hands in her pockets. Annie wondered if Megan knew this was the man who'd failed to find her.

The Sheriff reached them. Up close, Annie could see the lines around his eyes, the grey threaded through his brown hair.

"Folks," he said, the word falling flat and formal. His eyes moved from Annie to Ethan to Megan, assessing each in turn. "My God. Is that—."

"Yes," Annie said, understanding at once that he recognized her.

The Sheriff scanned her, something feral and broken in his eyes. "I see your Dad every now and then, Annie. Not much to say but I try."

"I appreciate that," Annie said, swallowing hard.

"They sent me over saying it was you who found the body but they must have made a mistake—."

"No mistake," Ethan said, removing his FBI credentials from his pocket and flashing them at Sheriff Homestadder. "We were here on official business. Seems someone got to Brenda before we could."

"Now, hold on," the Sheriff said, leaning back on his heels. "Little Ethan grew up to be a man of the law? I remember you, just a kid. Crying over your missing sister. I wished with everything I had we could have done more."

"Looks like Ethan didn't need your help," Megan said, stepping out from the shadows, where she'd been trying to blend into the night. "He found me all on his own."

The Sheriff clutched his chest as if his heart had stopped beating. "That can't be—."

"It's her," Ethan said, eager to skip the small-town theatrics. "And as much as we'd love to catch up, we're here on business."

The Sheriff squinted, offended Ethan couldn't give him the time to find closure on a cold case that had been in his files for years. Still, he nodded, adding: "Who am I to hold up the FBI? I'll help you however I can. But you need to tell me how Brenda was involved."

Annie exchanged a glance with Ethan. They'd discussed this in the car—how much to reveal, how much to hold back. The truth was always better, but the whole truth could be dangerous.

"Brenda had been in contact with someone who was gathering information on the murder of Annie's brother and the kidnapping of my sister—"

The Sheriff's pen stilled on the page. "She can't help you?" He said, motioning to Megan in disbelief. "You've got one of the victims right in front of you and she can't fill you in?"

"I don't remember much," Megan said, rage turning her cheeks red. "Was a little busy getting hit over the head that night."

"Sounds like the start of a terrible adventure," the Sheriff said, concerned understanding making him nod. He had seen a few cases like Megan's, and he couldn't help but think that — when a person disappeared for more than a decade— it was often because they wanted to stay gone.

The Sheriff closed his notebook with a decisive snap. "So you three come back to town after all these years, asking questions about a fifteen-year-old murder, and the very night you arrive, a teenage girl ends up dead." He looked at each of them in turn. "You can see how that might look suspicious to someone in my position."

Annie felt the accusation settle over them like a net. She'd expected this—the small-town sheriff protecting his territory, suspicious of outsiders and federal agents and anyone who might upset the careful order he'd established. But being expected didn't make it less uncomfortable.

"We arrived in town two hours ago," Annie said calmly. "We have gas station receipts, security footage, witnesses who can place us—"

"I'm sure you do," the Sheriff interrupted. "Still seems like quite a coincidence, don't you think?" He pulled a pack of cigarettes from his pocket, tapped one out. "Girl dies the same night you show up asking about her. Makes a man wonder. Especially a man like me, who cares about justice."

Ethan stepped forward, his FBI training evident in the controlled way he held himself. "We care about justice, too—."

"Do you?" The Sheriff asked earnestly, arching an eyebrow. He stepped closer to Ethan, pointing a finger at him. "You may not know this, seeing as you left town, but every one of these cases stays with me. I dedicated years of my life to finding your sister— never gave up on the case," he glanced at Megan. "And then she shows up here alive and well, and none of you bothered to inform the hardworking men and women in my department..."

"We only just found her," Annie said lightly.

The Sheriff ignored her. "And worst of all, you pull an innocent into your troublemaking? A fifteen-year-old girl who's dead now, because you got her all tied up in places she shouldn't be, chasing ghosts from the past." The Sheriff took a long drag on his cigarette. "Sure doesn't seem like justice to me."

"Well then," Annie said, gently breaking the tense silence with a calm smile. "It seems like you want to work together!"

"I—." The Sheriff stammered, taken aback by her breezy cadence.

"So in that case, given that you'd like us to be more forthcoming with our evidence and what we know—."

"Annie…" Ethan cautioned.

"I'd like to share a piece with you!" Annie continued. "Brenda was killed by the real estate ripper. I know because he left a note."

The Sheriff's expression shifted, surprise breaking through his strong facade. "What note?"

Annie pulled the folded paper from her pocket, careful to handle it only by the edges. She'd already photographed it with her phone, memorized every word and fold. "This was in her jacket pocket. It's addressed to me."

The Sheriff took the paper, reading the three words written there. His jaw tightened. "Welcome home, Annie," he read aloud. Then looked up at her with new wariness. "This is evidence in a potential homicide. You should have left it with the body."

"We needed to read it first," Annie said simply.

"That's tampering with—"

"We're aware," Ethan interjected. "We're also aware that time is critical in murder investigations. Every hour that passes, evidence disappears. Witnesses forget details. Killers establish alibis."

The Sheriff took a long drag from his cigarette, studying them through the smoke. Annie couldn't tell if he was angry or impressed or both. Before he could respond, another voice called out from across the scene.

"Sheriff! Sheriff Homestadter!"

They all turned. Mayor Bellows was approaching, his white button-down shirt glowing under the crime scene lights, a Cedarsburg High baseball cap on his head. He moved with the confident stride of someone used to being the most important person in any room, though Annie noticed the way his eyes darted nervously across the scene, taking in every detail.

"Excuse me," the Sheriff said, nodding at the group. "I'll bring the Mayor by. He'll want to hear from you—" The Sheriff left, moving to collect the Mayor, urgently whispering in his ear.

Next to Annie, Megan stiffened as she watched the two men talk. "I'm going to wait in the van," she said quietly, already backing away. "I think I've had enough of being recognized for one night."

"You sure?" Ethan asked, concern flickering across his face.

"Very sure. If the Mayor sees me, he'll want to parade me in front of the town as part of his re-election bid. I'm done being used," Megan said. She met Annie's eyes briefly, and Annie understood. Megan turned on her heel, marching to the black van with an urgent stride.

Moments later, Mayor Bellows appeared in her place—measured steps, careful smile, baseball cap tilted at an angle that suggested both authority and humility. A white button-down tucked neatly into his slacks, his silver hair peeking from beneath the cap's brim. He clapped the Sheriff on his back as if he'd brought him an award.

"Well, I'll be damned," Bellows said. "The Sheriff tells me I owe you a thank you," he extended his hand first to Ethan, then to Annie. His grip was firm and warm, the handshake of a man who'd perfected the art of physical reassurance over decades of town halls and ribbon cuttings. "Annie Hudson and Ethan Beckett. I'd recognize you two anywhere, though you've grown up quite a bit since last I saw you."

"Mayor Bellows," Ethan replied, his voice professionally neutral.

"Terrible circumstances, of course," Bellows continued, shaking his head with the slow gravity of a man who had attended too many funerals. "Just terrible. That girl—Brenda Welsh—her family's been in this town for generations. Good people." He paused, glancing back toward the water tower where crime scene technicians still worked under portable lights. "But I have to say, in spite of all this tragedy, it does my heart good to see you two back in Cedarsburg. After everything that happened—your brother, Annie, and your sister, Ethan—" He let the names hang in the air like offerings. "Well. I'm glad you came home. And am I to understand, Ethan, you found your sister?"

"We have," Ethan nodded, turning his eyes toward Annie, who the Mayor seemed happy to mostly ignore. "Annie's a great detective."

"Annie," the Mayor said, finally looking at Annie with eyes that seemed to see.

Annie studied his face, searching for something beneath the folksy warmth. The Mayor had been elected right after Joshua's murder, she remembered. He'd run on safety, on law and order— things that didn't mean much now.

"If she's open to it, I'd love to sit down with Megan," the Mayor said eagerly, practically salivating at the idea. "Where *is* she by the way?"

"Recovering," Annie said vaguely.

"Ah, of course, of course," the Mayor continued. "Maybe she'll feel well enough in a few days for a local news interview? We can tell everyone she's made it home safely. Maybe even bring the two of you in for an on-air interview as well!"

"Thanks, but we'd rather keep a low profile—" Ethan started to say, but he was interrupted by a faraway voice.

"Mayor Bellows!" The voice cut through the night, breathless and urgent. Annie turned to see a woman in business casual striding toward them, her light brown hair slightly disheveled, her cheeks flushed from either exertion or emotion. She wore high heels that clicked against the asphalt with purposeful rhythm— expensive leather pumps that seemed wildly impractical for a crime scene at two in the morning. "I just finished with the press. Channel 7 and the

Register. I think we should present a united front on this—join forces, show the town we're putting partisanship aside—"

The Mayor's expression barely flickered, but Annie caught the tightening around his mouth, the microsecond of displeasure before the professional mask reasserted itself. "That's a fine idea, Prim," he said smoothly. "But right now, I need to speak with the Sheriff about the investigation. You'll excuse us." It wasn't a question. He tipped his baseball cap and turned, falling into step with Homestadder as the two men retreated toward the police vehicles. The Sheriff dropped his cigarette and crushed it under his boot without breaking stride.

Prim watched them go, her jaw set with an irritation she didn't bother to hide. Then she turned, and her eyes landed on Annie and Ethan. The irritation vanished, replaced by something that looked like genuine shock.

"Oh my God," Prim breathed. "Annie? Ethan?" She covered her mouth with both hands, her eyes wide above her fingers. "Oh my God, it's really you."

Before Annie could respond, Prim closed the distance between them and wrapped her arms around Annie with a force that nearly knocked her backward. The hug was tight, earnest, and lasted several beats longer than Annie expected from someone she hadn't spoken to in over a decade. Prim released her only to seize Ethan in an equally fierce embrace, which he accepted with the stiff tolerance of a man unaccustomed to being grabbed by near-strangers.

"I can't believe you're here," Prim said, stepping back but keeping a hand on each of their arms, as if afraid they might evaporate. "Do you remember me? Of course you do, what am I saying. You were the girl with the perfect memory! I was in Joshua's class. And Megan's. We had AP History together — well, I had it *with* them, obviously, not with you two, you were younger—but still." She was talking fast, the words tumbling out with the breathless energy of someone who had too many things to say and not enough time to say them. "I'm running for Mayor against Bellows. Did you see my signs around town? I'm trying to change things here— *really* change them, not just rearrange the deck chairs, you know?" She straightened, lifting her chin with a pride that bordered on defiance. "It's my belief that Joshua and Megan would be proud to see one of their peers actually trying to make a difference in this place. Don't you think? I hope I can count on your support."

Annie absorbed the rush of words, processing each detail with the methodical patience that had served her through years of investigation. She tried to think of something to say, but nothing came to mind except:

"Those are lovely shoes," Annie said, nodding toward Prim's heels.

Prim glanced down, as if she'd forgotten what she was wearing. The left heel, Annie noticed, carried a faint crust of dried mud along its back edge—mud that matched the soil around the water tower's base with a dried, determined kind of set. The kind that couldn't have happened in the last few moments, but took time to crystallize and shed.

"Oh, these?" Prim said lightly, lifting one foot in a half-turn. "I didn't expect to be stomping through the mud tonight, but I care about Brenda. I care about our town. So I ran right out."

"The shoes suit you," Annie said simply.

Prim met her eyes, and something flickered there. "Annie Hudson," she said, her voice strained. "You never miss a thing, do you?"

Annie offered nothing in return but a pleasant expression that revealed exactly as much as she wanted it to—which was nothing at all.

Ethan touched Annie's elbow, redirecting her attention. "Over there," he said quietly.

Annie followed his gaze to a spot beyond the police tape

where a man in a fine leather coat knelt beside two figures on a bench— a man and a woman, both weeping openly. The woman's sobs carried across the night air, raw and guttural, the sound of a parent confronting the unthinkable. The man beside her sat rigid, staring at the ground, his hands clasped so tightly between his knees that his knuckles had gone white. Brenda's parents. The kneeling man held both of their hands, his head bowed, his lips moving in what Annie recognized as prayer.

"Do you remember Tim Erickson from high school?" Prim asked, following their gaze. Her voice softened with what sounded like genuine admiration. "He's a Pastor now, if you can believe it. He runs Renewed Hope— they're building an amphitheater church over on Elm. You wouldn't believe what he's done for this town despite our money troubles. Live concerts, community outreach, the whole thing. People drive in from three counties over for his services." She paused, adjusting a strand of hair behind her ear. "I've tapped into the Christian base, actually. A lot of his congregation supports my campaign. Tim and I have a good working relationship."

Annie watched the Pastor rise, give Brenda's father a firm clasp on the shoulder, and whisper something that made the man nod through his tears. Then, as if sensing their observation, Tim turned. His eyes found Annie and Ethan across the crime scene, and his face transformed—shock giving way to a wide, disbelieving smile that showed very white teeth.

The Pastor crossed the distance between them in long strides, his hands already outstretched. "Annie Hudson? Ethan Beckett?" He shook his head, running a hand through his slicked-back brown hair. Annie was surprised to see how many of their peers remembered them, but then reminded herself that both her and Ethan had been the talk of the town the year of the crimes. Their faces had been splashed across the papers and the nightly news. They were unwilling local celebrities, even so many years later. "I'm seeing ghosts

tonight," Pastor Tim continued. "What are you—*how* are you
—" He laughed, a warm, astonished sound, and pulled them
each into brief, strong embraces. "I can't believe I'm looking at
you two. After all these years."

"Tim," Annie said, and the name felt strange in her mouth
— this tall, polished man bearing almost no resemblance to
the shy boy she remembered from school. "It's been a long
time."

"Too long," he agreed, his charm so effortless it was almost
disarming. "Far too long."

The sound of footsteps—rapid, uneven—interrupted the
reunion. Annie turned to see a thin woman with dark brown
hair and strong eyebrows half-running across the parking
area, her purse bouncing against her hip, her breath coming
in visible clouds in the cold night air.

"Annie!" the woman called, waving one hand frantically.
"Annie Hudson!"

Zara Kane came to a halt a few feet away, pressing a hand
to her chest as she caught her breath. Her bird-like frame was
trembling— from the cold or from something deeper, Annie
couldn't tell.

"I saw you on the news," Zara managed between gasps. "I
had to come—I had to see for myself that it was really you."
Her eyes moved to Ethan. "Both of you." She swallowed hard,
steadying herself. "I don't know if you remember me..."

"Annie remembers *everyone*," Prim clucked, annoyed.
"She has an eidetic memory. It was all over town. She was
Josh's genius little sister."

"Right, right," Zara said, waving a hand in the air. "Annie,
I sell real estate now. I'm actually listing a commercial plot
just over there." She gestured vaguely toward the darkness
beyond the water tower, then seemed to realize how absurd it
was to mention a listing at a crime scene and dropped her
hand. "I almost quit, you know. After what happened to
Joshua. I almost gave up real estate entirely. You probably

don't know this, but I was the reason I got into the business in the first place." Her voice cracked on his name, and Annie felt the old familiar ache pulse beneath her ribs. Images flashed in Annie's mind: a young Zara, looking longingly at her brother during school dances. Annie couldn't remember that Josh had ever looked back at her.

"I'm glad you didn't quit," Annie said, and meant it.

The five of them stood in an uneven circle— Annie, Ethan, Prim, Tim, Zara—old classmates reunited by a dead girl and a town that had forgotten how to thrive. The red and blue lights from the police vehicles washed over their faces in alternating waves, lending the gathering the quality of a fever dream.

"Well, this is weird, isn't it?" Pastor Tim said, breaking the silence.

"Awful, is what it is," Annie said, her voice quiet. "A young girl is dead. Just like my brother. And I need your help."

Annie looked at each of them in turn. Then she spoke.

"What do you know about Brenda Welsh?"

The question landed like a stone in still water. Tim shifted his weight, his charming expression dimming. "She went to Cedarsburg High, just like us," he said. "Her family's been in my congregation since before I was ordained. She was quiet. Always taking notes." He glanced back toward the grieving parents. "Her parents said she did everything a good kid does. They're— they're crushed—"

"She was one of my interns," Prim added quickly, her voice carrying a note of pride she couldn't quite suppress. "My campaign uses a lot of young people—the youth in this town are hungry for change, and Brenda was one of the best. Sharp as a tack. Could build a database faster than my entire tech team." She paused, her expression sobering. "I can't imagine who would want to hurt her."

Zara said nothing, her arms crossed tightly over her thin

frame, her eyes darting between Annie and the crime scene tape.

Annie let the silence stretch for a moment, letting it do the work that words couldn't. She had learned, over years of investigation, that silence was the most honest interrogator— it didn't ask leading questions or offer comfortable exits. It simply waited.

"Ethan and I are here to find out who killed her," Annie said finally. The words were simple, declarative, and carried the weight of absolute certainty. "This wasn't an accident. And I'm going to need your assistance." She looked at each of them— Tim with his pastoral composure, Prim with her political calculations, Zara with her barely concealed fear. "All of you grew up here. You know this town, its people, its secrets. I'm sure I can count on you."

The silence that followed was heavy with things unsaid. Tim recovered first, offering a solemn nod. Prim opened her mouth, closed it, then nodded as well. Zara's arms tightened around herself, but she managed a small, jerky movement of her head that might have been an agreement.

"Good," Annie said. She touched Ethan's arm— a signal he understood without translation. "We'll be in touch."

They turned and walked back toward the SUV, its windows tinted black, its engine ticking softly in the cool night air. Behind them, Annie could feel the group watching — three sets of eyes tracking their departure, four minds turning over the implications of what she'd just asked. None of them could see through those darkened windows to where Megan sat in the backseat, very much alive, very much listening, and very much preparing for whatever came next.

Annie climbed into the passenger seat and closed the door. The sounds of the crime scene—the murmured conversations, the crackle of radios, the distant sobbing of Brenda's mother —fell away, muffled by glass and steel.

"Well?" Megan asked from the darkness behind her.

Annie stared through the windshield at the water tower, its silhouette rising against a sky just beginning to pale at the edges.

"One of them is lying," she said quietly. "Maybe all of them."

Ethan started the engine, and they pulled away from the scene, leaving Cedarsburg's past and present tangled together in the flashing lights behind them.

CHAPTER TWELVE

AS THE SUV— captained by Ethan's capable hands— curved around the barren streets of Cedarsburg, Annie studied Megan's profile in the backseat. The dim glow of the streetlights cascading through the vehicle's windows threw her features into sharp relief.

"You didn't want to see them," Annie asked quietly. "Prim. Zara. Pastor Tim. Not up for meeting old friends?"

Megan's jaw tightened as she caught Annie's eyes in the rearview mirror. "What are friends anyway?" she said, her voice flat. "None of them looked for me. Their lives didn't change one bit when I disappeared."

"That's not true," Ethan said from the backseat, a desperate tinge to his voice.

"Isn't it?" Megan glanced at him in the rearview mirror. "I've been gone fifteen years, Ethan. Fifteen years. And who looked for me besides you and Annie? What changed in Cedarsburg? What got better? What did anyone do differently because Megan Beckett vanished?" The vehicle made a sharp turn onto Main Street, the headlights sweeping across boarded-up storefronts. "Nothing. The world just went on like it was nothing."

"My world didn't," Ethan said.

Annie wanted to argue with Megan, because it was a thought too terrible to be true— that no one cared, that suffering hadn't led to change, or been put to good use to make the world better. But she didn't argue, because she knew on some level Megan was right. Megan's disappearance didn't bring the town together. There were no rallies held. No non-profits started. There was just a constant news cycle profiting from the bloodiness of it all— the tragedy of it, the shock. Annie had felt the same way about her brother's death. It had been made into a spectacle devoid of meaning— something everyone looked at, but nobody used for good. After a brief circus, the community had moved on. They had folded Megan's disappearance and Joshua's murder into a file marked "terrible" things that are over now," and then gone about their lives like none of it had mattered, having learned, well… absolutely nothing.

"The same thing will happen with Brenda," Megan continued, her voice taking on a bitter edge. "Watch. There'll be one late-night vigil. Flowers at the water tower. Her parents will cry and people will say how awful it is and how this sort of thing shouldn't happen in a place like Cedarsburg. And then, in a month or two, life will go back to normal. People will forget. They'll just carry on like it's nothing. They won't try to *do* anything about it."

The words hung in the air, heavy with truth that none of them wanted to acknowledge. Annie watched the streets of her hometown roll past, each one triggering memories she'd worked hard to bury. There was the corner store where she used to buy candy after school. The park where Joshua had pushed her on the swings. The library where she'd spent countless hours reading, trying to understand a world that had suddenly become incomprehensible.

"Turn left here," Annie said, directing Ethan toward her

father's neighborhood. "It's the blue house, three down on the right—"

"I remember," Ethan confirmed.

The house looked smaller than when Annie was young, its paint faded and peeling in spots, the front lawn overgrown. A single light burned in the front window, as if her father had been waiting up for her. Or maybe he'd just fallen asleep in front of the television again, which was more likely given his habits. Annie had called him from the road to let him know she was coming, but the conversation had been brief and awkward, both of them dancing around the real reason for her return.

Bill Hudson's car sat in the driveway, a twenty-year-old sedan that Annie remembered from her last visit home. It looked more worn now, like everything else in Cedarsburg.

Megan pulled the SUV to a stop at the curb. Annie sat for a moment, her hand on the door handle, gathering courage she didn't know she needed. This was *just* her father. Just home. But she'd been away so long that coming home felt like an event.

The front door opened before they'd even made it halfway up the walk. Bill Hudson stood in the doorway, backlit by the warm glow of the living room. He looked older than Annie had expected, his hair fully grey now, his shoulders slightly stooped. He wore jeans and a faded flannel shirt, feet bare despite the cool night air. The smell of whiskey wafted out from the house, familiar and disappointing.

"Annie," he said, and there was something in his voice that made her throat tight. Relief, maybe. Or regret. "Better late than never, huh?"

"Depends on who you ask," she said, climbing the porch steps. Ethan followed close behind, his hand briefly touching the small of her back in silent support.

Bill's eyes moved to Ethan, recognition flickering across

his face. "Beckett boy," he said with a nod. "Heard you made something of yourself. FBI, Annie told me."

"Yes, sir," Ethan replied.

Bill's gaze moved past them to where Megan stood at the bottom of the steps, her face half-shadowed. "And who's this?"

Annie took a breath. "You won't like the answer."

"Then maybe you shouldn't tell me."

"If I don't tell you, then I'd be doing you a disservice, Dad," Annie countered, weighing her options aloud. "You could be in danger. And you wouldn't even know why."

"Well, damnit Annie," Bill said, shaking his head. "Come inside and we'll—"

"I need you to know that letting us into this house might bring you into something dangerous," Annie interrupted. "You can still turn us away."

"I'm not turning my own daughter away!" Bill's cheeks flushed. He was used to entertaining Annie's preposterous ideas, but he wouldn't entertain this one.

"Then I guess I'll *have* to tell you what we're up to, even though I know you won't like it."

Bill rolled his eyes, glancing at Ethan. "She hasn't changed one bit, has she? My daughter, who talks in circles. You deal with this every day, huh?"

"It's my privilege," Ethan said generously.

Bill turned back to Annie. "Kid, just tell me what you've got to say. For once, don't make it a puzzle."

Annie pointed at Megan. "This is Ethan's sister. *This* is Megan Beckett. We found her, Dad. After all these years. She's *alive.*"

Bill Hudson's mouth dropped open. He stepped forward into the light of the porch, really looking— for the first time— at the woman before him. He remembered Megan Becket from the "missing" posters. Even in the midst of grieving his own son, Bill couldn't take his eyes off those posters. Megan had been younger, then. Her hair long and girlish. Now, there was a new hardness in her eyes— one he didn't recognize— but there was no denying it: the woman in front of him was Megan Beckett.

Bill clutched his head, reeling. "Annie, you— you *found* her ? —"

"We did. And next we're going to figure out who killed Joshua."

Bill's father's expression hardened immediately. "No," he said, shaking his head. "No, Annie. You leave that alone. You hear me? They'll just get you too."

"They won't—"

"You think you're the first person who wanted justice?" Bill's voice rose, roughened by years of drinking and disappointment. "We had half the county working to solve his murder, and they haven't found a thing. True crime groups on chat boards. Police across the nation. Now what does that tell you? Megan knows, doesn't she? I've always said there was more to this than one murder… one kidnapping. Sounded like a cartel. Or a crime ring." He looked at Megan for confirmation. "I'm right, aren't I?"

Megan's cheeks flushed. "You're pretty damn close, actually," she said, unable to deny the truth.

"Well, there you have it!" Bill threw his hands up in the air. "Megan herself agrees. And I bet she'd be the first to tell you, Annie, that drawing these people toward you will only end in suffering."

Megan didn't answer, but the flash of guilt across her eyes said it all: she had endured unspeakable horrors. Megan's expression wasn't lost on Bill.

"You might be smart, Annie, but you and I— we're just regular people. We can't fix the world. People like us can't change a damn thing when they're up against—" He broke off, gesturing vaguely at the night around them. "Whatever this is. This— evil."

Annie felt the familiar frustration rising in her chest, the same argument they'd had a dozen times over the years.

"But I don't want to live in a world like that," Annie whispered, looking at her Dad with wide open eyes. "So my only choice is to try and change it, even if it costs me everything.

When Bill looked back at Annie, there was something in his eyes she hadn't seen there since before her brother disappeared— something that might have been hope, or faith, or the distant memory of what it felt like to believe in good outcomes. Then, as quickly as it came, it was gone.

"Not you too, Annie," Bill said, his voice barely a whisper. "Go live your life. Leave this alone."

"I know nothing will bring Joshua back," Annie said softly. "But if Megan is alive after all this time, Dad, there's still hope. For answers. For justice. For making things right."

Bill looked like he wanted to say more, but then— as if it caused him physical pain— he just nodded slowly. Annie could sense the argument wasn't over— but her Dad had decided to leave it alone for the night. He looked at the three of them standing on his porch— his daughter who'd left and come back, the FBI agent who'd loved her, the girl who'd been dead and wasn't. The night air moved around them, carrying the scent of cut grass and distant rain.

"Come inside," he said finally, stepping back to hold the door open. "All of you. It's too cold to be standing out here." He paused, his eyes finding Annie's. "Your room is the same way you left it."

Annie's childhood bed was smaller than she remembered, the full-size mattress forcing her and Ethan to press close together in a way that would have scandalized her teenage self. The pizza boxes sat stacked on her old desk, grease already seeping through the cardboard in dark patches. Her father had ordered three large pizzas for the four of them, which was too much food, but Bill Hudson had always been the kind of man who expressed affection through excess when he couldn't find the words.

The room itself was a time capsule, preserved exactly as she'd left it so many years ago. Posters of bands she'd loved in high school still clung to the walls, their corners curling with age. Her bookshelf sagged under the weight of paperbacks she'd read and re-read, their spines cracked and faded. A bulletin board above her desk held ribbons from academic competitions, a dried corsage from prom, a photo of her and Joshua making silly faces at the camera. It was the last photo she'd taken with her brother before his murder. Neither of them had known that within a year, he'd be gone and she'd be someone else entirely.

The note found on Brenda's body sat on the desk next to the pizza boxes, its three words visible even from the bed. *Welcome home, Annie.* She'd placed it there deliberately, angled so she could see it whenever she looked up.

Ethan shifted beside her, his weight making the old mattress springs creak. "I wish you'd put that thing away," he said, not for the first time that evening. His eyes were on the note, his expression troubled. "Creeps me out."

"No," Annie said simply. "I'm still thinking about it."

"You're always thinking about it." But his tone was gentle, almost fond. He knew her well enough to recognize this habit, the way she needed to keep certain things visible, present, real. "You probably already know who did it anyway. You're just hiding the truth from me until you have enough facts to make your case airtight."

Annie turned to look at him. In the dim light from her bedside lamp, his features were soft, familiar, dear. "I have suspicions," she admitted. "But I need the entire case to fit together first. I need to understand what happened to Joshua all those years ago. How it connects to Brenda. How it all connects to The Collective." She paused, her fingers finding his under the blanket. "There are pieces I can see, but I can't make them whole yet."

Ethan squeezed her hand. "You will. You always do."

The certainty in his voice should have been comforting, but instead it triggered something in Annie that she'd been trying not to think about. A fear she'd carried for so long it had become part of her, like an extra organ she'd learned to function around.

"The thing that makes the least sense is thinking about *me*," Annie said quietly, the words coming out before she could stop them.

"You?"

"When I think about my own future," Annie continued. "I imagine how I'll feel if we solve the case. What I'll do after we figure out what happened to Joshua. I try to imagine where we live, or what my life is like. Even when I try, I just see... nothing. Or fog. Or question marks."

Ethan propped himself up on one elbow, looking down at her with concern. "Annie—"

"Don't worry," Annie smiled gently at Ethan. "You're always there when I imagine my future. You're in the fog with me."

"Well that's a relief," Ethan grinned gently. "I'm so happy I get to walk into the supernatural mist with you." He squeezed her hand. "You'll feel different when we solve the murder. When you've found justice. You'll be able to see the path forward then."

"But what if—" Annie swallowed hard. "What if we solve Joshua's murder and I still just see fog? What if getting the answers doesn't fix me like I thought it would? What if all that waits for me is the mist? I won't be of use to anyone anymore. I won't know who I am or what I'm for."

The silence that followed felt heavy, weighted with things neither of them wanted to examine too closely. Then Ethan leaned down and kissed her forehead, his lips warm against her skin.

"You'll be of use to me," he said simply. "Broken or whole or anything in between. You'll always be of use to me, Annie Hudson. That's not conditional on solving cases or getting justice or fixing whatever you think is wrong with you." He pulled back to meet her eyes. "You're not valuable because you're damaged. You're valuable because you're you."

Annie felt her throat tighten. She wanted to believe him, wanted to accept the simple truth he was offering. But fifteen years of defining herself by this quest, this mission, this need for answers— that wasn't something she could just set aside with pretty words and reassurance.

"After this," Ethan said, sensing her doubt and trying a different approach, "maybe we should live a quiet life. Find some small town that isn't haunted by murder and make a home there. Maybe get some goats. Or a chicken. I'll let you choose the animal, Hudson."

Annie studied his face, looking for certainty and finding instead what looked like hope dressed up as conviction. "You sure don't want to save the world anymore?"

Ethan snorted. "And what... become international crime fighters? Do what Megan wants and dedicate our lives to dismantling an organization so big and powerful that multiple governments can't touch it?" Ethan shook his head, his eyes darkening as he stared at the ceiling. "I've seen enough in my time at the FBI. Sometimes a man needs to pivot."

Annie rolled over, turning away from him.

"Not the answer you needed?" Ethan asked, worried.

"I don't know," Annie said honestly. "No answer seems quite right." She pulled the collar of her shirt over her chin, wishing she could disappear within it. The old T-shirt she'd found in her dresser—a relic from a high school math competition—was soft from years of washing. It felt like it was the wrong size, somehow, like it had stretched out over time. "Nothing seems to fit," she whispered.

Ethan stared at her for a long moment, something complicated passing across his features. Frustration, yes, but also admiration and fear and love all tangled together. "I just got you back," he said finally, his voice rough. "After everything we've been through, all the cases and dangers and close calls. I just want to keep you safe."

"I know," Annie said, and reached for his hand again.

They sat in silence, holding hands in Annie's childhood bedroom, the note on the desk watching them like an accusation or a promise or both. Outside, Cedarsburg slept its troubled sleep, unaware that in this small room, decisions were being made that would ripple far beyond its borders.

CHAPTER THIRTEEN

THE WELSH HOUSE sat on a street that still believed in lawn care. That was the first thing Annie noticed — the grass was cut, the hedges trimmed, the flower beds mulched and waiting for spring. In a town where half the porches sagged and half the paint peeled, this block had held the line. It reminded Annie of soldiers still standing at attention long after the war was lost.

Annie climbed out of the SUV, the morning air carrying the faint smell of coffee from somewhere down the street. She hadn't slept well. The note — *Welcome home, Annie* — had followed her into her dreams, the three words rearranging themselves into configurations she couldn't quite remember upon waking. Ethan had finally fallen asleep around four, his arm draped across her in a way that was both protective and unconscious. She'd lain awake listening to the sounds of her father's house settling around them, the old bones of the structure creaking and sighing like a living thing.

Now it was just past nine, and they stood on the sidewalk in front of a house where a family had been broken in half overnight.

"You sure you want to start with the family?" Ethan asked, adjusting the collar of his jacket. He looked tired too, though he wore it better than Annie felt she did. FBI training, probably. Or stubbornness.

"They need to know someone cares," Annie said. "And we need information. I want to know what Brenda didn't get to tell us."

Megan hung back by the SUV, her arms crossed, her expression guarded. She'd pulled her dark hair into a tight ponytail and wore a clean jacket she'd borrowed from Annie's old closet — a denim thing that was slightly too small in the shoulders but gave her the appearance of someone who belonged in this neighborhood. Someone normal. Blending in wasn't her strong suit, but Megan had tried.

"I'll follow your lead, Hudson," Megan said, nodding.

The front door opened before they reached the porch steps, as if someone had been watching from the window. A woman stood in the doorway — mid-forties, thin in a way that suggested she'd been thinner before yesterday and would be thinner still tomorrow. Her eyes were swollen and red, her hair unwashed, her bathrobe clutched at the throat with one white-knuckled hand. Behind her, in the dim hallway, Annie could see a man sitting at the kitchen table, staring at nothing. He didn't look up.

"Mrs. Welsh?" Annie said gently, stopping at the base of the porch steps to give the woman space. "My name is Annie Hudson. I'm a private investigator, and I'm looking into what happened to Brenda."

The woman's face tightened. "The police were here all night. You can talk to them," Her voice was raw, scraped clean of everything except exhaustion and the kind of anger that had nowhere to go. "I don't need another stranger telling me how sorry they are."

"I'm not a stranger," Annie said. "My brother was Joshua Hudson."

The name landed the way Annie knew it would — a key turning in a lock. Mrs. Welsh's expression shifted, the defensive wall cracking just enough to let something through. Recognition. Memory. The shared language of loss that no one wanted to speak but everyone who'd lived it understood. Annie didn't wait for her to say anything, but continued her sales pitch.

"I was fifteen when he was murdered," Annie said. "Brenda's age. And I know what your family is going through right now, because mine went through it too. We never *stopped* going through it."

The woman's chin trembled. She looked past Annie to Ethan, then to Megan, her gaze lingering on the unfamiliar face.

"This is my partner, FBI Agent Ethan Beckett," Annie continued. "His sister was the girl who went missing the same night my brother was killed."

Mrs. Welsh's hand went to her mouth. "The Beckett girl. Oh my God."

Megan stepped forward then, moving up the porch steps with a measured calm that Annie recognized as hard-won composure. "I'm Megan Beckett," she said simply. "I was taken that night. I survived. And I came back because I don't want what happened to me and to Joshua to keep happening to people in this town. Annie and Ethan found me," Megan nodded. "They can help you get justice for Brenda, if you'll let them."

Something broke behind Mrs. Welsh's eyes — not resistance, but the last thin membrane between grief and trust. She stepped aside, holding the door open with a hand that shook.

"Come in," she said. Then added: "Please."

The living room was small and immaculate, the kind of clean that came from a woman who controlled what she could because life had proven she couldn't control what mattered. Family photos lined the mantel — Brenda at various ages, gap-toothed and grinning, then serious and bespectacled, then the more recent version Annie had seen on the news: quiet eyes, silver nose ring, an expression that suggested she was always thinking about something she wasn't saying. Mr. Welsh had moved from the kitchen table to the couch, where he sat with his elbows on his knees and his head in his hands. He didn't speak when they entered. Annie didn't expect him to. She'd watched her own father sit in that same posture for years.

They settled into chairs that were offered with the automatic hospitality of people raised to be polite even in devastation. Mrs. Welsh brought out glasses of water no one had asked for. Mr. Welsh finally looked up, his eyes raw and searching.

"I'll get right to the point," Annie said carefully, once they were seated. "We believe Brenda may have discovered something." Something related to my brother's case and to what happened to Megan."

Mr. and Mrs. Welsh stared at her in disbelief. "Something about your brother's case?"

"Yes," Annie confirmed. "Can you tell us about her life? Was she working anywhere she would have used a computer?"

Mrs. Welsh glanced at her husband, who gave a barely perceptible nod. "She was interning for Prim Rosington's campaign," Mrs. Welsh said. "Building the website, managing the database. Prim was so impressed with her — called her a prodigy." A ghost of maternal pride crossed her face, then vanished. "But a few weeks ago, something changed. Brenda started coming home upset. Agitated. She wouldn't eat dinner. She'd go straight to her room and close the door."

"Did she say what was bothering her?" Annie asked.

"Not directly." Mrs. Welsh twisted a tissue between her fingers. "But she started saying things. Strange things. That the town was being 'stolen.' That people had a 'right to know.'

I thought it was just — you know, teenage passion. She cared so much about everything. Too much, maybe."

Mr. Welsh spoke for the first time, his voice a low rasp. "I told her to leave it alone. Whatever she'd found, just leave it alone. Or hand it over to the authorities and let the adults handle it." He stared at the carpet. "She said she couldn't. She said if the adults hadn't done anything so far, they weren't going to." He let his head fall into his hands. "I should have taken her more seriously. I just wanted to keep her safe."

The words hit Annie like a fist. She heard the echo of her father's voice in Mr. Welsh's grief. Brenda had been fifteen and already unwilling to look away. It was the bravest and most dangerous quality a person could have.

"Can we see her room?" Annie asked quietly.

The parents led them upstairs. Brenda's room was exactly what Annie expected — posters on the walls, books stacked on the nightstand, a bed that hadn't been made because its occupant had expected to come home and sleep in it again. The normalcy of it was the cruelest thing. A half-finished glass of water sat on the desk. A hoodie was draped over the chair. Evidence of a life interrupted mid-sentence.

The computer sat open on the desk, its screen dark. Annie touched the trackpad and the machine hummed to life, displaying a desktop that was completely empty. Too empty. No files. No folders. No browser history. Nothing. The hard drive had been wiped clean — not carelessly, but thoroughly, the kind of deletion that took deliberate effort and technical knowledge.

"What teenager do you know who has nothing on their computer?" Annie said, more to herself than to anyone else. She opened the file browser, the recycle bin, the system logs. All of it stripped bare. The computer was a shell, a body without organs.

"That's not—" Mr. Welsh's cheeks flushed. "Her *life* was on that thing. How could someone have—"

"A remote wipe," Megan said gently, shaking her head. "They were able to hack without stepping foot in your house."

Ethan leaned over her shoulder, his expression darkening as he clicked through empty directories. "It's all gone. Nothing."

"Did Brenda keep backups anywhere?" Annie asked, turning to the parents who stood in the doorway, hovering at the threshold of their daughter's room like they were afraid to enter. "A spare hard drive?"

Mrs. Welsh shook her head. "No, just—" She paused, thinking. "Well, there was the other computer. The laptop from the campaign."

Annie felt something tighten in her chest. "What laptop?"

"Prim gave her a laptop to use for campaign work," Mrs. Welsh explained. "Brenda used it for everything — not just the website, but her own projects too. She said it was faster than this old rock we bought her." She gestured at the gutted machine on the desk. "But last week, someone from Prim's team came by and took it back. Said they needed it for the campaign office."

"Before or after Brenda started acting upset?" Annie asked, though she already suspected the answer.

Mrs. Welsh's brow furrowed. "After," she said slowly, the implication dawning on her face like sunrise over bad news. "It was after."

Annie exchanged a glance with Ethan. The laptop — Brenda's real workspace, the device that held whatever she'd discovered about the town being "stolen" — was in Prim Rosington's possession. Whether Prim knew what was on it, or whether she'd taken it back precisely because she did, remained to be seen.

Annie was about to ask another question when the doorbell rang downstairs, its chime cutting through the house like an unwelcome alarm.

"Excuse me," Mrs. Welsh said, looking pained. "I have to get the door—"

"Probably another fucking lasagna," Mr. Welsh muttered as his wife disappeared down the stairs. "Everyone's been dropping off food as if we care whether we eat or not. Our daughter is gone," his voice trembled. "I don't know how she still answers the door—"

Just then, Annie heard the front door creak, then voices — one warm and practiced, the other low and professional. She didn't need to see them to know who had arrived.

"We should all go," Annie said, ushering Mr. Welsh down the stairs like it was her house and not his. She motioned to Ethan and Megan, who fell into line behind them. They reached the bottom of the stairs just as Mayor Bellows was stepping into the foyer, his baseball cap in his hand for once, pressed against his chest in a gesture of respect that looked rehearsed because it probably was. Behind him, Sheriff Homestadder filled the doorframe, his brown uniform crisp, his expression arranged into something that might have passed for sympathy if Annie hadn't been watching his eyes. His eyes were doing something else entirely — they were scanning the hallway, taking inventory of who was present and what they might have already learned.

"Vera," the Mayor was saying, clasping Mrs. Welsh's hands in both of his. "I am so, so sorry. The whole town is heartbroken. Lisa and I — rest her soul — well, she would have been here herself if she could. You know that." He spoke with the easy cadence of a man who had been comforting constituents for almost two decades, his voice pitched to that specific register between authority and tenderness that politicians spent entire careers trying to master. "I brought the Sheriff along because I know you want answers, and by God, we're going to get them for you."

Mrs. Welsh nodded, accepting the condolences with the

numb gratitude of someone too exhausted to evaluate their sincerity.

Sheriff Homestadder's gaze found Annie. His expression didn't change — that was the thing about Homestadder, Annie thought. His face was a locked room. But something shifted behind his eyes, a flicker of displeasure quickly buried under professional courtesy.

"Ms. Hudson," he said, tipping his head slightly. "Didn't expect to find you here quite so early. Most folks wait until after breakfast before they start investigating."

"I've never been much of a breakfast person," Annie replied evenly.

"She prefers to go twelve hours on coffee alone, then scarf down a cheeseburger," Ethan added. Annie appreciated the attempt at levity even as it landed nowhere.

The Sheriff studied Ethan for a beat, then let his gaze drift to Megan, who stood at the back of the hallway with the practiced stillness of someone trained to disappear in plain sight. If the Sheriff recognized her from the night before, he gave no indication. He simply returned his attention to Annie.

"I appreciate your concern for the family," he said, and his voice carried that helpful, earnest quality that made him so effective — the tone of a man who genuinely believed in justice, or at least wanted you to believe he did. "But this is an active investigation, and I'd hate for anyone to feel over- whelmed by too many visitors. I'm sure you understand."

"Of course," Annie said, and meant it — not because she agreed with his reasoning, but because staying would create a tug-of-war over the parents' attention that would serve no one. The Sheriff wanted them gone. The Mayor wanted the stage. And Annie had already gotten what she came for.

She turned to Mrs. Welsh. "Thank you for talking with us. If you think of anything else — anything at all — please don't hesitate to call." She pressed a card into the woman's hand, her fingers lingering for just a moment. Mrs. Welsh clutched it like a lifeline.

"Find out who did this," Mrs. Welsh whispered, her voice cracking on the last word.

"I will," Annie said. It wasn't a platitude. It was a contract.

They moved toward the door, Ethan and Megan falling into step behind her. The Mayor was already guiding the parents toward the sitting room, one hand on Mr. Welsh's back, his voice a steady murmur of reassurance and civic responsibility. The Sheriff held the door open for them with one hand, his other resting on his belt near the cigarette pack in his breast pocket. The gesture might have looked chivalrous to anyone who wasn't paying attention.

"We'll be in touch, Sheriff," Ethan said as they passed.

"Looking forward to it," Homestadder replied, and closed the door behind them.

———

The morning light felt too bright after the dimness of the grieving house. Annie squinted against it, the sun sitting low and harsh over the rooftops, casting long shadows down the street. The air was cool and smelled of damp earth and someone's dryer sheets from an open window. A normal morning in a normal neighborhood, except for the Sheriff's vehicle parked at the curb and the fact that nothing about any of this was normal.

"The laptop, right?" Ethan said as they walked toward the SUV. "That's our next move."

"And I want to talk to Prim," Megan interjected. "She took the laptop back. She knows something."

"We should get the laptop first so we can corner her with information," Ethan said gruffly. "It's an interrogation technique. We'll know as much as she does about what was on it and we can bait her into a trap—"

"Forget that!" Megan snorted. "I don't need to *bait* anyone. I'll just rough her up a little—"

"We don't do things that way out here!"

"Oh! I'm so sorry I'm not a big FBI agent like *somebody* else I know who follows all the rules and does everything perfectly *all* the time—"

"You take that back!" Ethan shouted.

"I will not!"

As the siblings bickered— presumably making up for the time they missed out on— Annie ignored them, silently turning the pieces of the case over in her mind. The campaign laptop. Brenda's wiped desktop. The timing of the repossession. There were threads here, fragile and half-visible, but threads nonetheless. She was reaching for the door to the SUV when a voice stopped her.

"Hey."

It was small and uncertain, the voice of someone who wasn't sure they should be speaking. Annie turned. Ethan and Megan stopped fighting, suddenly jogged back into the moment by the presence of a small boy they hadn't seen. Annie motioned at them to stay near the SUV and let her approach.

The little boy waved at her from the Welsh's lawn, where he peeked at them from behind the hedges that ran along the property line. He was about twelve, thin and serious, with the same blonde hair as Brenda and the same watchful eyes. He wore pajama bottoms and a sweatshirt that was too big for him, the sleeves pushed up past his wrists. His feet were bare on the cold grass. He'd been crying — Annie could see the tracks on his cheeks, still damp — but his jaw was set with a determination that seemed borrowed from someone older. Someone who wasn't here anymore.

Annie's chest tightened. She knew this boy. Not personally, not by name. But she knew him in the way that only someone who had been him could. *The younger sibling.* The one left behind. The one who would spend the rest of their life trying to make sense of an absence that had no sense in it.

His parents hadn't even bothered to introduce him. They'd left him in his room. They were certainly trying to shield him from everything, but Annie knew that was impossible. He probably felt forgotten in the midst of it all. Alone.

She walked toward him slowly, the way she'd approach a skittish witness. He didn't retreat. He stood his ground, his bare toes curling against the grass.

"You're the detective," he said. It wasn't a question. If Annie had to guess, she'd say he'd been listening from behind his bedroom door.

"I am," Annie said.

"The police don't care," the boy said, his voice wobbling on the edge of anger and grief. "The Mayor came last night and said a bunch of stuff about how sad it was and then he left. Now he's here again today but he doesn't care either. I can tell."

Annie knelt so they were eye-level. The grass was wet against her knee. She could feel Ethan and Megan watching from the SUV, giving her space, understanding without being told that this moment belonged to her.

"I care," Annie said quietly. "My brother was killed when I was a teenager. And I've spent my whole life trying to find out who did it. So I know what you're feeling right now, and I know that nothing anyone says is going to make it better. But I'm not going to give up on figuring out what happened to Brenda."

The boy's chin trembled. He looked down at his bare feet, then back up at Annie with eyes that were far too old for twelve.

"You wanted to see her computer?" he asked. Annie nodded. So he *had* been listening.

"She told me once she didn't trust her computer — said someone could wipe it remotely." He swallowed hard. "But she told me about her locker. She said she hid copies of all her files in her locker at school. She made me promise not to tell anyone." His voice broke. "But she's gone now, so the promise doesn't count anymore. Right?"

Annie felt something crack inside her. This boy, standing barefoot in the cold, was choosing to trust a stranger because his sister couldn't speak for herself anymore. It was the bravest thing she'd seen in a long time.

"The promise still counts," Annie said gently. "But I think Brenda would want you to tell me. I think that's exactly what she'd want."

The boy nodded, wiping his nose with his sleeve. "Locker 247. The combination is her birthday — 0-8-1-4." He hesitated, then added: "I know because I read her diary once. She got mad at me for it. I don't know if she'd still be mad."

Annie reached out and squeezed his shoulder — briefly, carefully, the way you'd hold something precious and fragile. "She would not be mad."

The little boy didn't respond. He just stood there, small and shivering. Annie leaned down and whispered to him: "Your parents are going to be very sad for awhile and they might act less interested in things— even you. But no matter what I need you to know they love you. And you are the most precious thing to them. You have to take care of yourself and be okay. Promise me you'll be okay?"

There was a long pause, then the little boy nodded. He watched as Annie rose and walked back to the SUV.

She climbed into the passenger seat and closed the door. Through the window, she could still see him — a boy in too-big clothes, standing guard over his sister's secrets in the morning light.

Ethan started the engine. "What did he say?"

"Cedarsburg High," Annie said, her voice steady despite the ache in her chest. "Locker 247. Brenda kept backups of everything."

Megan leaned forward from the backseat. "Smart girl."

"The smartest," Annie agreed. She looked out the window one last time as they pulled away. The boy had gone back inside, the hedges closing behind him like a curtain. Annie thought about promises, and how the ones we make to the dead are the only ones that truly bind us.

"Let's go back to school," she said.

CHAPTER FOURTEEN

THE MAYOR

AFTER SPENDING an hour with the Welsh family—assuring them of all the ways he was determined to find their daughter's killer— Mayor Bellows stood on the family's front lawn. The grass beneath his loafers was damp and impossibly green, and Bellows had the absurd thought that this was the nicest lawn in Cedarsburg. Possibly the nicest lawn left in the entire county. The Welsh family had maintained it with the kind of stubborn dedication that Bellows associated with people who believed that keeping your yard tidy was a form of prayer— a way of saying to the universe, *We haven't given up yet.*

He hated to think what that lawn would like in just a few months.

He adjusted his baseball cap and turned to find Sheriff Homestadder already behind him, having materialized on the porch steps with the quiet efficiency of a man who'd spent twenty years entering rooms and leaving them without anyone quite registering his movements. The Sheriff had his cigarette pack out, tapping the bottom with two practiced fingers until a single filter emerged.

"The Hudson girl sure doesn't miss a beat," The Mayor said, shaking his head.

"Noticed that." Homestadder placed the cigarette between his lips and cupped his hands around his lighter. The flame caught, and the tip glowed orange in the morning air, a small ember that looked almost cheerful against the blue sky. He took a long first drag, held it, then released a thin stream of smoke that drifted sideways in the breeze. "Offered you one?" he asked, extending the pack.

"No, thank you," Bellows said, the refusal automatic. He'd never been a smoker. His wife had hated the smell, and even though she'd been gone three years now, some of her preferences had calcified into his own habits, permanent as bone. "I'm trying to keep at least one vice off my resume."

The Sheriff's mouth twitched— not quite a smile, but a recognition of humor. He drew on the cigarette again and leaned against the family's front gate, the wood creaking softly under his weight.

"Those parents," Bellows said quietly, shaking his head. "Jesus. Did you see the father's face?"

"I saw it."

"Man hasn't said more than ten words since we arrived. Just sitting there, staring at the floor like he's waiting for someone to tell him it was a mistake. A mix-up at the hospital, wrong ID on the body, something. Anything." Bellows rubbed the back of his neck, feeling the tension that had settled there like a yoke since Marjorie's phone call. "I've done this too many times, you know. I'm getting tired of it."

"We all got things we're tired of," Homestadder shrugged, and the earnestness in his voice sounded genuine. "But we gotta keep on doing 'em, because our lives depend on it. These are lives we chose, and they come at a price."

"Very true," the Mayor agreed. "For years we've kept this town running. Kept it safe. Kept it together when every other small town in this part of the state was falling apart." He wasn't looking at the Sheriff when he said it. He was looking at the sky, the rooftops, the campaign sign three doors down that read *I'm Voting for Bellows.* "And now this. One bad night, and everything I've built is at risk."

The Sheriff exhaled smoke and studied the ember at the tip of his cigarette. "I think we both know who keeps this town safe," he said.

Bellows cleared his throat, forcing a chuckle that came out thinner than he intended, "I'd certainly appreciate it if we could get this wrapped up sooner rather than later. The election's coming up, and Prim Rosington is going to use this. You know she will. She'll be on every news channel saying the town isn't safe, saying the current leadership failed, saying we need new blood." He shook his head, his jaw tightening. "That woman has no idea what it takes to run a place like this. What it *actually* costs. But you and I know, wouldn't you agree?"

The Sheriff nodded. "I'm sure the election is safe," the Sheriff said. "If it isn't, you'll make sure of it." He didn't look at Bellows when he said it. He was watching a squirrel navigate the power line above the street, his expression mild, almost peaceful. But the words carried a weight that had nothing to do with polling numbers or campaign strategy. *I'm sure the election is safe.* Because it always was. Because it had been safe every cycle for fifteen years, safe in a way that had nothing to do with the will of the voters.

Bellows felt his throat constrict. He didn't like being reminded. .

"Well— of course it is—" Bellows started. "But there has to be enough popular support— to make it reasonable— to make it believable." He stopped. There was no point in clarifying. The Sheriff knew what he meant. The Sheriff always knew.

"I'll keep an eye on the Hudson girl," the Sheriff said. He ground the cigarette against the porch railing, then tucked the filter into his breast pocket— a small consideration for the Welsh family's lawn.

"The right kind of eye," Mayor Bellows pleaded.

"Whatever kind of eye I like," the Sheriff shrugged, then moved for his cruiser. He smiled at Bellows before opening the door and hopping in the driver's seat. "Good luck with your campaign."

He slammed the door shut and Bellows resisted the urge to shout at him. They had driven here together. The engine purred and the car moved into reverse. The Sheriff rolled down his window as he called out to Mayor Bellows: "Hope you don't mind. Just got an important call—"

With that, he sped away, leaving Bellows stranded. *Bastard*, Bellows thought. The nearest cafe was about a mile down the road. Bellows sighed and loosened his tie. Time to start walking.

CHAPTER FIFTEEN

THE REALTOR

ZARA COULDN'T STOP THINKING about Joshua Hudson.

Ever since she'd seen Annie at the water tower, something had come loose inside her — something old and carefully sealed. She'd driven home in a daze, the police lights still flashing behind her eyes, Annie's calm voice echoing in her ears:

"I'm glad you didn't quit."

Annie hadn't known what those words had meant to Zara when she'd said them at the water tower, only so many feet away from Brenda Welsh's body. And it wasn't just *what* she'd said— it was her tone. Annie's voice had sounded so much like Joshua's— the same deep, heavy timber made feminine in Annie. The sound made Zara feel like she'd met a ghost.

It was mid-afternoon and Zara should have been at work, but instead she was sitting on the edge of her bed, fully dressed, staring at the floor where the bed skirt failed to meet the carpet. The box was still there. Exactly where she'd left it.

Cardboard. Ordinary. Taped shut with yellowed packing tape. On the lid, written in a younger version of her handwriting, was a single letter surrounded by clumsily-doodled hearts:

♡ *J* ♡

Zara hadn't opened the box in years. She *shouldn't* open it. Obsessions were like beasts, and Zara had learned you shouldn't feed them. But then again, Zara couldn't deny her own obsession had made her who she was. Everything in Zara's life, every road she'd walked down and every door she'd opened and every listing she'd posted and every deal she'd closed, led back to that boy. That dead boy who'd been kind to her once in a high school cafeteria and had accidentally, carelessly, without any intention whatsoever, given her a reason to become herself.

Why *shouldn't* she open the box?

Zara reached under the bed.

The box was lighter than she remembered, which made sense because it was just paper and cardboard and a few small objects that weighed almost nothing individually. She set it on the bedspread and ran her finger along the tape, which fell to the side with ease. She removed the lid. The smell of her own perfume hit her first.

Then, the photographs. She picked up the first polaroid and set it under the bedside lamp.

Joshua Hudson, captured mid-laugh at what must have been the homecoming bonfire. He stood in a group of friends — boys in letter jackets, girls in oversized sweaters— but Zara's eye went where it always went: to his face, half-lit by the fire. Zara was in the picture too, but at the end of the group, her arm around some other boy whose name she could barely remember. She'd only gone to that party to see Joshua. They had friends in common, and she'd tried her best to win his love— but Joshua had never been hers.

She needed to say that clearly, even in the privacy of her own head, because the alternative was a delusion she couldn't afford. Joshua Hudson had been kind to Zara Kane in the way that some people are kind to everyone— generously, automatically, without ulterior motive or special intention. When she'd given her career presentation and stammered her way through an explanation of real estate licensing requirements, he'd been the one who'd clapped first. He'd found her afterward in the hallway and said, *That was really good, Zara. I'm going into real estate too. Maybe we'll be competitors someday.* And he'd smiled, and she'd died a small, silent death right there next to the trophy case, and that had been it.

She didn't dare tell him that she'd only done the presentation on real estate because she *knew* that was the field he planned to go into. She'd done it to get his attention. And it had worked.

It was the dumb idea of a teenage girl, and Zara had built a cathedral on it.

Beneath the photographs sat a diary. A small journal with a purple cover, the kind they sold at the dollar store in packs of three. Zara opened it to a random page, her handwriting leaping up at her in blue ink, round and eager and unmistakably young.

July 3— Josh said hi to me at the coffee shop today!! He said "Hey, Zara" and I said "Hey" back and my voice didn't even crack. Progress!!!!

She turned more pages. The entries were a catalogue of near-misses and imagined connections, each one recorded with the breathless conviction of a girl who had confused proximity with intimacy.

October 14— Saw Josh going to a listing. He was

carrying a *FOR SALE* sign to his car for practice listings. So unfair he graduated before me and I'm still training. I wanted to offer to help but couldn't make my feet move. He's going to be so good at this. He's going to be the best realtor in Indiana. I just know it. Maybe one day we'll work together and he'll finally *NOTICE* me.

December 8— Josh talked to everyone at the holiday party. I mean *EVERYONE.* He's that kind of person. But when he got to me he said "Merry Christmas, Zara, you look nice tonight." *YOU LOOK NICE TONIGHT.* I replayed it in my head the entire drive home. Seven times. Eight. I lost count.

December 18— He won't notice me. Not ever. I tried to catch him at the open house and invited him to get dinner with me. He said he was busy. How long can this go on? When will he see how hopelessly I love him. I love him. I love him.

And then, near the end of the journal, the entries changed. The ink got darker— a different pen, pressed harder into the page, as if the words were being carved rather than written.

January 3. He's gone. It's over. We are done. I don't have to suffer anymore, because he's not here. Joshua is dead. I will move on. I will never think about him again. He is dead, so my heart is free.

Everything will be okay now.

The entry stopped there. The rest of the page was blank. The rest of the journal was blank. Zara had never written in it again.

She set the diary down on the bed and wiped her face with the back of her hand. She hadn't realized she was crying until she felt the wetness on her wrist, warm and traitorous. She was thirty-seven years old and still crying over a boy from high school.

Don't be a sick fuck, Zara thought to herself. But she couldn't help it. That was one thing Zara knew about herself: she had *never* been able to help it.

She reached back into the box and found the last photograph— the one she always saved for last because it was the one that hurt the most and also the least. A group shot, taken at a school assembly. The kind of wide-angle photograph that tried to capture the entire gymnasium and succeeded only in making everyone look small and interchangeable. Joshua stood near the center, flanked by friends whose names Zara couldn't remember, his arm raised in what might have been a wave or a stretch. He was smiling— of course he was smiling, he was always smiling— and the gymnasium lights caught his dark hair and made it shine.

But it was the background that held Zara's attention now, the way it hadn't when she'd first cut the photo from the yearbook all those years ago. Off to the left, partially obscured by a taller student's shoulder, stood a girl. Small. Serious. Dark hair falling straight past her jaw. She wasn't looking at the camera. She was looking at her brother, watching him with the quiet, unblinking intensity of someone who was already cataloguing the world, already filing away every detail, already preparing for a future in which the ability to remember everything would be both her greatest gift and her heaviest burden.

Annie Hudson at fifteen. A girl who didn't yet know she was about to lose the person she loved most, but who— even then, even in this frozen moment of gymnasium fluorescence and teenage noise— looked like she was bracing for it anyway.

Zara stared at the young Annie's face and thought about the woman she'd seen tonight. The calm precision. The measuring eyes. The way she'd stood at the crime scene and looked at each of them.

She knows, Zara thought, unable to shake the feeling that Annie could see right through her. *She knows about me.*

Suddenly, Zara felt a wave of anger rip through her at the thought of Annie and what she'd built in her pain. She'd become a detective. A genius.

Zara envied her. Not for the loss— but for the clarity of purpose it had given her. Zara had spent years drifting through a career she'd chosen for the wrong reasons, in a town she stayed in because leaving felt like a betrayal of a memory that wasn't even hers to betray. She had no purpose. She had listings and commissions and late nights at the office uploading photographs of houses that wouldn't sell. She had a shadow buyer's email address saved in her contacts and a growing certainty that she'd wandered into something much larger and much darker than a simple arrangement to forward listings.

And she had this box. Zara shoved the little back over the cardboard frame.

She slid the box back under the bed, pushing it toward the wall until it sat between the boots and the duffel bag, invisible to anyone who didn't know to look for it. The bed skirt fell back into place like a curtain closing on a performance.

Zara closed her eyes. Behind her lids, Joshua Hudson smiled at her from across a career fair booth, a lifetime ago, and said nothing but her name: *Zara.* The words were warm and careless and perfectly kind, the way everything about him had been warm and careless and perfectly kind, and they meant nothing, and they meant everything, and they would never— not once in all the years she had left— stop echoing in the quiet rooms of her life.

Zara would never forget Joshua Hudson. As far as her heart was concerned, they had both died that day. His death had not set her free the way she'd thought it would— the way she'd promised it would, in her journal. Instead, it had trapped her, frozen her in time. And now, the past had come calling.

She pressed her face into the pillow and held very still, listening to the drip of the faucet and the hum of the refrigerator and the beating of her own stubborn, stupid, unrepentant heart.

CHAPTER SIXTEEN
THE ACTIVIST

PRIM ROSINGTON WAS fourteen minutes ahead of schedule, which meant she had exactly fourteen minutes to commit what might generously be called a misdemeanor. She gripped the steering wheel of her Audi— leased, not owned, though she'd never volunteer that distinction — and turned onto Maple Street, where Cedarsburg High School owned a full block of real estate. The building had the particular look of an institution that had stopped trying. Brick facade stained dark where the gutters leaked. Windows that were either cracked or boarded, depending on the floor. A marquee out front that read CONGRATUL TIONS WRESTLING TE M — missing letters like missing teeth, nobody bothering to fill them in because nobody was looking. There was no denying it: Prim's alma mater had gone down hill since she'd graduated.

Saturday morning. The parking lot was empty except for a rusted pickup near the dumpsters. Prim pulled her Audi into a spot near the side entrance, far enough from the main road that a passing car wouldn't register her presence. She put the car in park and sat for a moment, her hands still on the wheel, her eyes on the building.

I have to get to Brenda's locker before anyone else. That was the thought that had dragged her from bed at six-thirty, the thought that had followed her through her shower and her coffee and the careful selection of a navy blazer and cream blouse — rally attire, camera-ready, because Prim Rosington did not leave the house looking like anything less than a candidate.

The computer records had been clear. Prim had accessed Brenda's campaign laptop — the one she'd had her assistant retrieve from the Welsh house under the thin pretense of needing it back for "campaign data security" — and found exactly what she'd feared. The desktop wipe had been thorough, yes. With the help of another tech-savvy intern, Prim had handled that herself— remotely— using the administrative backdoor that Brenda had unwittingly installed when she'd synced the campaign's cloud storage to her personal machine. Every file, every folder, every breadcrumb of Brenda's private research had been scrubbed from the desktop at the Welsh house. Clean as a whistle.

But the system logs told a different story. Three days before her death, Brenda had connected an external drive — a USB device, logged as "LITTLEBUG_BACKUP" in the transfer history — and copied a substantial chunk of data to it. The transfer had taken forty-seven minutes, which meant it wasn't a few documents. It was *everything*. Brenda had backed up her entire investigation to a physical drive, and that drive was somewhere in the world, waiting to be found by someone who wasn't Prim. And Prim couldn't let that happen, because it would be evidence of a terrible fact:

That I am just as bad as the other guys, Prim thought to herself.

Prim had spent the rest of that night trying to determine where the drive might be. Brenda's bedroom was out — the police had already been through it, and besides, the parents were there, and after the laptop retrieval, showing up again would raise questions even a grief-stricken mother might think to ask. The campaign office was possible but unlikely; Brenda had been smart enough to keep her personal research separate from her campaign work, at least physically. Which left the places Brenda spent time outside of home and work. The library. A friend's house. The school.

And then, it had hit Prim: Brenda, in her ramblings, had mentioned her locker at school as "secure." She'd overheard Brenda chatting with the other interns about her "unbreakable locker." Like a true teenager, Brenda had hidden her drive in the most obvious place possible.

Prim opened the car door and stepped out into the cool morning. The air smelled like damp concrete and the vaguely chemical sweetness of the nearby recycling plant that the Mayor had approved three years ago over the objections of everyone who had to breathe. One of Prim's talking points, actually. Environmental justice. She'd used it at four separate town halls. It always got applause.

She smoothed her blazer and walked toward the side entrance, her heels clicking against the cracked asphalt with a rhythm that sounded more confident than she felt. The side door was a metal fire exit, the kind with a push bar on the inside and a keyhole on the outside. Prim didn't have a key.

She pushed, and the door gave with a grudging compliance. The hallway beyond was dark, lit only by the intermittent flicker of a fluorescent tube that buzzed like an insect. The air inside was different— stale and institutional.

Prim stood in the hallway and felt the familiar mixture of contempt and purpose that Cedarsburg High always triggered in her. She had walked these halls once. She remembered the gymnasium with its warped floor and the library with its outdated computers and the bathrooms where the soap dispensers were always empty. Even as a teenager, she had thought to herself: *This isn't good enough. We deserve better.*

She moved down the hallway with purpose, her heels

echoing in the emptiness. The sophomore lockers were in the east wing, past the main office and the trophy case — which still displayed awards from the eighties, their gold plating gone green — and through a set of double doors that groaned when she pushed them open. The sound bounced off the cinderblock walls and came back to her, distorted, like a voice she didn't recognize.

Locker 247. Prim knew the number because she'd grilled another intern on her campaign who went to high school with Brenda. That was the great thing about hiring young people: they were worshipful and afraid. Prim's army of interns did what she wanted, and kept their mouths shut.

The locker was halfway down the east corridor, sandwiched between 246 and 248, identical to every other locker in the row except for a small sticker on the door — a ladybug, red and round and slightly peeling at one edge. *Littlebug.*

Prim stared at the sticker and felt something cold move through her stomach. It wasn't guilt. It was the understanding that she could never turn back from this moment if she decided to continue. Prim took a deep breath and ignored the feeling.

She tried the combination — Brenda's birthday, 08-14, the same four digits the girl had used for everything because she was fifteen and hadn't yet learned that convenience and security were fundamentally opposed. The lock didn't respond. The dial was sticky, resistant, the tumblers grinding against each other with the exhausted reluctance of machinery past its service life. Prim tried again, slower this time, feeling for the click of each number falling into place. On the third attempt, the lock surrendered and the door swung open with a metallic squeal that made her flinch.

The interior of Brenda Welsh's locker was a portrait of a life in miniature. Two textbooks — biology and pre-calculus — stacked on the bottom shelf, their covers wrapped in brown paper bag material with doodles in the margins. A grey hoodie balled up and shoved into the top shelf, its hood spilling over the edge like a sleeping animal. Three pens clipped to the inside of the door with a magnetic strip. A photograph taped to the back wall: Brenda and a group of friends, arms around each other's shoulders, grinning in front of what appeared to be a computer coding competition banner. A small mirror, cracked in one corner. A tube of lip balm. Prim ignored it all. Her fingers moved through the contents with systematic precision.

No backup drive.

It wasn't there.

She checked the door itself, running her fingers along the ventilation slots at the top and bottom, feeling for anything that might have been wedged into the narrow openings. She removed the magnetic strip and the pens, examined the mirror, even pulled at the edges of the photograph to see if something had been tucked behind it. The photograph came away easily, revealing bare metal and a faded sticker from a band Prim didn't recognize.

Nothing.

Prim stepped back and stared at the open locker, her hands on her hips, her jaw tight. She thought about Brenda — really thought about her, not as an intern or a problem or a name on a form, but as a person. She didn't know much about Brenda, because she didn't pay that much attention to her interns as people. She knew Brenda had been careful. Brenda had been paranoid. Brenda had used the screen name "Littlebug2000." And… that was about it.

What did she do with it? Prim thought.

Her mind raced for answers. She could search the computer lab. The library. The bathrooms. But the clock on her phone read 8:47, and she was expected to attend a campaign rally that started at 9:30. Her absence would be suspicious, and Marcus had already sent three texts.

As if summoned by the thought, her phone buzzed in her

blazer pocket. She pulled it out and saw Marcus's name on the screen, the priority star blinking.

"I'm on my way," she said, answering before he could speak.

"On your way from *where*?" Marcus's voice was high-pitched and frantic. "The podium's set up, Channel 4 is here, the Register sent a photographer… I've got a mob of people standing in a park waiting for you to tell them about affordable housing. Where *are* you?"

"I had a personal errand," Prim said. "It's handled. I'll be there in fifteen minutes."

"Fifteen minutes!!! —"

"Twelve, if you stop talking."

She ended the call and slipped the phone back into her pocket. One last look at the locker. The ladybug sticker. The cracked mirror. The photograph of Brenda and her friends, all of them smiling like the future was something to look forward to. Stupid kids. They had no idea how difficult life became in the real world.

Prim swung the locker door shut. The slam echoed down the empty corridor. The force of it vibrated up through the metal and into her wrist, and even though she felt something give — a tiny tug, barely perceptible— Prim ignored the lightness on her right wrist. Her mind was already on the upcoming rally, rehearsing her opening remarks about the future Cedarsburg deserved. She didn't notice as the bracelet she was wearing— a thin, gold chain— yanked loose from her wrist, resting on the inside of Brenda's wide open locker.

The bracelet was a graduation gift from Prim's parents when she made it through her undergrad at Yale. It was a chain with a single charm in the shape of the letter *P*, made from a designer she had lusted after for years. At the time, the bracelet represented Prim's admission to the upper class. Now, it sat discarded inside a murdered girl's locker. Today—

even though Prim didn't know it yet— the bracelet represented her downfall.

Prim walked away. Her heels struck the linoleum in measured beats. She pushed through the double doors.

Outside, the morning had grown brighter. Prim got into her Audi and checked her reflection in the rearview mirror. Her hair was smooth. Her lipstick was intact. Her blazer showed no dust from the locker search. She looked exactly like what she was supposed to look like: a candidate. A reformer. A woman of progress and purpose. *Prim for Progress.* It was right there on the lawn signs, in red and blue letters, bold and clean and promising.

She put the car in gear and pulled out of the parking lot, leaving Cedarsburg High to its Saturday silence. *No one will know,* she thought of her recent escapades. *I'm safe.*

Inside locker 247, the gold chain caught the thin light that filtered through the door, which Prim had carelessly left ajar. The letter *P* glinted once, briefly. Then the light shifted, and the locker was just a locker once more — waiting quietly for someone who knew what they were looking for.

CHAPTER SEVENTEEN

THE PASTOR

IN THE SKELETON of what would become the greatest church amphitheater in southern Indiana, Pastor Tim Erickson stood on a concrete slab that smelled like wet cement and possibility… and felt absolutely nothing.

The structure rose around him, full of promise. Rebar jutted from half-formed walls. Construction had been underway for three months now. The foundation was solid, the framing nearly done, and on the eastern wall someone had bolted a massive vinyl banner that showed the finished product in full-color rendering: *Renewed Hope Amphitheater*, the banner proclaimed. It pictured a soaring glass facade and landscaped courtyard and the cross mounted on the roofline that would be visible, according to the architect's calculations, from four miles away. The rendering looked like something from a different country. A different economy. A place where buildings like this grew naturally from the ground because there was enough money and enough faith and enough of whatever else you needed to turn steel beams into something sacred.

Cedarsburg, Indiana, was not that place. Not anymore. Maybe not ever.

Tim stood at center stage— or what would *become* center stage, once the pouring was finished— and thought. He came here often and tried to feel the presence of God in the hollow spaces between the beams.

He used to feel God's presence everywhere. That was the part that scared him. When he'd first been called to ministry — a word he used carefully and sincerely, because it had been a calling, not a career choice— he had felt God in everything. In the creak of the wooden pews at the small church on Route 9 where he'd preached his first sermon to eleven people. In the morning light that came through the stained glass and landed on the hymnals. In the faces of the people who came to him broken and left, if not whole, then at least holding the pieces more carefully than before.

Now he stood in a two-million-dollar construction site and felt… nothing. Not emptiness, exactly. More like the echo of something that had been there once and had quietly, without announcement or ceremony— stepped out.

"Pastor Tim?"

The voice belonged to his assistant— a young man in his mid-twenties, earnest as a golden retriever, perpetually holding a clipboard. He appeared at the edge of the concrete slab, picking his way through a gap in the temporary fencing.

"I just got off the phone with the folks at Christian Today. They want to do a *feature*. A feature, Pastor Tim. Full spread! Photos of the construction, an interview with you. They said it's one of the most exciting church-building stories in the country right now."

Tim turned toward him and produced a false smile based on something he didn't feel.

"That's wonderful," Tim said. The words came out perfectly pitched. "God has blessed us."

"Yes," the assistant corrected, grinning. "And that's not even the best part. I reached out to a producer at one of the Christian cable networks— you know, the one that does the live worship specials?— and she said they'd be interested in covering the grand opening. Live. On television." He paused to let the word settle. "Can you imagine, Pastor Tim? Renewed Hope, broadcast coast to coast. People in California watching our choir. People in New York hearing your message. This could put Cedarsburg on the map."

Tim nodded. He was supposed to feel thrilled. He was supposed to feel the way the assistant felt.

Instead, Tim looked up at the open sky through the unfinished roof and thought about Brenda Welsh's mother.

He'd knelt beside her the night her daughter died— on the cold ground near the water tower, the police lights turning everything red and blue. He'd held both of her hands and prayed with her, his lips forming words he'd spoken a thousand times over grieving parents and hospital bedsides and funeral parlors. *Lord, we don't understand your plan, but we trust in your love. We ask for your comfort in this hour of darkness. We ask for your peace that surpasseth all understanding.*

The words had come easily, and for the first time in a long time— he had felt the spirit of God again. Why couldn't he feel it here?

The assistant was still talking— something about stage dimensions and seating capacity and the possibility of a café in the lobby— but Tim had stopped listening. He knew why he didn't feel the presence of God in this place.

It was because he had walked the wrong path to build it.

God had not provided this amphitheater. Mayor Bellows had.

The cashier's check had arrived six months ago, delivered not by mail but by hand, in a manila envelope with no return address. Tim had opened it in his office at the old church— the small one on Route 9, the one with the eleven-person congregation that had since grown to four hundred— and stared at the number for a long time. It was more money than he'd ever seen in one place. More money than the entire church budget for three years.

The check came with a note. Two sentences, handwritten on plain white paper: *For Renewed Hope. With gratitude for your endorsement.*

Tim had known what it meant. He'd known when the Mayor's office first approached him about the endorsement, three months before the check arrived. The pitch had been simple, delivered over coffee at the diner on Main Street by a man from the Mayor's re-election committee who wore a suit that was too expensive for Cedarsburg. The Mayor wanted the endorsement of the most popular pastor in the county. In exchange, the Mayor would ensure that Renewed Hope received a "community development grant" sufficient to begin construction on the amphitheater.

Tim had asked, once, where the money would come from. The man in the expensive suit had smiled and said: "The Mayor has friends… who take care of *his* friends."

Tim knew right then the money was tainted. He should have said no.

But he'd thought about the town. He'd thought about the empty storefronts on Main Street and the families leaving for Indianapolis and Columbus and anywhere that wasn't here. The people needed this church. He told himself God worked in mysterious ways, which was true.

But now, being honest with himself, Pastor Tim was forced to admit— it was excitement at his own advancement that made him take the deal. He'd pictured exactly this moment: his own face on banners and television screens. And that's why he'd said yes.

Now, he was standing in the bones of a building bought with money he was increasingly certain had been stolen.

He'd done the math. Not the exact math— he didn't have the numbers for that— but the rough, intuitive math. The money came too fast— delivered within weeks of his endorsement of the Mayor. Which left one possibility that Tim could see: the money had come from somewhere it shouldn't have. And the most likely somewhere, given the timing and the source, was the Mayor's campaign fund.

Campaign contributions used for personal benefit— or redirected to third parties— was illegal. Tim knew this because he'd looked it up, late at night, in the privacy of his study, while his wife slept in the next room.

He hadn't told anyone.

"Pastor Tim?" The assistant had stopped talking. He was looking at Tim with the particular expression of someone who had just realized that the person they were speaking to had left the conversation several minutes ago. "Everything okay?"

"Fine," Tim said. The smile again. Automatic. "Just thinking about the sermon for tomorrow."

"Oh, great," the assistant said, visibly relieved. "I'll write back to the cable television network and tell them we want to firm up plans." He nodded, scribbled something on his clipboard. Then, a voice emerged from behind him:

"I wouldn't. Not yet," the woman said. Tim's wife stood at the entrance to the construction site, her coat pulled tight against the morning chill, her dark hair lifted slightly. She had a travel mug in one hand and her car keys in the other. She was watching him the way she always watched him when something was wrong.

"I'm sorry— ma'am—" the intern started to say as Tim's wife held up a hand.

"Can you give us a moment?" she said to the intern. He dismissed himself at once.

"Honey," Tim smiled at her, ready to convince her of the best. "What are you doing here so earl—"

"Don't," she said, cutting him off. She crossed the concrete slab toward him, her boots leaving faint prints in the construction dust. "Don't do that thing where you pretend everything is fine and then preach your way around whatever's actually happening. I can see it, Tim. I've been able to see it for weeks."

He looked at her— really looked, past the comfortable familiarity of marriage and into the specific, irreplaceable person she was. She had never been fooled by the smile. Not once, in all their years together.

"Tell me what it is," she said.

"This place feels empty," Tim answered painfully.

His wife glanced around at the steel beams, the concrete, the banner with its glossy rendering. "It's a construction site, Tim. It's supposed to feel empty. It's not done yet. Now... what do you really mean to say?"

Tim stared up at the windows, so much promise in their half-built frames. "I mean here." He pressed a fist against his chest, his voice quiet. "This place. Inside me. It's gone quiet." He moved to a nearby folding chair and collapsed into it, as if the weight of saying what was on his mind had made him heavier somehow.

His wife set her travel mug on the ground and sat down on the concrete beside the folding chair, cross-legged, her coat pooling around her. She didn't touch him. She didn't need to. Her presence was enough— the quiet, unmovable fact of her, sitting on cold concrete in a half-built church because her husband needed to say something he'd been choking on for months.

"Sometimes God is silent so we can make our own decisions," she said after a moment in which she'd gathered her thoughts. "God allows us to tread our own path so we can decide who we want to be, even when his voice is harder to hear." She paused, looking at Tim with a steady gaze. "What path are you walking, Tim?"

"A bad one," Time said. The words came out rough, stripped of the practiced smoothness that characterized everything else he said.

"You can reverse," his wife said, nodding. "You can

always change direction." She reached out and touched his hand. "What is it?"

"The amphitheater. The endorsement. The money. All of it." He swallowed. "I wanted so badly to help this town. I watched Cedarsburg dying— year after year, store after store closing, families leaving, kids growing up with nothing to hope for— and I thought, if I could just build something."

Tim paused. His wife waited. Waited for him to get to the truth.

"But if I'm being honest—" Tim continued. "I was seduced by my own success. The idea of my face on a television screen. Being the town's hero. Being known as a great man who changed everything. I allowed myself to sell out. For vanity."

"How much trouble are we in, Tim?" His wife said, arching a concerned eyebrow.

"I don't know," Tim said honestly. "The money came from the Mayor. A cashier's check. No paper trail, no legitimate funding source, just— here's your money, thanks for the endorsement, don't ask questions." He ran both hands through his slicked-back hair, disrupting it for the first time all morning. "And I didn't ask questions. Because asking questions would have meant hearing answers I didn't want to hear, and hearing those answers would have meant giving the money back, and giving the money back would have meant —" He gestured at the steel beams, the banner, the chalk-marked stage. "No amphitheater. No national media. No television broadcast. No saving Cedarsburg." His voice cracked on the town's name. "So I took the money and I kept my mouth shut and I preached prosperity gospel every Sunday like a man who had the right to tell other people how to live, while I—"

He stopped. The sentence had nowhere good to go.

"I see," his wife nodded, understanding.

"While you what?" she asked gently.

"Every beam is a lie," Tim sighed. "And I've been standing up there every Sunday, in the old church, telling people that God rewards faithfulness, while I've been faithless in the one way that matters most."

His wife was quiet for a long moment. The wind moved through the open structure, carrying the distant sound of traffic on the highway and the closer sound of a bird that had found a perch on one of the I-beams and was singing with the indifferent cheerfulness of a creature that had no concept of moral compromise.

"So we find a new path," his wife said, shrugging as if the answer was simple and had been there all along.

Tim felt something shift inside his chest— not a dramatic collapse, but something quieter and more permanent. A realignment, maybe. Like a compass needle that had been spinning for months finally finding north.

"I need to talk to someone," he agreed, his voice steadier now. "Zara Kane."

Tim's wife nodded. She, too, had gone to high school with Zara. The woman had brokered the land deal for them— the one in which they purchased a plot to build the amphitheatre on.

"She knows something," Tim said, shaking his head. "I can feel this goes deeper than just one check, one offer. And whatever it is, Zara knows."

His wife looked up at him. "You trust her?"

Tim considered the question. He thought about Zara Kane — the thin, dark-haired woman he'd known since elementary school, who'd always been a little nervous, a little too eager.

"I don't think it matters," Tim said. "I need to get to the bottom of whatever I'm tangled up in."

He looked one last time at the amphitheater skeleton— the steel ribs, the chalk lines. For three months he'd looked at this structure and seen salvation.

Now he saw what it actually was: bones. Just bones.

His wife rose from the concrete and took his hand. Her fingers were cold from the morning air, and he wrapped his around them. They stood together in the unfinished church, two small figures dwarfed by steel.

"First steps on a new path," his wife said, nodding. "I'm with you."

"I'll call Zara this afternoon," Tim answered.

His wife squeezed his hand.

They walked out of the amphitheater together, determined to begin again.

CHAPTER EIGHTEEN

CEDARSBURG HIGH WAS an empty shell of the place Annie remembered. She walked through empty halls with Ethan and Megan by her side, their footsteps echoing off the cinderblock walls with a hollow percussion.

"Changed, hasn't it?" Ethan said, his voice too loud in the empty building.

The fluorescent lights overhead buzzed as if in warning. Annie walked fast. She'd been walking fast since they'd slipped through the side entrance. Annie couldn't explain it, but a strange feeling was pushing her forward: the feeling of being second to arrive.

"Changed? This place somehow got worse," Megan said from beside Annie, her voice flat with the particular disappointment of someone revisiting a memory and finding it diminished. A denim jacket she'd borrowed from Annie made a soft sound as she moved, too small in the shoulders. "I didn't think that was possible."

Ethan said nothing. He was scanning the hallway the way he scanned every room he entered— systematically, left to right, top to bottom, his FBI training running the show. His hand wasn't on his weapon, but it was near enough to suggest he hadn't ruled out the need for it.

They passed the trophy case first. It sat against the wall near the main office, its glass smudged with fingerprints from students who had pressed their faces against it to see the relics inside— or, more likely, from custodial staff who had cleaned the exterior and never bothered with the interior, because the trophies themselves hadn't been updated since the early 2000s. The gold plating had gone green in places, giving the figures atop each column— wrestlers and runners and debaters— a diseased, swamp-creature quality that undermined whatever glory they'd originally been meant to represent.

Annie saw the name before she was ready for it. Third shelf, second from the left, on a wrestling trophy whose plastic base had cracked along one side: *Joshua Hudson, Regional Champion, 2008.* The letters were small and engraved on a brass plate that had tarnished to the color of old pennies. She stopped walking. The halt was involuntary, a full-body response to five syllables that still, after fifteen years, could reach into her chest and squeeze.

Ethan's hand found the small of her back. He didn't speak. He'd learned, over the years they'd known each other, that there were moments when Annie needed touch more than language, and this was one of them. She let herself look at the trophy for three seconds— counting them, because counting was control and control was what kept her moving— and then she stepped forward again, leaving Joshua on his shelf, frozen mid-grapple, forever seventeen.

"Annie." Megan's voice had changed. Softer now, surprised.

Annie turned. Megan had stopped a few feet behind, her face angled toward the lower shelf of the trophy case, where a smaller trophy sat partially hidden behind a basketball team photo. Track and field. *Megan Beckett, 200m, District Finals,*

*2007.** The figure on top was a runner, one leg extended, arms pumping, captured in a stride that would never finish.

Megan stared at it the way you stare at a photograph of someone who died— except the someone was herself, a younger version, the girl she'd been before she became whoever she was now. Her jaw worked. She didn't touch the glass.

"It's me," she said quietly. "It's me before they took me. I forgot I was fast."

They moved on. Past the main office with its dark windows and its hand-lettered sign reminding students that TARDINESS IS A CHOICE, past the bathrooms with their perpetually broken soap dispensers, past a long hallway display case that Annie almost walked by before the photographs inside caught her peripheral vision and pulled her to a stop.

Class photos. Arranged by year, each one a grid of small faces smiling. Annie's eyes found the year that mattered— the year Megan had been taken. She found Megan's class, noticing a younger version of the woman beside her surrounded by a group of familiar faces.

There was Tim Erickson, his hair not yet slicked back, but his smile was already disarmingly kind. He had the kind of goodness about him that could make a person believe. Annie could help but think he was born to be a Pastor. Beside him, Prim Rosington, light brown hair pulled into a severe ponytail, her chin slightly lifted even at twelve, already composing the version of herself she intended to present to the world. A couple rows back was Zara Kane, dark-browed and thin, her eyes looking slightly past the camera as if she'd been watching something more interesting just off-frame. And Megan— young Megan, long-haired and bright-eyed, grinning with the uncomplicated joy of a girl who had not yet learned what the world was capable of taking from her.

"Funny thing about childhood friends," Megan said,

studying the photograph with an expression that was closer to anthropological interest than nostalgia. "You think those connections are the realest things in the world. You think they're permanent." She touched the glass with one finger, tracing the row of faces. "But they're not concrete. They're chalk on a sidewalk. First hard rain and they're gone, and everyone just walks over the spot where they used to be like nothing was ever there."

The words settled in the hallway like dust. Annie let them. She understood what Megan meant, even if she wanted to argue with the bleakness of it. Some connections *did* last. Hers and Ethan's had lasted. But Megan hadn't been given the chance to test that theory— she'd been ripped away at an age when friendship was still a thing you assumed would continue forever.

"East wing," Annie said, redirecting them. "Sophomore lockers."

They pushed through the double doors. The groan of the hinges filled the corridor. The east hallway stretched ahead of them, rows of dented lockers lining both walls, their ventilation slots like narrow eyes squinting in the fluorescent half-light. Numbers counted upward as they walked. 230. 235. 240.

Annie saw it from twenty feet away and felt the temperature of her blood change.

Locker 247 was open.

Not ajar— open. The door hung at a forty-five-degree angle, the combination lock dangling from the latch like a pendant on a broken chain. The ladybug sticker on the door— *Littlebug*— caught the light and held it, red and round and absurdly cheerful against the grey metal.

Annie approached slowly. Ethan had his hand on his sidearm now, his eyes sweeping the empty hallway in both directions. Megan pressed her back against the opposite wall of lockers, giving herself a line of sight to the corridor's far end.

Inside the locker, discarded textbooks were still there. A hoodie. A collection of pens on their magnetic strip. A cracked mirror. A photograph of Brenda and her friends. All of it untouched, undisturbed, except for one addition: a small white card, placed on top of the biology textbook with the deliberate precision of someone who wanted it found.

Three words, printed in block letters:

YOU'RE TOO LATE.

Annie's eyes moved across the locker's contents with the systematic patience of a woman who had trained herself to see what wasn't supposed to be there. The card was three words, just like the note left with Brenda's body. The untouched belongings. The absence of any backup drive, which proved nothing except that whoever left the note had been looking for the same thing they were. And then— there. Caught in the ventilation slot near the bottom of the door, glinting like a small bright accusation: a thin gold chain. A bracelet. Delicate, broken at the clasp, with a single charm dangling from one of the links.

The letter *P*.

Annie's hand moved toward it, then stopped. She studied the bracelet without touching it, cataloguing every detail— the style of the chain, the weight of the charm, the way the clasp had snapped cleanly, suggesting it had been torn away by force or caught on something during a hasty departure. The letter *P*. A common enough initial. It could belong to anyone. But Annie's mind, which never stopped filing and sorting and cross-referencing, had already placed it alongside a specific person, a specific wrist, a specific habit of wearing gold jewelry that was tasteful and expensive. It was precisely the kind of thing you'd buy with a Yale education.

Prim had been here. Annie was sure of it.

Annie said nothing. She memorized the bracelet's position, its angle, its relationship to the other items in the locker, and then she stepped back and let the information settle into the locked room of her mind where she kept things that weren't ready to be shared. Then, she picked up the bracelet and slid it into her pocket.

"Someone got here first," Ethan said, his voice tight. He was reading the note over her shoulder, his jaw set in the particular way that meant he was angry and trying not to show it. "Does that mean they got her backups?"

Annie considered the question. She thought about the note — its brevity, its confidence, its deliberate theatricality. Someone who had found what they were looking for wouldn't leave a taunt. They'd leave nothing. The note was a performance, designed to discourage pursuit. Which meant—

"No," Annie said. "We only know they've been looking for the backup, same as us. Not that they found it." She turned from the locker, her eyes moving down the empty hallway, following a line of thought that was assembling itself in real time. "Brenda's brother said she kept a backup in her locker. But what if it wasn't *this* locker?" She paused, the idea sharpening. "What if it wasn't a locker at all? Not a physical one. What if it was a *digital* locker?"

Megan pushed off the wall, her expression shifting from vigilance to recognition. "A *cyber*locker," she said, nodding. "Encrypted cloud storage. A dead drop for files. Brenda was a computer genius— she'd know how to set one up. And she'd access it from a machine she trusted."

"A machine at school," Annie finished. "Somewhere she went every day. Somewhere no one would think to look."

The three of them stood in the empty hallway, the open locker behind them a gaping maw, mocking them. Prim's gold bracelet smiled up at Annie, and she knew— somewhere in this building— in a classroom or a lab or a workstation that bore Brenda Welsh's name— the truth was waiting, patient as a held breath, for someone who knew what they were looking for.

The records office was three doors down from the principal's, its door helpfully labeled *STUDENT RECORDS* in block letters that had been stenciled by someone who believed in capitals but not in locking doors. Annie tried the handle and it gave immediately, swinging inward onto a room the size of a generous closet, crammed with filing cabinets that looked like they'd been purchased during the Reagan administration and hadn't been reorganized since. The air inside was thick with the particular smell of old paper— not unpleasant, exactly, but dense.

"Brenda Welsh," Annie said, pulling open the cabinet marked W-Z. "Current sophomore. I need her class schedule."

It took less than a minute. The folder was thin— a single sheet of paper listing Brenda's courses for the semester, her homeroom assignment, her locker number. Annie's eyes ran down the schedule and stopped on the fourth period listing. Technology Applications. Room 114. Every day, 11:15 to 12:05.

"Technology lab," Annie said, holding up the sheet. "Room 114. Let's go."

Room 114 was in the basement. Of course it was. The school's technology investment had been literally buried— placed underground, in a windowless rectangle of cinderblock that the architects had probably intended as storage. The lights here were worse than upstairs, half the fluorescent tubes dead or dying, casting the room in a sickly yellow-grey pallor that made everything look like it was being viewed through dirty water. Twenty computer workstations sat in rows, each one separated from its neighbor by a thin particleboard divider. Helpfully, each station was labeled with a small laminated card bearing a student's name.

Annie moved down the rows. The workstations were ancient— bulky monitors, keyboards with missing keys, towers humming faintly beneath the desks. She read the names as she passed. *Henderson. Cho. Paulson. Dietrich.*

"Here," Megan said, two rows ahead. She was standing at a workstation near the back corner, its laminated card reading *Welsh, B.* in careful handwriting. A small ladybug sticker had been pressed onto the monitor's bezel— the same sticker, or its twin, that had marked locker 247 upstairs. Brenda's signature. Her mark on the places she claimed as her own.

Megan sat down and touched the mouse. The monitor flickered to life, its screen casting blue light across her face, turning her features sharp and spectral. The desktop loaded slowly, flashing an image of the school mascot— an ironically appropriate, battered-looking eagle. Megan's hands moved across the keyboard with the fluid authority of someone who had navigated systems far more complex and dangerous than a high school computer.

"There," Megan murmured. She pointed at the browser bookmarks. Annie and Ethan leaned in to make sense of her discovery. Saved links appeared on screen. A pre-calculus tutoring website. A robotics forum. And then— a ladybug emoji. Megan clicked it. A login screen appeared, minimal and encrypted.

"That's it," Annie nodded, appreciating that Brenda had created a bland interface meant to be invisible to anyone who didn't know its importance.

"Username," Megan said, typing. *Littlebug2000.* Password. She tried Brenda's birthday— 0814— and the screen rejected it. She tried it again with the year— 081407. Rejected. Annie watched Megan's fingers hover above the keys, thinking, calculating.

"Try it backward," Annie said quietly.

Megan typed: *7041080.* The screen unlocked.

"How'd you know?" Megan asked, surprised.

"The ladybug emoji," Annie shrugged. "It goes the opposite direction of the sticker."

The cyberlocker opened like a door into another world. Folders upon folders, nested and organized with meticulous precision. Annie leaned in, reading the folder names over Megan's shoulder. *Shell_Companies.* *Property_Records.* *Campaign_Finance.* *Collective_Connections.* *Sheriff_Incident_Reports.* Each one a thread in the web that Brenda had been painstakingly mapping before someone threw her from a water tower. Her last revenge.

"My God," Ethan breathed from behind them. "She documented everything."

"She was trying to save her hometown," Annie said, and the words felt true in a way that hurt. Brenda had done what all of them should have done years ago, and she'd been fifteen, and she'd been alone— and it had killed her.

"No," Megan said, shaking her head and pointing at a file labeled *The Collective__All.* "She was trying to save the world. She knew about them. I wonder how much she got…"

Megan was already reaching into her jacket pocket. She produced a thumb drive— small, black, nondescript— and plugged it into the tower beneath the desk. Her fingers flew across the keyboard, initiating a bulk transfer. A progress bar appeared on screen: *Copying files... 2% complete. Estimated time: 4 minutes.*

Four minutes. In an empty building on a Saturday morning, four minutes should have felt like nothing.

Annie smelled it before she saw it.

Smoke. Not the stale, institutional staleness of the basement air she'd been breathing since they descended the stairs. This was different— acrid, chemical, the sharp bite of something burning. It hit the back of her throat and she coughed, once, her hand going to her mouth.

"Ethan," she said.

He was already moving. He crossed the lab in three strides and pressed his palm flat against the door they'd come through. He pulled it back immediately.

"Hot," he said. His voice had dropped into the register Annie associated with operational mode— low, clipped, stripped of everything except necessary information. "We're in trouble, Hudson."

Annie looked at the gap beneath the door. Grey smoke was curling underneath it, sliding across the linoleum as if it were alive. The wisps thickened, layering over one another, building density. Through the narrow window in the classroom door— reinforced glass, wired through with mesh— she could see the hallway filling with a thick fog.

"Almost there!" Megan shouted from the computer station. Her voice was steady but her eyes had gone hard. She looked at the progress bar. *18% complete. Estimated time: 3 minutes 12 seconds.*

"We need to find another way out," Ethan said. He'd drawn his weapon, not because a gun would help against fire but because the fire meant someone else was here, or had been here, and a gun helped against that. "Now."

"Not without the drive," Megan said.

"Megan—"

"Not. Without. The drive." She didn't look up from the screen. "Brenda died because of what's on this computer. I'm not leaving it behind."

"I said *now!*" Ethan called back.

"I didn't escape The Collective just to let my little brother boss me around!" Megan shouted, standing.

Annie thought she heard Ethan mutter something about stubborn, pain-in-the-ass people, but she blocked out his mumbles. Her eyes were already scanning the room for alternatives to the door. No windows— they were underground, the walls solid cinderblock on all four sides. One door, the one they'd come through, the one that was now radiating heat like a furnace grate. She looked at the ceiling. Acoustic tiles, suspended from a metal grid, the kind found in every institutional basement in America. Above them would be ductwork, pipes, the building's mechanical guts. None of it passable. None of it an exit.

She turned to the back wall. A second door— she'd missed it when they entered, partially hidden behind a rolling whiteboard. She shoved the whiteboard aside and tried the handle. Locked. A deadbolt, keyed from both sides, the kind installed to keep students from wandering into restricted areas of the building.

"Ethan," she said.

He was beside her in a second, shouldering the door with the full force of his frame. The wood shuddered but held. He hit it again. The deadbolt rattled in its housing but the frame was metal, set into cinderblock, built for an era when school security meant keeping doors closed rather than keeping people alive.

The smoke was thicker now. It had filled the space between the floor and Annie's knees, a grey tide rising with the patient inevitability of water. The chemical smell had intensified, joined by something warmer and more organic— wood burning, maybe, or paper, the school's decades of accumulated records feeding the fire above them like kindling. The fluorescent lights flickered, buzzed, and two of the four tubes went dark, plunging the far side of the lab into shadow.

Annie pulled her shirt over her nose and mouth. The fabric was thin— it wouldn't help for long. She looked at Megan, still seated at the workstation, her face lit by the monitor's blue glow as smoke curled around her.

34% complete. Estimated time: 2 minutes 28 seconds.

Ethan hit the door again. Something cracked— wood or bone, Annie couldn't tell— and he stepped back, his shoulder dropping, pain flashing across his face before he composed it away. The door had splintered near the handle but the deadbolt held, indifferent to desperation, doing exactly what it had been designed to do.

The smoke reached Annie's waist. She could feel the heat

now, pressing down from the ceiling, radiating through the walls, the building contracting around them like a fist closing. Somewhere above— one floor up, maybe two— something collapsed with a sound like thunder rolling through the bones of the earth, and the lights went out entirely, leaving only the blue glow of Brenda Welsh's computer screen, steady and bright in the rising dark, its progress bar inching forward with the maddening patience of a thing that did not know it was running out of time.

With a choking sound, Annie lunged toward the door and kicked at the deadbolt one last time. She couldn't breathe. When her lungs tried, they burned. She kicked and prayed.

Then, a wall collapsed, and the world went black.

CHAPTER NINETEEN

THE REALTOR

THE COFFEE SHOP on Third Street was called Common Grounds, which was either a pun or a warning, depending on how generous you were feeling. Zara Kane was not feeling generous. She sat in the back booth with both hands wrapped around a mug she hadn't sipped from, watching the door with fixed attention.

Zara had arrived twenty minutes early because being early was the only form of control available to a person who had lost control of everything else. She'd chosen this booth because it was farthest from the windows and closest to the back exit. She could leave if she needed to, she told herself.

Tim's call had come at nine the previous night. She'd been sitting on her bed, the box freshly re-sealed and pushed back into its hiding place, her face still damp from the crying she'd done over photographs of a dead boy and the diary of a girl she no longer recognized as herself. The phone had buzzed and she'd seen the name— Pastor Tim Erickson, stored in her contacts under the professional heading she gave to anyone associated with a closed transaction— and her stomach had dropped.

"Zara," he'd said. No pleasantries. No warmth. Just her

name. Tim Erickson without his charm was like a church without its stained glass— frighteningly stone. "I need to talk to you."

"So we're talking," Zara said, trying to sound pleasant.

"Not on the phone. In person."

"About what?" she'd asked, though she'd already known. The deal for the land the amphitheatre was built on wasn't the first one that had been arranged by her anonymous benefactor.

"You know what," Tim had said, and hung up.

Now she sat in Common Grounds and waited for Tim to walk through the door. The coffee in her mug had gone luke-warm. The barista wiped the counter in slow circles and stared at her phone.

The bell above the door chimed, and Tim Erickson walked in.

The first thing Zara noticed was that his hair was wrong. Not dramatically wrong— not unwashed or uncombed— but softer than usual, lacking the architectural rigidity of the slicked-back style he wore like armor on Sundays. It fell across his forehead in a way that made him look younger and less certain, closer to the shy boy she remembered from school. The second thing she noticed was that he wasn't smiling.

He slid into the booth across from her without stopping at the counter. No coffee. No small talk. No pastoral warmth deployed like a handshake. He just sat down and looked at her.

"Thank you for coming," he said.

"You didn't give me much choice." She meant it to sound light. It came out thin and defensive.

Tim leaned forward, his forearms on the table, his hands clasped in a posture that could have been prayer but wasn't. "I'm going to say some things," he said, "and I need you to let me finish before you respond. Can you do that?"

Zara nodded, because her throat had closed and nodding was all she could manage.

"I know you *know*," Tim said. The four words landed on the table between them like stones placed in a row. "I know you didn't become the number-one commercial real estate agent in Cedarsburg by accident. Not in this market. Not in this economy. Not when every other agent in the county is scrambling for residential listings that barely cover their gas money." He paused, watching her face for confirmation. "Someone helped you. Someone directed business your way — commercial deals, land acquisitions, transactions that were too big and too clean for a town this size. And in exchange, you did things for them, didn't you? Small things. Things that didn't feel like crimes because nobody was bleeding."

Zara's fingers tightened around the mug. The ceramic was barely warm now, the heat having leached away while she wasn't paying attention.

"Tim—"

"I'm not judging you because I did it too."

Zara closed her mouth.

Tim ran a hand through his unstyled hair. Seeing him like this— raw, uncertain, his white teeth hidden behind a mouth that had forgotten how to smile— made Zara realize what a mess she'd gotten herself into.

"I don't know their name," he continued. "Whoever is behind this. I know they're connected to the Mayor. I know they have a lot of money. I'm almost sure they've come by it through illegal activities. I've been trying to piece it together. The group. The organization. Whatever they are. I've been trying to figure it out since—" He stopped. Swallowed. "Since Brenda."

The name fell between them and neither of them moved. Outside, a car passed on Third Street, its engine loud in the morning quiet.

"When I wanted to build the amphitheater," Tim said, his

voice lower now, almost confessional— "I went to Mayor Bellows. I told him what I wanted to do for this town. And he listened— he's good at listening. He listens and he nods and he makes you feel like you're the most important person in the room."

Zara knew. She'd sat across from the Mayor herself, in his office with its baseball cap hung on a hook and its framed photographs of Cedarsburg from better decades, and she'd felt exactly what Tim was describing— the gravitational pull of a man who made you believe he was on your side, even as the ground beneath you shifted in ways you couldn't see.

"He said he'd help," Tim went on. "And three weeks later, I received a cashier's check. Anonymous. No paper trail. No funding source. Just— money. Enough to break ground." His hands unclasped and he laid them flat on the table, palms down, as if he were trying to steady himself against something that was moving beneath him. "I told myself it was a blessing. That God works through imperfect vessels. That the money's origin didn't matter because its purpose was righteous." He looked at her. "You can justify anything if you try hard enough. I'm sure you know that too."

She did. God help her, she did. She'd been justifying the shadow buyer's emails for years— the forwarded listings, the shell company offers, the steady erosion of Cedarsburg's property map into something that looked less like a town and more like a portfolio. She'd told herself she was just doing her job. She was just a realtor. She was just following instructions. She was just trying to survive in a market that didn't leave room for questions.

"After the check," Tim said, "the calls started. Small favors. That's what they called them— *favors*. Could I share some information about a particular church patron? His financial situation, his family circumstances, whether he might be open to selling his property. Could I encourage a certain family to attend a town council meeting? Could I mention, from the

pulpit, that certain businesses in town were worth support-
ing." He pressed his palms harder against the table. "None of
it felt like harm. That was the trick. Each favor was so small,
so reasonable, so easy to rationalize, that by the time I looked
up and saw the whole picture— by the time I understood that
I was a tool being used by people I'd never met to do things I
didn't understand— I was already in too deep to climb out."

Zara was gripping the mug so tightly now that her
knuckles had gone white. The barista had stopped wiping the
counter and was stacking cups.

"And then Brenda died," Tim said. His voice cracked on
the girl's name, the first fracture in what had been, until that
moment, a controlled delivery. He pressed his fist against his
mouth for a beat, composing himself. "A fifteen-year-old girl.
Dead. And I'm standing at the water tower holding her mother's hands and praying— *praying*, Zara— and the whole time
I'm thinking: This is connected. There's something wrong in
this town. And I've known it for a long time. Did the people
who sent me that check, the people who called me for favors,
did they—" He couldn't finish the sentence.

"Tim," Zara whispered.

"You brokered the amphitheater land deal." He said it
flatly, without accusation, but the words carried the weight of
a fact that had been established and could not be retracted.
"You came to *me*," Tim said, his voice shaking. "You were the
one who put the idea for an amphitheater in my head. You
said you had the perfect land, owned by a shell company I
didn't need to worry about. You handled the paperwork. The
title transfer, the deed, the sale records. You said I could get
the land cheap and the money to build would present itself.
And then it did. You're the one who gave me the idea. But
you got it from someone else… didn't you?

Zara felt the tears come before she could stop them. They
came fast and hot and blurred her vision until Tim became a
smear of brown hair and tired eyes across the table. She

pressed both hands over her face and made a sound that she hadn't heard herself make since the day Joshua died. It was the sound of two parts of her— the best and the worst— converging.

"You knew," Tim said. Not a question.

Zara nodded behind her hands. The gesture felt like signing a document. Like closing a deal she could never reopen.

"They asked me to plant the idea in your head," Zara said quietly. "And like you, I always do what they ask."

Tim was quiet for a long moment. The couple near the window glanced their way, then politely returned to their muffin. The barista put in earbuds. Outside, Cedarsburg went about the business of being a town— cars moving, lights changing, the machinery of normalcy grinding forward over whatever was rotting underneath.

"Does the Mayor know?" Tim asked. "How deep does this go?"

Zara lowered her hands. Her mascara had run— she could feel it, the damp tracks on her cheeks, the rawness around her eyes— and she didn't care, because vanity required a kind of energy she no longer had. She looked at Tim Erickson, this man she'd known since childhood. They were the same. Both of them had wanted so badly to matter in a town that was disappearing that they'd made deals with people who were causing the disappearance.

"The Mayor knows," she said. Her voice was wrecked. "He's known from the beginning. He's part of it. How deep it goes— Tim, I don't think you understand. I don't think either *one of us* understands. I've been forwarding listings to a shadow buyer for years. Every property that comes on the market in Cedarsburg, I send to an email address before it goes public. And they buy. Through shell companies. Through intermediaries. Half the commercial real estate in this town is owned by people who don't exist— companies, fake names on paper, nothing more. And I made it happen. I brokered the deals. I cashed the commissions. I told myself it was just business."

She reached for a napkin from the dispenser on the table and pressed it against her eyes. When she pulled it away, it was streaked with black.

"You need to be careful," she said. "You're dealing with something so much bigger than both of us. Bigger than the Mayor. Bigger than the amphitheater. Bigger than this town." She leaned forward, and her voice dropped to barely a whisper. "They have a name. The group. The people behind all of it. I'm not supposed to know it but I've been digging and I've learned—"

Tim's eyes were fixed on her face. He wasn't breathing.

"The Collective," Zara said.

The word sat between them on the table like a thing that had been uncaged. Two syllables. Clean and corporate and utterly devoid of the violence that lived inside them.

"That's all I know," Zara said. She was already reaching for her purse, already sliding toward the edge of the booth. "And knowing even that much is dangerous. For both of us. I shouldn't have said anything… If anyone told you it was me, I'll deny it."

She stood. Her legs felt unreliable— the kind of shaky that came after adrenaline had burned through the body and left behind only the residue of what it had cost. She looked down at Tim, still seated, still processing, his unstyled hair falling across his forehead, his white teeth invisible behind a mouth that had forgotten every sermon it had ever delivered.

"Be careful, Tim," she said again.

She walked out of Common Grounds without looking back. The bell above the door chimed behind her— a bright, ridiculous sound.

The storefronts stretched away from her in both directions, half of them occupied, half of them dark. A campaign sign stood in a planter box across the street— *"I'm Voting for Bellows!"*— its colors faded by the weather.

Zara stared at it and thought about the tangled mess she'd found herself in: all of it because she'd dared to love a boy named Joshua Hudson, who wasn't even here anymore.

She'd given Tim the name. The Collective. She couldn't take it back. The seal was broken, and whatever happened next— to Tim, to her, to the amphitheater, to the Mayor, to all of them— had already been set in motion.

Zara walked to her car and opened the door, sliding into the driver's seat before starting the engine. She drove as normal, hoping that life would let her forget what had just happened— even though she knew, from experience, it wouldn't.

CHAPTER TWENTY

DESPITE ALL ODDS, Annie was alive.

She was seated on the rear bumper of Fire Engine 7, a wool blanket draped across her shoulders. She stared across the parking lot, watching the last tendrils of smoke rise from Cedarsburg High's east wing in thin grey columns. Her lungs felt scraped— raw, from inhaling ash and soot. Ethan sat beside her, his right shoulder held at an angle that told her his attempts to break down the door had only broken him. Megan was on her other side, cross-legged on the truck's running board, her borrowed denim jacket streaked with soot. She held the thumb drive between her fingers.

"That building's been trying to die for decades," Annie said cheerfully, nodding at the limp form of Cedarsburg High. "Seems like with someone's help, it's gotten its wish!"

"So glad we could be present for the funeral," Megan snorted, rolling her eyes.

They'd gotten out through the ceiling. That was the part Annie's mind kept circling back to, not because it was heroic but because it was stupid. A wall had collapsed and landed on Annie, who was only protected by Ethan's lumbering frame. His body covered her as the world went dark for a moment, which was when Annie managed to shout, "We have to go up!" Ethan had smashed through the acoustic tiles with the folding chair, and Megan had found a maintenance shaft above the drop ceiling that ran laterally toward the building's west side, away from the fire. The three of them had crawled through ductwork that wasn't designed to hold their weight, listening to the building groan beneath. Annie had torn the knee of her pants on a riveted seam. Ethan had lost his tie somewhere in the shaft— the kind of detail that would be funny later, maybe, if later turned out to be the kind of time where things could be funny. The progress bar had been at eighty-one percent when Megan pulled the drive. Not everything. But enough, maybe. Enough to be worth almost dying for.

Two fire engines, an ambulance, and a Cedarsburg Police cruiser occupied the parking lot in loose formation. The EMTs had already checked them over— vitals, pupils, lungs— and had cleared them with the mild disapproval of medical professionals who believed that people had no business being inside burning buildings. A small crowd had gathered beyond the orange cones— Saturday morning bystanders who materialized at every crisis with their phones raised. Cedarsburg loved a spectacle. There wasn't much else to love.

Annie heard him before she saw him. The click of a lighter, distinctive and unhurried, followed by the creak of leather. Sheriff Homestadder came around the front of the engine truck. He was in uniform— he was *always* in uniform. Annie hadn't seen the man in civilian clothes even once since they'd been here. His brown hair was neat despite the hour, his posture easy.

"Lord," the Sheriff said, looking at the three of them on the truck bumper like they were lost feral cats. "You all look like you crawled out of a chimney." He held up a hand before anyone could respond. "Don't get up. EMTs told me you're cleared, but cleared and fine are two different things, and I'd rather you sit for a minute. Can I get you water? There's a case in the cruiser."

"We're okay," Annie said.

"You're *okay*," the Sheriff repeated, nodding slowly, as if testing the word. He drew on the cigarette he'd lit during his approach. The ember flared orange in the morning air— a cruel joke after the fire they'd just escaped. "Here's what I'm trying to figure out," he said, and his voice was the voice of a man who genuinely wanted to help, who stayed up at night worrying about the people in his jurisdiction, "Three of you come back into town— and I'm glad you're back, don't misunderstand me, especially you, Megan— but since you've been here, we've had a girl fall from a water tower and a fire set at the high school. In the same building where you happened to be."

He let the observation hang.

"We didn't set the fire, Sheriff," Ethan said. His voice was hoarse from the smoke, stripped of its usual measured precision.

"Didn't say you did." Homestadder held up his free hand — palm out, a gesture of peace. "I'm just saying it seems like trouble follows you folks around. Like a dog that won't stay home." He smiled, but the feeling didn't reach his eyes. "And I worry about that. For your sake and for the town's. I've spent twenty years keeping this place safe. Twenty years making sure the wheels keep turning the way they should. Been doing this since I was a young man. And when things start going sideways—" He shrugged, the gesture encompassing the smoldering building, the fire trucks, the crowd of gawkers. "Well. I take it personally."

Annie studied his face. She had a habit of watching people the way a jeweler watches light pass through a stone, looking for the flaws that revealed its true composition. The Sheriff's face was good. Very good. The concern registered as genuine. The eyes were warm and direct. She couldn't find the seam. It bothered her. Everyone had a seam.

"We appreciate your concern," Annie said, and the words came out with the professional neutrality she deployed when she wanted to end a conversation without appearing to end it. "And we appreciate the fire department's response. We'll be happy to give statements about what happened."

"Of course, of course." The Sheriff waved the offer away. "No rush. Get yourselves sorted first. You've had a morning." He took another drag— long and deliberate. "Tell you what, though," he said, exhaling a thin stream that caught the light and turned briefly silver before the breeze dismantled it. "You three keep going this way, I'll be through a pack a day again." He tapped the cigarette against his thumb, dislodging ash that fell and scattered on the asphalt. "I tried to quit, you know. Must have been— what, over a decade ago? Patches, gum, the whole routine. Lasted less than a year." He looked at the cigarette between his fingers with the fond resignation of a man who loved his vices. "Some habits, I guess, you just learn to live with. You all got any of those? Vices that you just can't quit? Can't walk away from?"

He raised the cigarette to his lips, and Megan shuddered. It was a small gesture, but Annie noticed it. Filed it away.

"We do," Annie said, nodding seriously. "We do have our vices. And I think it's clear what they are." Annie motioned at the broken building laid bare behind the Sheriff. "Getting into trouble. Being too curious. Holding the guilty to account. It's an addiction I suppose, finding justice," she smiled at him brightly. "One I just can't quit."

The Sheriff scanned Annie from head to toe, then stepped toward her, close enough for her to see the pockmarks on his cheeks. "Then— as your elder— I have to warn you, young lady. Vices always catch up with a person. Maybe not today. Maybe not tomorrow. But they do." He took another long, slow drag on his cigarette. "Be careful yours don't eat you up, you hear?"

"Too late," Annie said as if no further explanation were necessary.

The Sheriff nodded. Good enough. "Well," he said, straightening his belt in a reflexive motion. "I'll let you folks rest. But do me a favor— stay out of trouble. I feel responsible for justice in this town, and I intend to make sure things operate the way they should." He touched the brim of an imaginary hat— he wasn't wearing one, but the gesture made a point— and turned away, disappearing into his police cruiser.

They watched him go. The cigarette trailed a thin line of smoke behind him, a grey thread connecting the Sheriff to the space he'd just occupied.

"I hate that guy," Megan said.

The words came out flat and immediate. She wasn't looking at the cruiser. She was looking at the thumb drive in her hands, turning it over and over, her jaw set in a way that Annie recognized from Ethan— the family resemblance surfacing not in their features but in the architecture of their anger.

"Yeah," Annie said quietly, something in her hurting in a new, delicate way. "Me too."

She didn't elaborate. There would be time for elaboration later. But right now, sitting on the bumper of a fire truck with soot in her hair and smoke in her lungs, all Annie could offer was agreement.

Ethan shifted beside her, wincing as his shoulder protested the movement. He nodded toward the thumb drive in Megan's hands. "We need to look at that. Whatever Brenda found— whoever she was tracking— the answers are on that drive."

"Eighty-one percent," Megan said, holding up the small black rectangle. "Not everything. But close."

"Close might be enough," Annie said. She believed it. She had to. Annie had meant it when she'd told the Sheriff justice was her addiction. And like all great addicts, Annie wasn't about to quit before she got her hit. "We'll look at the drive tonight, at my Dad's house, away from prying eyes. As for tomorrow, I'd like everyone to add this special event to their calendars."

She reached into the pocket of her jacket. Her fingers found paper. She pulled it out: a flyer, creased and slightly damp, that she'd picked up from a bench in the town square two days ago and had been carrying around since, the way she carried everything, because Annie Hudson did not throw things away until she understood why she'd picked them up in the first place.

She unfolded it and held it up. Red and blue lettering on white paper— the universal color scheme of American politics, of people who wanted to be in charge and believed that primary colors communicated trustworthiness. The text read: *CEDARSBURG MAYORAL DEBATE. Mayor Bellows vs. Prim Rosington. Tomorrow, 7 PM, Town Hall. The Future of Cedarsburg — YOU Decide!*

"Now that we almost burned down the town, anyone feel like getting political?" Annie asked.

Ethan looked at the flyer. Then he looked at her— the careful, searching look he gave her when he was trying to determine whether she was serious or deflecting, because with Annie the distinction was often academic. She was always serious. Even when she was deflecting.

"A debate?" Ethan said.

"A debate tomorrow," Annie confirmed. "Every person of interest in this town, in one place, on a stage, under pressure. The Mayor. Prim. Probably the Sheriff in the audience. Probably Tim Erickson— I doubt he'd miss a chance to mingle with his congregation. Probably half the people Brenda was investigating." She folded the flyer and tucked it back into her pocket. "People reveal themselves when they're performing. They think the performance is the mask, but it's the opposite. The performance is where the truth leaks through."

Megan looked at her with something that was close to admiration. "You sound like a spy," she said.

"I sound like an investigator," Annie corrected. "Spies create chaos. Investigators watch chaos happen and take notes."

"Who knows," Annie smiled, reaching into her pocket and pulling out the bracelet with its letter P on the surface. She let it dangle in the air, sun glinting off the charm. "Maybe we can even be good samaritans and return *this* to its owner. I'm sure Prim will be thrilled."

Ethan and Megan exchanged a glance, their raised eyebrows making the same delighted arch. They were close to finding answers. All three of them could feel it.

Behind them, the high school continued its slow exhalation of smoke and ruin, the east wing's windows dark and broken, the brickwork stained with soot in patterns that looked, from the right angle, like something written in a language no one had taught Annie to read. But she was learning. Every hour in this town, she was learning.

CHAPTER TWENTY-ONE
THE ACTIVIST

THE LIVING ROOM of Prim's parents' house on Birch Court had been converted into something between a war room and a disaster area. Prim Rosington sat at the center of it — a general who had misplaced her army and found, in its place, a collection of twenty-three-year-olds minions who called themselves "interns" and were eager to do her bidding. Campaign posters covered every horizontal surface— the coffee table, the dining table her mother had begrudgingly surrendered, the floor in front of the television that hadn't been turned on in weeks because the television was buried under a mountain of flyers that read *Prim for Progress* in red and blue lettering. The overhead light was off. Nobody had turned it on. The room was lit instead by the blue glow of three laptop screens and the intermittent flash of phone notifications, giving the whole scene the quality of a situation room — purposeful, urgent, and slightly claustrophobic.

Four interns. She'd started with seven, but two had dropped out after midterms, for which Prim privately labeled them as "slackers." Then, of course, there was Brenda, who had been murdered, but Prim was trying very hard not to think about that. The remaining four interns were good.

Earnest. Relentless in the way that only people under twenty-five could be relentless, their energy sourced from some renewable well of idealism that Prim remembered having once, at Yale, before she'd learned that idealism didn't move a person forward.

The one with the glasses— Eric, her communications intern who drafted her social media posts— was pacing behind the couch with a tablet in his hand. "The numbers are good," Eric said, not for the first time. He'd said it when he arrived. He'd said it during the pizza. He'd said it while organizing the stack of opposition research folders that now sat on the arm of Prim's chair. "Really good. The Register poll has you within three points, and that was before the school fire. People are scared. Scared people want change."

Prim said nothing. She was looking at the opposition research folder. It was blue— the color had been her choice, because blue suggested authority and calm. Inside were forty-seven pages of documentation: campaign finance discrepancies, municipal contract irregularities, a pattern of zoning decisions that benefited shell companies over local businesses, and— the centerpiece, the bomb, the thing her interns had been circling all evening— evidence that Mayor Bellows had redirected campaign contributions to fund private projects, including a two-million-dollar cashier's check with no legitimate paper trail.

The bomb. That was what Prim's team was calling it. Her interns used the word with the giddy anticipation of people who had never seen the consequences of an *actual* bomb.

"So tomorrow night," said the intern whose name Prim could never get right. Was it Mary or Marie? Whoever she was, she was sitting cross-legged on the floor, surrounded by a semicircle of printed debate prep questions she'd been sorting into categories labeled ECONOMY, INFRASTRUCTURE, and KILL SHOT. "When do we deploy the bomb? Opening statement? Or do we wait for him to say

something about fiscal responsibility and then— boom?!"
Maybe-Mary made an explosion gesture with both hands,
fingers splaying outward.

Prim looked at the girl's hands and thought about Brenda
Welsh's hands.

She hadn't meant to think about them. She'd been disci-
plined about that all day— pushing the image back each time
it surfaced, the way you push a door shut against wind. But
the girl's gesture— the splaying fingers, separated and stocky
— had opened the door, and now Brenda was in the room
with her, fifteen years old and blonde and dead at the bottom
of a water tower with bruises that told a story nobody in this
town seemed interested in reading.

Brenda, who had been her intern. Her volunteer. A girl
who had walked into Prim's campaign office four months ago
with a laptop bag over one shoulder and a quiet ferocity in
her eyes that Prim had recognized because she'd seen it in her
own mirror, years ago, before Yale had taught her to dress it
up in policy language and strategic ambiguity. Brenda had
wanted to make a difference. She'd said those exact words— *I
want to make a difference*— and Prim had smiled and handed
her a volunteer form and put her to work on data entry, never
once suspecting that the girl's definition of "making a difference" extended far beyond stuffing envelopes and knocking
on doors.

She was like me, Prim thought, swallowing hard. And
look at what happened to her. *She was like me before I
changed.*

Brenda had been brave enough to take on the establish-
ment. Prim *wanted* to do the same, but throughout this
campaign she'd slowly realized the only way to win was to
become a part of the beast. And now Brenda was dead.

Prim had found her first note left on the doorstep of this
very house, six months ago. It read, simply: *Find Bellows'
Secret.*

She had ignored the first note. Then, a second had arrived. Again, only three letters long, it said: *"Winners are ours."*

Then, the emails had arrived. One by one, they crowded her inbox, all of them from no-reply, proxy-routed anonymous accounts. And these? These were longer than three letters. The emails told Prim the future was hers to have, if she earned it by destroying her competition. The election was no longer hers to win or lose. It was being given to her. Handed over, like a key, by people who would expect her to open whatever doors they pointed to.

She'd told herself she could handle it. She'd told herself that accepting help wasn't the same as being controlled, that she could take their assistance and still govern on her own terms, that the voting machines and the assured victory were just tools and tools were neutral and it was the hand that wielded them that determined their morality. She'd told herself this at Yale, too, when she'd written a thesis on the ethical compromises of revolutionary movements and concluded, with the confidence of someone who had never been tested, that pragmatism and principle could coexist if you were smart enough to manage the tension.

Now, Prim realized, she wasn't smart enough. Nobody was.

"Prim?" The communications intern had stopped pacing. All four of them were looking at her now, their faces blue-lit and expectant. "Are you ready? For tomorrow? The bomb?"

Prim looked at the folder on the arm of her chair. Forty-seven pages. Campaign finance violations. Shell companies. It would end Bellows' career. It would be historic— at least by the standards of a town where "historic" meant anything more interesting than a new Walmart. It would make her the reformer she'd always claimed to be, the Yale-educated activist who came home to root out corruption and give Cedarsburg back to its people.

And it would work. She would win. She'd been *told* she

would win. The notes had said so. The people behind the notes had promised it with the calm certainty of those who did not make promises they couldn't keep, because they had access to the machines that counted the votes and the will to use them. She would win regardless of what she said at the debate tomorrow, regardless of the bomb, regardless of the forty-seven pages. She would win because she'd been chosen, the same way Bellows had been chosen before her, and the price of being chosen was doing what they asked when they asked it, and the price of refusing was—

Brenda's face. The water tower. The bruises.

Prim swallowed.

She could walk away. She could do that. It was an option.

Prim picked up the blue folder. She opened it. The pages were crisp and orderly.

"Yes," she said. Her voice was steady. Her voice was always steady— she'd learned that at Yale, in debate practice, in seminar rooms where the ability to sound certain was more valuable than the ability to be right. "We're going forward as planned. Tomorrow night, when he talks about fiscal responsibility, I drop it. All of it. Every page."

The room erupted. Eric, the communications intern pumped his fist. The girl on the floor gathered her KILL SHOT questions with renewed purpose. Someone opened a laptop and began drafting press-ready excerpts.

Prim watched them work and felt nothing. Not triumph. Not relief.

Outside, Cedarsburg was dark and quiet. Tomorrow would be the day. The day from which Prim could never turn back.

CHAPTER TWENTY-TWO

THE MAYOR

THE WAREHOUSE on County Road 12 had been a grain storage facility once, back when Cedarsburg grew things instead of losing them. Mayor Bellows parked his Lincoln in the gravel lot beside it and sat for a moment with the engine running. He felt like he was going to a dentist's appointment — he knew this was necessary, but also that it would hurt.

Bellows was sixty-two years old. He'd been doing this thing so long— corruption, running games— you'd think the pain would lessen. But it never did. He wore a white button-down tucked into khakis and a baseball cap from the Cedarsburg Rotary Club that he kept on the passenger seat for occasions when he needed to look like one of the people, which was most occasions, because Mayor Bellows had built his entire career winning the trust of the people. The cap was slightly sweat-stained along the brim. He'd never replaced it. Replacing it would have made it new, and new was the opposite of what the cap was supposed to communicate. The cap said: *I've been here. I've put in the work. I'm one of you.*

But he wasn't one of them.

He turned off the engine. The silence that replaced it was deafening. The warehouse sat fifty yards from the road, separated from it by the gravel lot and a chain-link fence that had been cut open and never repaired. Severed links curled back like fingers recoiling from something hot. Beyond the fence, cornfields stretched into darkness so complete that the horizon was theoretical. No streetlights out here. No houses. Just the warehouse and the Lincoln and the sky, which was overcast and starless.

Bellows got out of the car. The gravel crunched under his loafers.

The warehouse door was open. Not wide— just enough to suggest invitation. Bellows accepted, slipping through the crack and sucking in a little to fit.

Inside, the air smelled like machine oil and cardboard. The overhead fluorescents were on— half of them, anyway. The warehouse floor was concrete, cracked and stained, and on it sat four pallets arranged in a neat row, each one stacked with machines that Bellows recognized immediately because he'd seen them every two years for the last decade and a half, in gymnasiums and community centers and church basements across the county:

Voting machines.

Touchscreen models, their casings a neutral grey, their screens dark, their power cords coiled on top like sleeping snakes. He counted quickly, coming up with forty-eight. Forty-eight machines that would be distributed across Cedarsburg's polling locations in time for Tuesday's election, each one carrying inside its circuits the invisible machinery of a democracy that had stopped being one years ago— and nobody had noticed yet.

Or maybe people *had* noticed but had decided, the way Cedarsburg decided most things, that noticing was too expensive and ignorance was a kind of insurance policy against having to act. That's fine. Indifference only helped Bellows' cause.

The man was already there.

Bellows had never learned his name. Tonight, the man wore a dark jacket over a dark shirt— no tie, no insignia, nothing that would survive a witness description with any specificity. He was of medium height and medium build and medium age, somewhere between thirty-five and fifty-five, with features so deliberately unremarkable that looking at him was like looking at a composite sketch of no one in particular. He stood near the first pallet of voting machines with one hand resting on a grey casing.

"Mayor," the man said. The single word carried an unmistakable irony.

"Evening." Bellows nodded. He stopped walking about six feet from the man, then glanced at the voting machines. "They're ready."

"Tuesday morning. Six a.m. They'll go out on county trucks, same as always." The man patted the machine casing like it was a dependable animal. "The satellite signal interruption is already configured. It's a sixty-second window during the upload phase— when the machines transmit their tallies to the county server. During those sixty seconds, the feed reroutes through a relay that adjusts the count before it reaches the central database. Clean insertion. No digital fingerprints. The county's own audit software will confirm the adjusted numbers as legitimate because the adjustment happens before the audit checkpoint." He said all of this the way a mechanic might explain an oil change.

Bellows felt the thing he always felt at these meetings— not relief, not gratitude. Just— a trip to the dentist.

"Seven points," he repeated.

"Seven points," the man confirmed. "Prim Rosington will lose. Gracefully, if she's smart. Less gracefully if she isn't."

"You're sure?" Bellows said, an edge to his voice.

"Of course I'm sure," the man said, but a knowing smile played on his lips. "Unless you know something I don't know?"

"What I know is that The Collective likes to run us all around like rats," Bellows said, trying to keep his tone even. "Wouldn't surprise me if you were playing Prim against me and me against her, and all kinds of promises were made every which way."

"That sounds like an excellent strategy," the man nodded. "Just in case, let us say, something went wrong with the voting machines. If— despite our best efforts— you were to lose the election, perhaps because our technological attempts at subversion were intercepted, it would be excellent if Prim Rosington were *also* our acquaintance. If she believed she won *because* of us, not in spite of us. Then we'd still have a friend in office. What an excellent idea," the man pretended to stroke his chin. "I'll have to pass it along to my supervisor."

"You're bastards, everyone of you," Bellows said, shaking his head.

The man shrugged and smiled. "Maybe we just like making friends."

"I've done everything you want, for years."

"Then you have no reason to be concerned," the man answered, patting the voting machine again. "You know how the game goes"

Five times. Twenty years. Bellows had been elected— if that was the right word, and it wasn't— again and again. The first election had been the hardest. Not because the race was close— The Collective had handled that— but because Bellows had still, at that point, possessed the residual capacity for shame. He'd stood in the shower the morning after his first "victory" and let the water run hot enough to redden his skin and thought about the man he'd been before the deal.

"There's something else," the man said.

There was always something else. Bellows had learned this the way you learn any recurring pattern— through repetition, through the slow, grinding accumulation of instances that eventually formed a rule. The Collective never called a meeting to deliver good news. Good news came by itself, quietly, in the form of things going the way they were supposed to go..

"The three investigators," the man said. He didn't use their names. He never used names when functions would suffice. "The private investigator, the FBI agent, and the sister. They survived the fire."

Bellows knew this. He'd seen the news. He'd also seen the fire trucks from his office window and felt, briefly, the particular cold that settled in his chest whenever The Collective's operations became visible to the public— the cold of a man standing on a stage whose machinery was showing through the floorboards.

"They got data from the school," the man continued. "From the girl's computer. We don't know how much. Enough to be a problem."

The girl. Brenda Welsh. Fifteen years old. Dead at the bottom of a water tower because she'd been too smart and too brave and too young to understand that bravery without power was just a more scenic route to the same cliff everyone else eventually reached. Bellows hadn't known she was going to die. He hadn't ordered it. He hadn't been consulted. He'd learned about it the way the rest of Cedarsburg had learned about it— from the sirens, from the whispered phone calls, from the particular quality of silence that settled over a town when something happened that was too terrible to discuss and too important to ignore. But he'd known, the moment he heard, that The Collective was involved. The same way he'd known fifteen years ago, when Joshua Hudson's body was found and Megan Beckett disappeared, that the violence bearing down on his town wasn't random— it was structural. It was the cost of the system he'd agreed to maintain.

"What do you need?" Bellows asked. The question came out flat, drained of everything except the weary pragmatism of a man who had stopped pretending there was a version of this conversation that ended with him saying no.

The man reached into his jacket and produced an envelope. White. Letter-sized. Unsealed. He held it the way you'd hold something that was both valuable and dangerous— with care, with awareness, with the implicit understanding that its contents would rearrange whatever situation they were introduced to.

"New evidence," the man said. "In an old case."

Bellows looked at the envelope. His hands stayed at his sides.

"The Hudson murder," the man continued. "And the Beckett disappearance. A source of ongoing pain for this community and, more recently, a source of ongoing interference from the people who keep digging into it." He tapped the envelope against his palm, twice, the sound soft and rhythmic in the warehouse's hollow air. "What's in this envelope solves both cases. Definitively. A suspect. Physical evidence. You'll announce it at the debate tomorrow," the man said. "You'll stand at a microphone and you tell this town that the case has been solved. That the person responsible for Joshua Hudson's death and Megan Beckett's disappearance has been identified. That you— personally, tirelessly, at great cost to your own peace of mind— ensured that justice was finally done."

Bellows stared at the envelope. His mind was doing the math. He would be a hero. The man who solved the case that had haunted Cedarsburg for a generation.

It was a beautiful story. It was exactly the kind of story that Cedarsburg wanted to believe. And it was, of course, a lie. The same way everything The Collective constructed was a lie

"The suspect in the envelope," Bellows said carefully. "Who is it?"

The man didn't answer. He let the silence hang in the air,

waiting instead for Bellows to ask a question that actually mattered.

"I'll need the Sheriff on board—" Bellows started to say.

"You know of course, he is," the man confirmed.

"We'll need a chain of custody, procedural legitimacy— it has to come through the Sheriff's office or it won't hold up."

"It's all there," the man agreed. Then, he turned and walked toward the warehouse's far exit, where a vehicle was presumably waiting in the darkness beyond the building's back wall. He called over his shoulder, "Good luck, tomorrow."

The warehouse door closed behind him. The sound was small, but in the empty space it carried the finality of something much larger. Bellows stood alone among the voting machines, forty-eight grey sentinels arranged on their pallets, their screens dark, their circuitry patient, waiting for Tuesday the way a trap waits for its spring. He tucked the envelope in the breast pocket of his jacket. It sat against his chest, thin as a promise, like the one he'd fifteen years ago and still hadn't figured out how to end.

CHAPTER TWENTY-THREE

AT HER FATHER'S HOUSE, Annie sat at the table with her hands wrapped around a mug of coffee she'd made herself. The mug was chipped. Everything in this kitchen was chipped, or cracked, or held together with a pragmatism that had long ago replaced any impulse toward repair.

Bill Hudson stood at the sink with his sleeves pushed to his elbows, washing the dinner plates by hand. He didn't own a dishwasher. He'd never owned a dishwasher. Annie suspected this was less about frugality and more about the fact that dishwashers were efficient, and efficiency implied a life that was moving forward at a pace worth optimizing, and her father's life had not been moving forward in any meaningful direction since the night his son had died. He washed the plates the way he did everything now— slowly, thoroughly, and only because he had to.

From the next room, Megan's voice drifted through the doorway, low and clipped, punctuated by the occasional murmur from Ethan that was too quiet to decode. The house was small enough that conversations in one room were overheard in every other.

"Heard about the school," Annie's father said. He didn't

turn from the sink. "Fire department was there all morning. Helen from next door called to tell me. She calls to tell me everything. I think she thinks I'm lonely."

"You're fine," Annie said, knowing that her father didn't *get* lonely anymore.

"Exactly right," he nodded, agreeing with his daughter. "But are you?"

"Dad—"

"You were in a burning building, Annie. A building that someone set on fire. On purpose. While you were inside it." He paused. The water ran. The faucet dripped. "That's not fine. That's the opposite of *fine*. I told you not to play around with things that are bigger than us. I can't lose you too," he said. "Joshua is gone. Your mother is gone. You're what I have, Annie. You and this house and the fact that you call me every day and I get to hear your voice and know you're still somewhere in the world being alive." He turned off the water. The silence that followed was louder than the faucet had been. "Don't take that away from me. Please. Just— leave it alone. Let the police handle it. Let the FBI handle it. Let someone with a badge and a pension handle it. You don't have to save everybody."

"I'm not trying to save everybody."

"Then what are you trying to do?" He turned from the sink. The towel in his hands was damp and he twisted it between his fingers. "You're trying to find who killed your brother. I know that. I've always known that. But Annie— sometimes the world just takes from you and doesn't explain why, and the bravest thing you can do is accept that and keep living. Little people don't win. We don't. We survive. That's the best we get."

Annie set down the coffee mug, ready to make a point. She sat up straight, ready to tell her father what she'd been thinking for a long time:

"There's no such thing as a little person, Dad."

Bill Hudson looked at her. The towel went still in his hands.

"Brenda Welsh was fifteen years old," Annie said. "She had a laptop and a nose ring and an internet name and zero authority. Nobody gave her a badge. Nobody gave her a pension. She sat in a basement computer lab at a high school that couldn't afford to fix its own lights, and she mapped the entire structure of the thing that's been eating this town for fifteen years. By herself. Because she decided that someone should, and no one else was." Annie paused. The overhead light buzzed. The faucet dripped. "She was a little person. By every measure you're using, she was the littlest person in the room. And she found the truth. And the people who are afraid of the truth killed her for it, which tells you everything you need to know about how much little people matter."

Her father's jaw worked. The expression on his face was the one she'd grown up watching— the mixture of love and frustration and fear that he wore whenever she demonstrated, through word or action, that she was not the kind of daughter who would stay safe because safety was comfortable. She was the kind who ran toward the thing that was burning. She always had been. He'd known it since she was nine years old and had climbed the water tower on a dare, and he'd known it when she'd left Cedarsburg to become an investigator, and he knew it now, standing in his crumbling kitchen with a dish towel in his hands and the sound of the faucet keeping its sad, steady time behind him.

He nodded. Not agreement, but acceptance. He'd been letting go of things for fifteen years. His son. His wife. His house, piece by piece, to the slow erosion of neglect. His belief that the world was fair, or at least comprehensible. Now he was letting go of the last illusion he'd been holding— that he could keep his daughter safe by asking her to be someone she wasn't.

Annie stood. She crossed the small kitchen. She pulled her father into a hug.

"Be careful, Annie," he asked her one last time.

Then his hand dropped and he turned back to the sink and picked up another plate, and the water ran, and the faucet dripped, and Annie walked through the doorway toward the sound of Megan's voice and the work that was waiting for her in the next room.

———

Bill Hudson's office was the kind of room that had given up on being a room and was now, more accurately, a symptom— the physical manifestation of a man who had stopped filing, stopped organizing, and stopped performing. Boxes lined the walls in stacks that had no discernible system. A filing cabinet stood in one corner with its middle drawer permanently half-open, the track bent or broken. The desk was red oak, and it was lined with different bottles of half-drunk liquor— evidence that Bill Hudson's only current occupation was grieving.

They'd cleared enough space for three folding chairs and two devices. Megan sat at the desk, her fingers resting on the keyboard. Ethan leaned against the filing cabinet, his injured shoulder held carefully away from the metal. Annie leaned over Megan, hunching herself over the desk so she could better see the screen.

Megan held up both devices. In her left hand, the small black thumb drive they'd pulled from the school— eighty-one percent of Brenda Welsh's life's work, the data inside it waiting with the silent patience of testimony that has not yet been called to the stand. In her right hand, the hard drive from Russel Grey's compound— heavier, older, its casing scratched. They had seen some of its contents in the caves, but hadn't had an opportunity to review it all in the middle of the chaos that came after Brenda's murder.

"Which one first?" Megan asked.

Annie looked at the thumb drive. She thought about Brenda's locker and the ladybug sticker. She thought about Joshua's trophy in the display case, the brass plate tarnished to the color of old pennies, his name in small letters on a shelf in a building that had burned. She thought about the fifteen years between his death and this moment.

"Annie—" Megan started to say as if she could read Annie's mind, and knew what she was about to choose.

"The thumb drive," Annie said.

"But the hard drive could tell us The Collective's global reach—" Megan exclaimed.

"I need to give Joshua his justice before we look at anything else."

Megan's face shifted— a flicker of something that might have been disappointment, quickly banked, replaced by the professional neutrality of a woman who understood priorities even when they weren't her own. She set the hard drive on the desk beside the lamp and plugged the thumb drive into the computer's USB port. The machine wheezed to life with labored enthusiasm.

The files loaded. Megan navigated through the folder structure with quick, lateral movements. Annie watched over her shoulder as the folders opened, one inside another, the nested architecture of Brenda's research revealing itself layer by layer.

The first layer was campaign work. Opposition research files organized by category: *Bellows_Finance*, *Bellows_Contracts*, *Bellows_Zoning*, *Bellows_Personal*. Each folder was dense with documents— scanned receipts, screenshot captures of public records, spreadsheets cross-referencing municipal expenditures with dates and amounts that didn't match the city's published budget. It was meticulous. It was also, Annie realized as she read the file names and recognized the format, illegal. A fifteen-year-old had hacked into protected government databases and private financial accounts to gather opposition research for a political campaign.

Annie pointed at a folder labeled *PR_Deliverables*. Megan opened it. Inside were dated files— weekly reports, formatted with headers and summaries and action items. Each report was addressed to the same recipient, identified only by initials: *P.R.*

"That's evidence she did all this for Prim," Annie said, thinking about the bracelet they'd found with the letter "P" on it.

"And Prim had her killed for it to cover their tracks?" Ethan thought out loud.

Annie didn't confirm or deny his theory. But it was clear— Prim Rosington had weaponized a child.

"Look at this," Megan said. She'd navigated deeper, past the campaign deliverables, into a folder that Brenda had labeled with a single word: *More*. Inside were files that had nothing to do with Prim Rosington's campaign. These were different— rawer, less organized, the work of a girl who had been following one thread and stumbled onto another, darker thread tangled beneath it. Financial records that connected Bellows's campaign fund to shell companies. Shell companies that connected to property transactions. Property transactions that connected to names Annie didn't recognize but that triggered something in the architecture of her thinking, the way a wrong note triggers something in a musician— not a conscious identification, but a felt wrongness, a dissonance that demanded resolution.

"Brenda found out about The Collective while researching Bellows," Annie said. "She didn't mean to find them, but their claws are so deep in this town she couldn't help it." She paused, watching Megan scroll through files documenting real estate transactions. A familiar name popped up on the screen: Zara Kane.

"The Collective owns over half the town," Ethan said, letting out a low whistle.

"And all of it was brokered by Zara Kane," Annie agreed.

Megan turned and looked over her shoulder at Annie, a smile playing at her lips. "See why I don't keep old friends, Annie? They only manage to disappoint you."

Annie nodded, watching as Megan turned back to the screen and scrolled through files that grew progressively more complex, the spreadsheets giving way to network diagrams, connection maps. It was the visual grammar of conspiracy rendered in the clean lines of a girl who was trying to make sense of it all. "That's what turned Brenda," Annie said. She went from doing opposition research to investigating The Collective because Bellows's corruption was the door and the door was open and she walked through it."

Megan had stopped scrolling. She was staring at the screen with a focused stillness. "Guys," she said. "Look…"

The folder was labeled "VF." *Voter fraud.* Inside were email exchanges— not originals but screenshots, captured from an account that Brenda had accessed through means that Annie preferred not to speculate about. The emails were between an address she recognized as Bellows's private account and an anonymous sender routed through a proxy, the kind of layered encryption that existed specifically to make identification impossible. The content was brief and transactional, the language of people who understood that every written word was a potential exhibit.

Machines will be configured for a seven-point margin. Distribution follows standard county protocol. No action required on your end. Results will be confirmed by midnight.

Confirmed. Same arrangement as previous cycle. Appreciate the partnership.

Partnership. The word sat on the screen like a confession.

Annie read the exchanges twice. She swallowed. The sound was loud in the quiet room, louder than it should have been, and she felt Ethan's eyes on her from the filing cabinet, watching her face the way he always watched her face when he suspected she'd arrived at a conclusion she wasn't sharing.

She didn't share it. Not yet. The conclusion was still forming— still cooling, still hardening from liquid thought into solid understanding— and saying it aloud too soon would jinx the thing. But the shape was there, visible through the scaffolding: Mayor Bellows wasn't just corrupt. He wasn't a politician who'd made bad deals and taken dirty money. He was a part of the machine. Installed, maintained, and operated by the same people who had killed a fifteen-year-old girl — and, maybe, her brother.

"The hard drive," Megan said. She'd turned in the chair to face Ethan, her expression carrying the particular intensity of someone who has been patient long enough. "We need to look at what Russel left us."

Ethan shook his head. Not a refusal— not yet— but a plea. "I didn't bring it up earlier when you two were debating which drive to start with because I didn't want to rain on your parade—"

"That sure doesn't sound like you! Refusing to rain on a parade?" Megan jabbed, ignoring the corresponding eye roll from Ethan, who simply continued on as if she hadn't spoken.

"— but if that drive is tagged... if there's *any* kind of tracking embedded in the files, plugging it into a connected machine could lead them right here. Right to this house. To Annie's father and all of us."

"Ethan," Megan's voice hardened, the frustration breaking through the professional surface. She stood from the chair, the movement sharp, and faced her brother across the cluttered room. "Don't you get it? They're *already* here. They've been here for at least fifteen years, maybe more. They own the Mayor. They own the voting machines. They set a building on fire to destroy evidence. At some point we have to come face to face with them if we want anything to change! We can't run forever. Annie—" She turned. "Tell him."

Annie looked at Ethan. His face was set in the expression she knew best— the one he wore when his training and his instinct were pulling in opposite directions. She saw the exhaustion in the lines around his eyes, the cost of the day written in his body.

"Ethan," Annie said gently. "At some point we will have to face this—"

"What do you two want me to do?" Ethan said, throwing his hands in the air. "Agree to take on a shadow criminal organization with just the three of us? We need other agents we trust— the CIA— the FBI—"

"They're infiltrated," Megan said, looking away in disgust. "We don't know who we can count on—"

"Then give me time to figure it out! We can't just rush into something this big without a plan—"

"We could miss our chance—" Megan countered, but Ethan cut her off, his voice rising.

"I'm not getting the one person who stood beside me while you were missing *killed* because you refuse to slow down and make a plan!" Ethan shouted.

Annie cleared her throat, and suddenly both siblings looked at her as if they'd only just remembered she was even standing there.

"Megan is right," Annie said quietly. Then, because she saw the hurt in Ethan's eyes, she added: "Partially, anyway. The town isn't just compromised. It's owned. Every institution— the Mayor's office, the Sheriff, the elections themselves — it's all part of the same system. And we could miss a chance to take them down if we don't move now. But Ethan's right, too. We can't just take on a group this sophisticated without a plan. Alternatively, Ethan," Annie cringed as she looked at him. "I don't see a way to make a plan without knowing as much as we can about The Collective. And I'm pretty sure they already *know* we're here. Which brings me back to the drive."

The silence that followed lasted four seconds. Annie counted them. Then Ethan uncrossed his arms and nodded— a tight, controlled nod.

"Fine. Do it."

Without waiting a second more, Megan plugged in the hard drive.

Russel Grey's files were different from Brenda's. Where Brenda's work had been the urgent, instinctive mapping of a teenager who'd stumbled onto something enormous, Russel's was the accumulated intelligence of a man who'd spent years — decades, possibly— watching and documenting from inside the belly of the thing he was studying. The files were organized not by topic but by geography. Folders named for cities: *Cedarsburg. Terre Haute. Louisville. Denver. Phoenix.* Then states. Then countries. *United Kingdom. Brazil. South Africa. Indonesia.* Each folder contained operational plans, financial networks, personnel structures, communication protocols— the architecture of an organization that was not one thing in one place but many things in many places, connected by a logic that revealed itself like a satellite image showing patterns that were invisible from the ground.

Annie felt the temperature of the room change.

"One area at a time," Megan said, scrolling through the city folders, her voice flat. "That's their strategy. They find a town— a town like this one, small, struggling, forgotten by everyone who could help it— and they move in like water filling cracks. They buy the property. *They* install the officials. *They* control the elections. And then they move to the next one. And the next. Town by town, city by city, country by country. Shadow government. No flags, no borders, no visibility. It's—" She gestured at the screen, at the sprawling map of connections and operations that covered the globe like a web whose spider had never been photographed. "A hostile takeover. And no one knows it's happening."

She turned from the computer. Her eyes moved from Ethan to Annie and back. For a second, Megan looked like the girl Annie had once known— the one with stringy hair and wide eyes.

"This is evidence," Megan said. "*Real* evidence. This is what Russel died for. What Brenda died for." She stepped toward Ethan, her voice gaining the texture of conviction, the sound of a person who has found the hill they intend to die on and is no longer interested in looking for a safer one. "We have to do something."

"I can call my direct report at the bureau—" Ethan started to say, but Megan waved him away.

"So he can sit on this information while people die?" Megan said. "The FBI, the CIA, every agency in every country — they're already inside. They're already compromised. The only people who can take The Collective down are people like *us*. People who are already outside the system. Rogue agents. Vigilantes, if that's what you want to call it." Her jaw set. "The innocents of the world are at stake, Ethan. Not just Cedarsburg. Not just America. Everywhere. They've started here, but they're absorbing every criminal network on the planet. If we don't stop them—"

"No."

The word came from Ethan like a door closing.

He straightened from the filing cabinet, his good hand rising to his injured shoulder. His face was composed, but Annie could see the fracture lines beneath the surface. It was an exhaustion that went deeper than one bad day— the accumulated fatigue of a man who had spent his entire adult life inside institutions that he'd believed in and that had failed him, one by one, until belief itself had become a luxury he could no longer afford.

"I've been through enough," he said. His eyes found

Annie's. "I've given everything I have to this work. My career. My trust. Fifteen years of not knowing where my sister was." His voice was steady but thin, stretched taut over something that would break if he pushed it any further. "I'm done, Megan. I'm done being a soldier in someone else's war. I want—"

He stopped. The sentence hung in the air, unfinished, and Annie watched him decide whether to complete it.

"I want a simple life," he said. "With Annie. That's it. That's everything."

The room was quiet. The computer hummed. Russel's files glowed on the screen.

Megan didn't say anything. She just stared at her brother as if— somewhere out there— she was still missing, and he wasn't searching for her.

"You're giving up on me," Megan said, her lower lip trembling despite herself.

"No, Megan," Ethan said, kneeling down and taking her hands in his. "I'm trying to live. To live with *you*. Don't you want a normal life? We could be the way we used to. Family dinners on Sundays. Maybe you could be an aunt if Annie and I have kids, or you could have your own kids, or, I don't know—" Ethan threw his hands in the air— "teach teens to drive or something, since you seem to have gotten pretty good at evasive maneuvers. I don't know what you want from your life, but you can have it. You can find a different purpose."

"This *is* my purpose," Megan said, her eyes taking on a faraway look. "You've stopped looking for me."

"Megan," Ethan said, pleading with her. "I found you. You're right here. You're *here*."

"No," Megan shook her head. "Part of me is still out there. And I won't find her again until The Collective is dead."

"Then you'll be searching forever," Ethan countered.

Megan blinked and looked at Annie for support. Annie

knew what she meant— she, too, was searching, and couldn't stop until the job was done.

"Ethan," Annie said. "That's enough."

The three of them sat in silence for a moment. Down the hall, the faucet dripped in the kitchen. Bill Hudon's footsteps creaked on the floorboards as he moved through the house, performing the small rituals of a man preparing for sleep in a home he'd stopped maintaining but hadn't stopped loving.

"We'll sort this out," Annie said, not sure she believed the words even as they left her mouth. "Just not tonight."

With that, the group departed to their separate rooms. As Annie walked down the hall, she tried to think about how far someone should go in the face of such evil. Was it the right choice to live, or to fight, or some mixture of both? She couldn't puzzle out an answer. All she could calculate was that there was a certain distance between what the world took from you and what you chose to take back— which was, she suspected, the only distance that mattered.

CHAPTER TWENTY-FOUR

LATER THAT NIGHT— after retreating to Annie's childhood bedroom— Annie and Ethan lay curled in her old bed, staring at the ancient boy-band posters still decorating her blue walls. Annie noticed how the paint had faded. It was a color she'd chosen herself— a robin's egg blue to adorn the bedroom— and here it was, fading without her permission. *Rude of the paint*, Annie thought

Ethan rolled over so his injured shoulder faced the ceiling, the rest of him facing Annie in the narrow bed that had been designed for one teenager and was now holding two adults with grudging tolerance. The house had finally gone quiet except for the dripping kitchen faucet— always the faucet, that three-second metronome. Megan was in the guest room, either sleeping or staring at the ceiling.

"She's not going to let it go," Ethan said to Annie, keeping his voice soft. He knew how easily whispers travelled in houses like this one.

"No," Annie agreed. "She's not."

"And you?" His voice was low, roughened by smoke damage that the EMTs had said would clear in a few days. "What do *you* want to do? After this. After Cedarsburg."

Annie considered the question. She considered it the way she considered evidence— not rushing toward a conclusion but letting the pieces arrange themselves, trusting that the shape would emerge if she gave it enough silence and enough time. "I don't know yet," she said, which was honest, but costly in the dark of night, when she could tell how her answer would land.

Ethan shifted, the bed protesting beneath him with a creak. "Can I ask you something?"

"You're going to anyway."

"Who are your suspects? Right now. Top of the list." He paused. "And why aren't you out there interviewing them? That's what you do. You sit people down and you ask questions until the questions become answers. But you've been— waiting. Watching."

Annie looked at the ceiling. A water stain in the corner had been there since she was fourteen, shaped like nothing, meaning nothing, but familiar in the way that only the imperfections of childhood spaces could be familiar.

"They'll come to me," she said.

"What makes you so sure?"

"Because this town is small, and the people in it have known each other their whole lives, and that kind of bond doesn't break clean." She turned her head on the pillow to look at him. His face was close— close enough that she could see the fine lines around his eyes. The lines hadn't been there when they'd first met, and Annie knew how they'd been earned. "Old friends carry each other's weight whether they want to or not. Guilt is heavy. Secrets are heavy. And when the ground starts shaking— when the thing you've been standing on starts to crack— you don't run to strangers. You run to the people who knew you before. The people who remember who you were when you were still someone you recognized." She paused. "They'll come. They're already coming. I can feel it."

The faucet dripped. The house settled. Somewhere outside, the wind moved through the trees on the street where Annie had grown up— not a rustle but a whisper, the sound of something empty being asked to speak.

"Can I ask *you* something?" Annie said.

"You're going to anyway."

She almost smiled. "My dad. He said something to me in the kitchen. About little people. About how ordinary people can't do anything about the injustice in the world— they just have to accept it and survive." She felt the question forming, rising from the place where she kept the things she was afraid to examine. "Do you think he's right?"

Ethan was quiet for a long time. Long enough that the faucet dripped four times, maybe five, each drop marking a second in which he was deciding something.

"I would've said no ten years ago I wouldn't have joined the FBI if I didn't think I could make the world better."

"And now?"

"Now I've seen too much," Ethan answered, running a hand through his hair. "I've seen the machinery. I've been inside it. I know how big it is and how small we are and how the math doesn't work no matter how you run the numbers. There's always someone with power who doesn't deserve it trying to steal from the rest of us. I'd agree with your Dad if it weren't for—"

He paused and reached for her hand. His fingers found hers in the dark with the accuracy of someone who had memorized a distance.

"For what?" Annie asked.

"For you. The only thing that makes me believe differently," he said, "is you."

Outside, Cedarsburg slept. The streetlights on her father's block cast their pale circles on pavement that had been cracked and patched and cracked again, the endless maintenance of a town that kept repairing itself without ever asking why it kept breaking. Tomorrow there would be a debate. Tomorrow there would be lies told into microphones and truths hidden in pockets and the slow, tightening spiral of a reckoning that had been years in the making. But tonight there was this— a narrow bed in a blue room in a house that was falling apart, and two people holding onto each other in the dark, and the stubborn, irrational, evidence-defying belief that holding on was enough.

The faucet dripped. Annie closed her eyes. And the night went on without them, patient and indifferent and full of things that would look different in the morning.

CHAPTER TWENTY-FIVE

THE NEXT MORNING, it was the day of the big debate. After a rushed exit marked by a few squabbles, warm coffee, and donuts, Annie, Ethan, and Megan had hopped in her father's old car. Her father drove them because he *"didn't want them causing a scene without me there,"* and together, they all clanged their way down the road to Cedarsburg's village square.

The village square had been optimistic once— back in the 1920s, it was designed to conform to the best of Americana design. A bench, a fountain, and a few well-placed trees were reminders of the promise the park once held. Now, it told a different story. The fountain hadn't worked since the Reagan administration. Two of the trees had been removed after a storm and never replanted, leaving stumps that the parks department had painted white for reasons no one could explain. But the square was still there, occupying the center of town with stubborn permanence. Today, it was dressed for a holiday— bunting, folding chairs, a portable stage with two podiums, a microphone system that a volunteer was testing with escalating concern, and a projection screen behind the stage that currently displayed nothing except a blue rectangle and the logo of the Cedarsburg Register. The planners had expected a crowd, and they'd been right: the crowd had come. Half the town had turned out to hear the debate.

Annie stood near the back of the crowd with Ethan on her right and Megan on her left and her father behind her, the four of them arranged in the loose formation of people who were together but not relaxed about it. Bill Hudson had put on a clean shirt and was holding a paper cup of coffee from Common Grounds that he hadn't sipped, the cup serving the same function as a prop in a play. He'd come because Annie had asked him to come, and he had hoped to keep her out of trouble— a cause he knew was destined to fail.

"You 'gonna tell me what you're planning, Annie?" Bill Hudson whispered, leaning over to his daughter as he spoke out of the side of his mouth.

"I don't know what you're talking about, Dad," Annie said brightly. "I'm just a passionate lover of politics coming to watch a lively debate."

Bill huffed and shook his head— he'd find out soon enough why his daughter had insisted on attending. He always *did* find out eventually.

Annie scanned the square. Some people in the crowd stood— like Annie— at the back of the event, while others had arrived early enough to win a seat on a section of folding chairs. The chairs were arranged in rows of twenty, twelve rows deep, and most of them were occupied. Annie spotted Zara Kane in the seventh row, near the center aisle. The realtor sat with her hands in her lap, her dark brown hair pulled back in a clip that exposed the angular architecture of her face. She was sitting still, and the stillness looked wrong on her, like a costume that didn't fit.

"You were right," Ethan tapped Annie on the shoulder, signaling her to look toward the front of the crowd. "Everyone is here."

Annie looked at where Etahn pointed— Pastor Tim

Erickson occupied a seat in the front row, which was, Annie supposed, where a man of his stature in the community would be expected to sit. His hair was slicked back today, the architectural rigidity restored, the charm redeployed. He wore a jacket that looked expensive from a distance and probably looked more expensive up close, and his smile was in place. But Annie watched his hands where they rested on his thighs, and the hands were telling a different story than the smile. His fingers were interlocked. Tight. The knuckles pale beneath the skin.

And there— at the perimeter, where the folding chairs ended and the open square began— stood Sheriff Homestadder. In uniform. Of course in uniform. Annie had begun to suspect the man slept in it. He leaned against the base of the defunct fountain with a cigarette between his fingers, the smoke curling upward in a lazy spiral that the morning breeze bent and scattered. His posture was relaxed. His eyes were not. They moved across the crowd with patient, tracking attention. When they passed over Annie's group, they paused — a fraction of a second, no more, the briefest hitch in the sweep. Annie nodded at him. The Sheriff looked away.

The debate began at ten o'clock, as promised.

Prim Rosington stood at the right podium and looked like the future. Light brown hair, business casual, the Yale education visible not in any single detail but in the overall composition. Across from her, Bellows took the stage, looking like one of the people in his burnished baseball cap. Annie doubted he ever wore that hat outside of official business.

The moderator— a woman from the Register— introduced the format, the rules, the topics. Economy. Infrastructure. Public safety. But Annie barely listened. She was waiting for something specific to happen. Something she had suspected for some time *would* happen. And Annie loved nothing more than being proven right.

Bellows spoke first. He talked about stability. He talked

about keeping the town running. He talked about the importance of proven leadership.

Prim spoke next. She talked about stagnation. She talked about a town that was shrinking, losing its young people, losing its businesses, losing the very thing that made it a community rather than a collection of addresses.

Annie watched. And waited.

Thankfully, she didn't have to wait long.

The question was about fiscal responsibility. The moderator asked it with the neutral delivery of someone reading from a card, and Bellows opened his mouth to answer, and Prim interrupted him.

She didn't shout.. She simply turned from the moderator to the crowd and said, in the steady, measured voice of a woman who had been rehearsing this moment in her parents' living room: "Before the Mayor addresses fiscal responsibility, I think this town deserves to know what fiscal responsibility looks like in his administration."

The crowd murmured.

Prim reached beneath her podium. Annie saw the blue folder emerge and watched Prim open it with steady hands.

"I have evidence," Prim said, "that Mayor Bellows has redirected campaign funds for personal use. Specifically—" She lifted a page, held it up, let the crowd see the numbers even though they were too small to read from the folding chairs. The gesture was theater. The words were the weapon. "Specifically, a two-million-dollar cashier's check, drawn from campaign accounts, directed to a shell company with no public record, used to finance private construction projects that were presented to this community as charitable development."

The crowd made a sound. Not a gasp— Cedarsburg was too midwestern for gasping— but a collective intake of breath, a murmur that started in the front rows and traveled backward through the chairs like a wave running up a beach.

Someone in the fourth row said *"shit"* loud enough to be heard from where Annie stood, and the word carried across the square with the particular resonance of profanity deployed in proximity to a pastor.

Annie watched Bellows. His face did not change.

He's letting her talk, Annie thought, and the thought arrived with the cold clarity of a woman who was watching a chess game and had just seen the next three moves. *He's letting her talk because what comes next makes this irrelevant.*

Prim was still speaking— reading figures, citing dates, building the case. The crowd was with her.

Then Bellows raised his hand.

The gesture was simple. One hand, palm out, held at shoulder height. The crowd quieted.

"I appreciate Ms. Rosington's concerns," Bellows said. His voice was low and steady. "And I assure this community that every question about campaign finances will be addressed transparently, through the proper channels, with the full cooperation of my office." He paused. The microphone hummed. The crowd waited. "But I didn't come here today to talk about money."

He turned to the projection screen behind the stage. The blue rectangle and the Register logo disappeared, replaced by a photograph— a photograph Annie recognized with the immediate, visceral certainty of someone seeing a face they had loved.

Joshua. Her brother. Seventeen years old, smiling in the sunlight, the photograph taken at a family barbecue that Annie remembered attending though she couldn't remember the year.

Beside Annie, her father gasped. She knew how it felt. Seeing Joshua's picture without expecting it was a punch to the gut. "Annie—" Bill Hudson said. "What's happening?"

"I'm not exactly sure," Annie said honestly.

The air left Annie's lungs. Onstage, Bellows continued on

"The death of Brenda Welsh shook this town," Bellows said. Annie could tell he had rehearsed this speech and had rehearsed it well, the pauses placed with the precision of a craftsman. "It shook me. It made me look back at other tragedies— other losses that this community has never been able to put to rest. Specifically, the murder of Joshua Hudson and the disappearance of young Megan Beckett, fifteen years ago."

Annie felt Megan go rigid. She reached sideways without looking and found Megan's wrist, her fingers closing around it, holding on, because holding on was the only thing she could do

"Ethan—" Megan said, trying to make herself smaller.

"It's okay," Ethan whispered, their prior sibling squabbles forgotten. "You're alright, Megan, we're here, just don't do any—"

"I'm pleased to announce," Bellows continued, "that Megan Beckett has been found. She's alive. She's here tonight, in this very crowd."

Two hundred heads turned. The movement was synchronized. Two hundred pairs of eyes swept the square, searching, and found what they were looking for in approximately three seconds, because Cedarsburg was small and the people in it had known each other their whole lives and the woman standing beside Annie Hudson with her jacket collar pulled up and her face gone the color of chalk was the right age and the right build.

Megan didn't move. She stood in the gaze of the town that had lost her and let it land on her, and Annie felt the wrist beneath her fingers trembling— not with fear, exactly, but with the trembling of a person who had once been invisible and was now made visible to everyone she'd ever known.

"And," Bellows said— and the *and* was the hinge, the moment where the door swung open and whatever was behind it came through— "through diligent investigation and the tireless work of our Sheriff's office, we have identified a new suspect in the murder of Joshua Hudson."

Annie reeled. Her father stared at her, betrayed.

"Dad, I didn't know—" Annie said. *They couldn't have solved his case before me,* Annie thought to herself, surprised at her own arrogance.

New images appeared on the screen. Photographs— Zara Kane and Joshua, together, at what looked like a school event. A yearbook page with handwriting in the margins, the looping script of a teenage girl, Joshua's name circled and underscored. A printed email, the text too small to read from the chairs but the heading visible: *RE: I need to talk to you.*

Then, diary entries. Page after page outlining Zara's love for Joshua, taken from a personal journal.

In the seventh row, Zara Kane looked mortified, as if she were watching her own execution— which, in a way, she was. Zara's mouth opened and no sound came out, and her hands came up from her lap in a gesture that was half-denial and half-surrender. The shock on her face told Annie Zara still wasn't entirely sure what she was being accused of— not something so big, so horrible, as killing Joshua Hudson. It couldn't possibly be.

"Based on this new evidence, law enforcement believes," Bellows said, his voice carrying across the square, "that Zara Kane murdered Joshua Hudson out of obsessive jealousy. And I have asked Sheriff Homestadder to act on this evidence immediately."

The Sheriff was already moving. Annie watched him separate from the fountain with an efficient, purposeful stride. The crowd parted for him, the collective body making room for authority.

Zara was on her feet by the time he reached her. She was shaking her head— a continuous oscillation that looked involuntary, the body's protest against a reality the mind hadn't finished processing. "No," she said, and the word was audible from where Annie stood, which meant it was either very loud or the crowd had gone very quiet, and Annie suspected it was the latter.

"*No!*" Zara said again, and this time the word broke apart on its way out, splitting into syllables that didn't quite fit together. "Those aren't— that's not— how did he *get* those?"

The last four words were different. They came out as a confession.

Zara tried to run, but the Sheriff was there. His hand closed around her wrist— not roughly, not with the performative force that Annie had seen in other arrests, the theatrical slam of a body against a hood or a wall. Homestadder's grip was careful. Almost gentle. He produced handcuffs from his belt and the metal caught the light as it closed around Zara's wrists— a small, bright flash, like a camera going off. There. It was done.

"Zara Kane," the Sheriff said, and his voice was the voice he always used— helpful, concerned, even as he sentenced Zara to a life of pain. "You're under arrest for the murder of Joshua Hudson."

The name hit Annie like a hand against her sternum. Not because she hadn't been expecting it— she had. But hearing it spoken aloud, in the Sheriff's steady baritone, in the square where she'd played as a child, in front of a crowd that included her father— threatened to break her. She looked over at her father, whose paper cup of coffee had slipped from his fingers and was now lying on its side at his feet, the brown liquid spreading across the pavement in a slow, dark stain that no one was looking at because everyone was looking at Zara.

The Sheriff led Zara through the crowd. The crowd parted again— the same instinctive yielding to uniform. Zara walked. Her shoulders were shaking. Her head was still moving in that small, continuous oscillation— no, no, no— the body's protest continuing. She passed within ten feet of

Annie, and for a single second their eyes met, and what Annie saw in Zara's face was not guilt but the particular anguish of a woman who understood that the same system she had helped build was the system that was destroying her.

On the stage, Mayor Bellows stood behind his podium with his hands clasped and shoulders back. He looked like a leader. He looked, Annie thought, like the most dangerous kind of liar— the kind who had told the lie so many times, to so many people, for so many years, that it had become the truth.

The blue folder sat abandoned on Prim's podium. The bomb that was supposed to end Bellows's career lay open and irrelevant, its forty-seven pages fluttering slightly in the morning breeze, the campaign finance evidence that had taken months to assemble rendered meaningless in approximately ninety seconds. A group of Prim's interns were gathered at the bottom of the stage, engaged in desperate whispers. They turned to Prim, pleading with her to do *something*.

Prim left the stage. She didn't try to regain the audience's attention. Instead, she descended the portable stairs, pushed through the first row of chairs— the row where Tim Erickson was already on his feet. Tim grabbed her by the elbow and whispered something in her ear. Prim paused for a second, then nodded, allowing him to pull her away from the crowd. The crowd had become a mob, and now everyone was on their feet, a mulling churning mess.

Prim reached Annie first. She was breathing hard. Behind her, Pastor Tim Erickson caught up.

"Tell her," the Pastor urged Prim. His white teeth were invisible behind a mouth pressed into a thin line

"They're wrong," Prim said sharply. The words came out fast, clipped, stripped of the measured rhetoric she'd been deploying from the podium minutes earlier. "Annie— Zara didn't do this. She couldn't have. I've known her since we were children. She *loved* Joshua. Everyone loved Joshua. But she didn't—" She stopped, swallowed, started again. "She didn't kill him. Bellows is using this to distract me from telling everyone about his campaign finances…"

"You mean the information that got Brenda Welsh killed?" Annie asked, her words coming out slow and even.

"Yes," Prim said, her lower lip trembling. "And there's more. There's more about Brenda."

"I was with Zara yesterday," Tim said. "She's scared. She's involved in things she shouldn't be involved in— we *both* are — but she's not a killer. We planned to come talk to you together, Annie, and now this happens—"

"I need to tell you something, Annie," Prim said, shaking now from her head to her feet. "About how Brenda Welsh died. I was there that night. I saw it. And Zara has nothing to do with any of this."

"I know," Annie said.

Prim looked like she might collapse. Waves of grief washed across her face. She was relieved, and also— somehow— disgusted with herself. She'd been running around town, believing she was safe beneath the weight of her own secret. But Annie Hudson had known all along.

"How could you—" Prim started to say.

"Your shoes. That night at the water tower," Annie offered. "They had mud on them. You came back to the scene of the crime to have a reason your prints would be in the area. I saw the prints before you even got to the crime scene. It was clearly a woman's high heel— something Brenda would never wear. I wondered why a woman would be in the area wearing such impractical shoes. What kind of person, I asked myself, would do such an impractical thing. And then," Annie smiled, "Very helpfully, *you* showed up."

Prim nodded. She was in trouble. She knew that. But Annie seemed as if she were— on her side, somehow. Prim had no choice but to trust it.

"I'll tell you everything," Prim said.

"You will," Annie agreed. "But not now. Not here."

"But—" Prim started to say.

"At the right time," Annie assured her. "At the right place. There's too many ears and eyes here." Annie put a hand on Prim's arm. "I trust you," she said simply. "I don't believe you're a flight risk. Can I count on you to do the right thing?"

"I'll be there," Prim said reluctantly. "When you tell me it's time."

Annie turned. Ethan was beside her, his hand still in hers, his injured shoulder held at the angle that had become his default. Megan stood rigid, her jacket collar still up, her face still pale, the town's gaze still on her even as the crowd's attention had shifted to Zara and the cruiser and the aftermath. She looked like a woman who had been made visible against her will and was calculating the cost.

And her father. Bill Hudson stood behind her with coffee spreading at his feet and his face open in a way Annie hadn't seen in years.

"Dad," Annie said. She said it gently, the way you say a word that is about to be followed by something that hurts. "They've got the wrong person."

His face didn't change. He looked at her, and she looked at him. Of course Bill Hudson *wanted* to believe his son had found justice. But he believed in Annie more. "Whatever you say, Annie," Bill nodded. "That's the truth."

Annie turned back to all of them— Ethan, Megan, Prim, Tim, her father. Five faces, five different versions of fear and hope and exhaustion, five people standing in a village square while the crowd milled around them and the Mayor accepted handshakes on the stage and the Sheriff's cruiser pulled away from the curb with a woman inside it who was not a murderer but who would, by tomorrow morning, be one in the eyes of every person in Cedarsburg who wanted to believe that the worst was over.

"Zara Kane did not kill my brother," Annie said. Her voice was steady. "This entire performance was designed to close the case before we could open it any further, and I am not going to let that happen. I'm going to prove it. But I need both of *you*—" she looked at Prim and the Pastor — "to tell me everything you know, at the proper time. Perhaps publicly."

They both nodded.

Annie felt a familiar chill run up her spine. They were close to solving this case. All that needed to be done was to tie up a few loose ends.

"Good," Annie said, satisfied. "But before we get to details… I want to talk to Zara."

"But, the Sheriff has her," Prim said. "She'll be in a cell by now."

"Then I guess we'll have to pay him a visit," Annie smiled.

CHAPTER TWENTY-SIX

THE CEDARSBURG SHERIFF'S station was cold, unforgiving, and the last place Annie wanted to be. She stood outside its imposing form, flanked on either side by Ethan and Megan.

"You sure about this, Hudson?" Ethan asked.

In answer, Annie pushed through the door and stepped into air that smelled like industrial cleaner and burnt coffee. The front desk was staffed by a deputy who looked up with a wary blankness. Behind the deputy, a hallway stretched toward the back of the building, fluorescent-lit.

Sheriff Homestadder appeared from the hallway before the deputy could speak. His eyes found Annie's group in the lobby— Annie, Ethan at her right shoulder, Megan slightly behind and to the left in the formation that had become their default, a triangle with Annie at the point. The muscles around his mouth tightened in the tiniest amount that was visible only to someone who was looking for it— and Annie was always looking for it.

"Agent Beckett," the Sheriff said, addressing Ethan as he looked completely past Annie and Megan, as if they didn't exist. "I got the call from your field office."

"Good," Ethan said simply, preferring not to elaborate

"I want you to know—" The Sheriff paused. He placed his hands on his belt, thumbs hooked over the leather. "I wouldn't be allowing this if it were up to me. A suspect in custody, not even a few hours after arrest, no attorney present — this isn't how I run my station. I believe in *process*. I believe in doing things the right way." He looked at Annie when he said this, as if he knew this whole mess were her fault. "But the order came from the FBI, and I respect federal authority, even when I disagree with it."

"It's good, then," Ethan said, "that you don't get to have your way."

The words landed in the lobby with the clean, quiet impact of something that had been precisely aimed. The deputy at the front desk looked up. Megan didn't move. Annie watched the Sheriff's jaw shift— a lateral motion, small, the mandible sliding sideways and back, the involuntary mechanics of a man swallowing a response he would have preferred to deliver.

Then the Sheriff smiled.

"Follow me," he said. He turned and walked toward the hallway without checking to see if they followed.

The hallway was narrow, the fluorescent tubes overhead creating an alien glow. Bulletin boards on the walls held layers of notices— wanted posters, community safety bulletins, a flyer for the Cedarsburg Rotary Club's annual pancake breakfast. The Sheriff walked ahead of them with a measured, unhurried stride, the smell of cigarettes wafting behind him.

The holding area was at the back of the station— two cells, separated by a cinderblock wall, each one equipped with a metal bench bolted to the floor and a humble toilet. One cell was empty. In the other, Zara Kane sat on the metal bench with her knees drawn up and her arms wrapped around them. She looked small. Her bird-like frame— which looked elegant in a blazer at an open house— seemed, behind bars, simply fragile.

"You've got ten minutes," the Sheriff said. Then, he turned and walked back up the hallway, his boots marking their unhurried rhythm on the linoleum.

Annie turned to the cell. Zara's dark brown hair was loose now, the clip gone, the strands hanging around her face in a way that softened the angular architecture Annie remembered. Her strong eyebrows, usually the most assertive feature on her face— were drawn together now, not in anger but in fear.

"Zara," Annie said. She said it the way she said everything during an interview— measured, precise, each syllable placed with intention, the verbal equivalent of putting a hand on a table rather than slapping it. "How are you?"

Zara looked at her through the bars. Her eyes were red-rimmed but dry. She'd been crying earlier— the evidence was on her face.

"How do you think," Zara said. Her voice was hoarse. Flattened. "They're saying I killed Joshua. I didn't kill Joshua, Annie. I didn't. I *loved*—" She stopped. The sentence broke in the middle. Zara couldn't say more.

Annie gave her the silence. Silence was a tool— she'd learned this early in her career, back when she was still young enough to believe that the right question, asked at the right moment, would produce the truth the way a correct key produces an open lock.

"You have to know," Zara said, avoiding Annie's eyes. "I *loved* him."

"Here's what I find interesting," Annie said. "You're the only realtor in Cedarsburg who's having any success. The economy in this town is—" She paused. "Contracted. Businesses are closing. Properties are losing value. The automobile plant left. The big-box stores moved in. Every economic indicator points in the same direction, which is down. And yet." She let the conjunction sit. "Zara Kane, realtor, is closing deals. Moving properties. Functioning— thriving, even— in a market that shouldn't be able to support a lemonade stand, let alone a real estate practice."

Zara's eyes came back from the wall. They found Annie's face and stayed there.

"Do you know what they called Joshua's murderer?" Annie asked quietly. "The real estate ripper."

Annie let the information settle.

"Isn't it funny that you loved him, and you work in real estate?"

"I only started because of *him,* because of Joshua—"

"Love quickly turns to obsession," Annie suggested. "And obsession to rage—"

"Annie," Megan whispered quietly in her ear. "Zara *couldn't* have been the killer. Whoever kidnapped me hit me over the head. They would have to have been bigger than me to drag me out of there. She's so small…"

Annie waved Megan away. Of course, she knew everything Megan was saying to be true. But this was her brother's justice at stake. She had to test Zara— she had to push her— to break her, just a little— so she would tell Annie everything she knew.

"I didn't kill him!" Zara shouted. She was standing now, clutching the metal bars so hard her fingers turned white.

"There was the smell of mint, Annie," Megan reminded her. "Zara doesn't smell like anything."

Annie turned, staring at Megan with a knowing look. "Funny, how the body remembers, isn't it?" She turned her attention back to Zara. "You may not have killed Joshua directly, but you've been involved with a group— a shadow organization— that's been helping you. Not out of charity, not because they care about your career, but because you're useful to them. Because a realtor in a dying town who has access to every listing before it hits the market is a tool, and tools get used. You *did* kill him Zara. Not with your own hands, but by working with the people who did. By being a cog in their machine."

The sound Zara made was not a word. It was the sound of something giving way— a structural sound, the sound of a load-bearing wall accepting the one additional pound that exceeds its tolerance. Her hands came up to her face, pressing against her eyes, her fingers spread.

"You've been working with a group called The Collective, haven't you?" Annie pressed.

"Yes," she said, the word emerging from behind her hands. She released her fingers from around her eyes, and her face was wet. "Yes. There's a group. I don't know everything about them— I don't think anyone does, anyone who works with them at my level— but I know enough. I know what they've done to this town."

She stood from the bench. The movement was sudden.

"They have their claws in every part of Cedarsburg," Zara said. Her voice was low, pitched for the three of them alone. "Every part. The city contracts. The zoning board. The property market— that's me, that's my piece of it. They gave me an email address. A dead drop. Every listing that comes through my office— every single one— goes to that address before it goes to the MLS, before it goes to market, before anyone in the public even knows the property exists. And then the offers come in. Shell companies. Names I've never heard of. They buy everything. Half the land in this town is owned by entities that don't exist as anything other than paperwork and a P.O. box."

She paused. Her fingers tightened on the bars again.

"And it's not just here they're doing this. It's in thousands of towns across the country. I don't know everyone they control," Zara continued. "But I can guess. The Mayor— obviously the Mayor, anyone who's paying attention can see the Mayor. The Sheriff—" Her voice dropped further, barely a whisper now, the word *Sheriff* handled the way you handle something that might detonate. "I don't know what he does for them. I don't want to know. But he's in it. You can feel it. The way nothing in this town ever gets investigated. The way every bad thing that happens gets explained away." She swallowed. "Brenda Welsh didn't fall off a water tower. Everyone knows that. Nobody says it. And… Annie, you won't believe me, but all this happened right as I was planning to come to you and tell you everything."

"I actually do believe that," Annie nodded.

"You do?" Zara didn't try to hide her surprise.

"The timing makes perfect sense. Of course The Collective would want you out of the way if you were planning on turning on them." Annie paused. "What made you decide to tell me?"

"Pastor Tim," Zara admitted. "I met with him the other day about the amphitheatre. His church— Renewed Hope— they've been trying to build a new space to expand the ministry. Tim wanted it more than anything. He believed it could save Cedarsburg. Give people something to come together for, something to hope about." Her mouth twisted. "I helped broker the deal. That's how— that's how Tim got pulled in. The Collective offered to fund the amphitheatre through the Mayor's office. A cashier's check. Enough money to build the whole thing. And Tim..." She trailed off, but Annie could see the rest of the sentence in her face. "Tim endorsed the Mayor," Zara said quietly. "In exchange for the funding. He threw his support behind a man he knew was wrong because the money was right, and I was the one who made the introduction. I was the bridge." She pressed her forehead against the bars. The metal made a soft sound against her skin. "That's how they work. They get one person, and then they use that person to get the next one, and the next one uses the next one, and before you know it the whole town is chained together and everyone is holding everyone else's leash and nobody can let go because letting go means everyone falls." She lifted her head. "That's how they got me. Someone I trusted introduced me. Someone they trusted introduced them. It goes back— I don't know how far. Years. Decades, maybe. It's a chain, Annie. And every link thinks they're the only one. But I didn't know they killed Joshua. You have to believe me, Annie. I would never have accepted their offer if I'd known."

The holding cell was quiet. The fluorescent tubes hummed their unending hum. Somewhere down the hallway, a country song had been replaced by a commercial for an auto dealership in Carver County.

Annie looked at Ethan. He met her eyes, and what she saw in his face was the expression she'd come to rely on— the expression that said he'd heard what she'd heard and was thinking what she was thinking and was waiting for her to say it first.

She turned back to Zara.

"I'm going to post your bail," Annie said.

Zara's face did something complicated. The fear didn't leave— it was too deep for that. But something else arrived alongside it. Hope, maybe, or something close.

"But I need something from you," Annie continued. Her voice was steady. "I need you to help us. Not from in here— out there. In the town. With the people you know and the connections you have and the things you've seen that nobody else has seen."

Zara stared at her. "You want me to— what? Testify? Go public?"

"I want you to help me get to the bottom of this," Annie said. "All of it. The Mayor. The Sheriff. The land deals. The elections. Everything Brenda Welsh was tracking before she died, and everything Russel Grey documented before they killed him. The whole chain, Zara. Every link." She paused. "But not alone. The Collective found their power by using one person to get to the next. Now, I need all of you to work together to stop them." She let the words settle. "Old friends, Zara. People who grew up here together. People who went to school together and remember each other before any of this happened— before the deals and the compromises and the chains. You're not the only person here who's made mistakes. Now it's up to all of us to fix it, together. For Joshua. And for Megan." Annie nodded at Megan, who stood behind her in the shadows. "I think we owe them that."

The cell was quiet. Zara's fingers were still wrapped around the bars, her bird-like frame held upright by the metal she was gripping as much as by anything inside her. She looked at Annie for a long moment.

Then, Zara nodded. It was a small motion— barely a dip of the chin.

"Okay," she said. The word came out rough, scraped raw by crying. "Whatever you want. Okay."

Footsteps in the hallway. The Sheriff's boots, returning with the measured, unhurried cadence of a man who had given them ten minutes and had been counting each one. Annie heard them approach and straightened from the bars, her hand releasing the metal railing she hadn't realized she'd been gripping. Ethan shifted beside her, his body angling slightly toward the hallway in the unconscious orientation of defense.

"Time," the Sheriff said, appearing at the end of the hallway. He stood with his thumbs hooked over his belt, the posture identical to the one he'd struck in the lobby. His eyes swept the scene— Annie at the bars, Zara inside, Ethan and Megan at the edges— and whatever he saw, he processed it quickly, then let it go.

"Thank you, Sheriff," Annie said. The words cost her nothing, and yet she hated to offer them.

They walked back through the hallway. Annie pushed through the front door and stepped into daylight that felt, after the fluorescent interior, like emerging from underwater — the sudden brightness, the warmth, the air.

She stood on the sidewalk and looked at the town. Main Street stretched in both directions, its storefronts a mix of open and shuttered.

"We need Pastor Tim," Annie said to Ethan and Megan. "And we need Prim. And we need them in a room together with Zara, telling the truth, all of it, at the same time. Because they've been holding each other's chains for years, and the only way to break a chain is for everyone to let go at once."

Ethan looked at her. Megan looked at her. The breeze moved through Main Street, and somewhere down the block, a shop owner was unlocking a door and turning a sign from CLOSED to OPEN, performing the small, stubborn act of commerce that kept a dying town alive one day at a time.

Annie took a breath. She started walking.

CHAPTER TWENTY-SEVEN

THE LIVING ROOM in Bill Hudson's house had not been designed to hold six people and the truth at the same time. It could manage three comfortably— Bill in his recliner, the television on, the leaky faucet providing its accompaniment from the kitchen— and four with negotiation. But six was too many.

Annie stood by the window. She'd chosen the position deliberately— not sitting, not joining the arrangement of bodies on the couch. Ethan sat closest to her, looking as if he trusted Annie's judgment while reserving the right to intervene. Megan occupied the corner of the couch with her legs crossed and her jacket still on.

Zara sat in the chair nearest the door— the chair Bill usually reserved for company he expected to leave quickly— and her thin fingers were wrapped around a glass of water she hadn't touched. They had posted her bail. She owed them this. She was a free woman, at least, for now.

The knock came at seven-fourteen. Annie had told them seven. They were late, which Annie hated— their tardiness had made her wonder if she'd been wrong to trust. Annie crossed the room and opened the door, and there they were:

Prim Rosington in her business casual, and Pastor Tim Erickson, half a step behind her.

"Come in," Annie said.

They came in. The room rearranged itself to accommodate them— Tim taking the remaining kitchen chair, Prim perching on the arm of the couch near Megan, the two women acknowledging each other with the brief, loaded glance of people who had not been in the same room since childhood and were now sharing furniture. Bill hovered in the kitchen doorway, feeling like his home was harboring fugitives.

"I asked you all here," Annie said quickly, "because every person in this room is holding a piece of something, and the pieces don't work alone. They never did. That's how The Collective designed it— one person, one piece of information, everyone isolated, everyone afraid, everyone believing they're the only one." She looked at each of them in turn. "You're not the only one."

Annie turned to Zara. "Zara, let's start with you. Tell them everything you told me."

Zara took a deep breath in, then exhaled. She shared her story with the group, and it left her mouth the way water leaves a cracked dam. She told them everything. The shadow buyers. The email addresses. The shell companies. The listings she'd funneled before they hit the market, property after property disappearing into the architecture of an organization that owned half the town through names that existed only as signatures on paperwork. "After Joshua died, I felt lost in my career," Zara admitted. "They made it easy. They made me the biggest realtor in three counties. I didn't really know what I was saying yes too until it was too late, and I was in too deep, and I— I didn't want to lose what I had." She slowed only when she got to Tim's amphitheater. "They made me bring Tim in," Zara said, ashamed. "But maybe—"

"It's Tim's story to tell," Annie nodded. "Tim, do you want to tell the group how The Collective first found you?"

Tim nodded. "It's funny," he said. "I usually take the confessions of others. I guess it's my turn now. You'll excuse me if I'm rusty." Then, he told them everything. He told them about Zara giving him the idea for the amphitheater, and what it led to. The cashiers check. The mayor's office. The favors that were asked of him, all of them delivered in the middle of the night, through a blocked call. "All I wanted was a place where the town could gather and find God," he said. "But when Brenda died, I realized I'd lost sight of my mission. I let my own desire to be celebrated— to be famous — get in the way of what God was really asking me to do. So I'm here," Tim said to the group. "And I want to make it right. Especially for you, Megan." He nodded at Megan, who simply looked away.

"While we're on the subject of losing sight of one's mission," Prim said, rising from her seat and folding her arms around herself. "I guess I should go next." Prim cleared her throat. "Brenda was my intern."

Looks were exchanged among the group.

"… and it's my fault she's dead. I asked her to do opposition research on Bellows. To find information we could use against him. And she did it. But she also found something else. Something about a shadow group that had taken over the town…" She told them about Brenda. The weekly reports. The internet research that left a trail. "All of it brought me to the night Brenda was killed—" Prim said, her voice failing her, a choking sound behind every word. "I was— I was there when she died… I know who killed her, but I was too afraid to say anything."

Murmurs echoed through the group. Zara put a hand over her mouth, horrified. Pastor Tim looked at the ground, as if he were ashamed on Zara's behalf.

"You were afraid because The Collective got to you, too, isn't that right?"

"They started by sending me three word notes," Prim answered. "They were harmless at first, but then they came with instructions. Phone calls from blocked numbers. Emails." Prim paused, chewing on the idea. "I don't think they really wanted to help me win the election," Prim said. "It was more like they wanted me to *believe* they would help me, just in case I won."

"Did they tell you to light Cedarsburg high on fire when Ethan and Megan and I were inside?" Annie asked.

Prim looked confused for a moment, as if Annie had hit her. "What? No— no— I—"

Annie reached into her jacket pocket. She produced the bracelet they'd found with the letter P on a dangling charm.

"We found this in Brenda's locker, right before someone lit the school on fire and tried to kill us," Annie said, passing the bracelet to Prim. "It's yours isn't it?"

Prim's face collapsed. She took the bracelet from Annie and held it as if it might burn her.

"I went to Brenda's locker to try to destroy the evidence of the opposition research I asked her to do. I didn't want to be implicated in her murder. It was wrong, but Annie, I didn't light the school on fire."

"But you were at the water tower the night Brenda was killed," Annie said, pacing in a small, uneven oval shape across the living room's old shag carpet. "You've confessed to that already, and the mud on your shoes that night—"

"I was there," Prim agreed. She put her hands over her face again as if she wished she could disappear, then looked up at the group, her eyes wide and horrified. "I went to the water tower that night to tell Brenda to stop. To drop it. She'd gotten out of control! She went way beyond the scope of what I was asking her to do! They sent me a note. Three letters. It said "Stop the kid." I *knew* they meant Brenda because she was obsessed— *obsessed* with bringing down The Collective. I saw in her calendar that she had a meeting planned with an informant at the water tower. We had access to all her work emails and I saw her reminder to herself come through— I went there to tell her to stop talking to Russel, to stop investigating The Collective, to stop— being brave! Because I wasn't brave. I knew what she'd found and I knew what they were capable of and I told her it wasn't safe, and she—" Prim's hands came down. Her face was wet. "She told me she didn't care. She said someone had to do something."

The room held its breath. The faucet dripped.

"We fought at the top of the water tower, shouting at each other. I followed her up there to try and convince her to leave. And then *he* came," Prim whispered. "And I thought maybe he was there to help us— it never occurred to me he was part of their group— I didn't know. I thought he was going to make her get down and instead, instead…" Prim was sobbing now, unable to catch her breath. "He pushed her. He *pushed* her and she screamed and went over the edge. It all happened so fast. Then he looked at me— he looked at me and he didn't say anything. He just put a hand to his lips," Prim mirrored the movement, making the gesture for *shhh*. "And I knew right then if I said anything he'd kill me too. Then he left. And I was all alone on the water tower, trying to figure out what to do. I couldn't go to the police, obviously, because—"

"Because The Collective has infiltrated law enforcement," Annie said.

"Yes," Prim nodded. "I realized while I was standing up there that if I said anything, this would end my campaign. And that would have been fine! I would have ended it all if it meant justice for Brenda but… what about my *life*? They'd kill me next, I knew it for sure. And it hit me, standing up there in the cold, that there wasn't anyone I could talk to. It was only *then* I realized that The Collective has so many people working for them. Who could I trust? The answer was no one," Prim looked at Annie. "Until *you* came into town."

Annie let the confession settle. She let it find its weight in the room. Then she said, quietly: "Brenda found more than you knew, Prim"

Prim stared at her. "More?"

"The voting machines," Annie said. "The Collective has rigged them for Bellows. You were never going to win that election."

Prim stared at her. The stare was the stare of a woman watching the last wall fall.

"Why didn't she tell me?" Prim's voice was small. Smaller than Yale. Smaller than the signatures she'd gathered and the speeches she'd written and the future she'd imagined from the doorstep of a campaign office.

"Because you'd already shown her what you'd *do* with dangerous information," Annie said, and the words were not cruel but they were not gentle either— they were precise, which was the thing Annie's words became when precision was the only kindness available. "You'd hide it. She couldn't afford to have you hide this."

The silence that followed lasted long enough for the faucet to drip seven times. Annie counted. She always counted.

"Every person in this room," Annie said, "made a deal they shouldn't have made. Every person in this room kept a secret they shouldn't have kept. And because you did— because we *all* did, because this town did— The Collective was able to do what it does. One person at a time. One compromise at a time. One silence at a time." She looked around the room— at Zara's bird-like frame gripping the water glass, at Tim's bare face with its demolished smile, at Prim's wet cheeks and Megan's rigid posture and Ethan's steady, watching eyes. "But tomorrow is the election. And I have a plan. And the plan requires every person in this room to do the thing they should have done years ago, which is trust each other. Not The

Collective. Not the Mayor. Not law enforcement. Not the system that's been rigged against you since before you knew it was rigged. *Each other*. The way we trusted each other when we were all kids playing in the same school yard… and the world was something we believed we could change."

She waited. The room waited with her. And then, one by one, they nodded— Zara first, the small dip of a chin that Annie recognized from the holding cell. Tim next, his nod carrying the weight of a man who had spent a decade building the wrong thing and was ready to build something else. Prim last, her nod repeating and unending, as if she were apologizing again and again— for Brenda— in the only way she could.

Then a voice from the kitchen doorway.

"I'll help too."

Bill Hudson stood where he'd been standing— dishrag in hand. He shrugged at Annie as if they were simply discussing the weather

"Maybe ordinary people can make a difference," he said. The words cost him something— Annie could see it in the way his hand tightened on the dishrag. "Maybe they just need to be in the same room when they try."

The faucet dripped. Annie looked at her father and felt something move in her chest that was not evidence and could not be catalogued.

"I know who killed my brother," Annie said, returning her gaze to the group. "And I know who killed Brenda," Annie continued. She glanced at Megan who up until now had been quiet, sitting on the edge of the couch and observing the scene as if it were unfolding on television and not in real life. "Megan?" Annie asked. Megan jumped at the sound of her name.

"Yes?"

"I need you to tell me again. The night you were taken— the night Joshua was killed," Annie swallowed at the word *killed.* It still felt strange to say, in relation to her brother. "The person who hit you over the head and took you from that house." Annie paused. The faucet dripped. The house held. "You remembered one thing about them. What was that one thing?"

Megan's eyes met Annie's. In them was the fifteen-year depth of a memory that had been examined and re-examined and turned over and held up to every kind of light.

"That they smelled like mint," Megan said quietly.

Annie nodded, then turned back to the group. "Tomorrow, we're going to arrest the Real Estate Ripper. And we're going to send The Collective a message: that our town is not for sale. Tomorrow, The Collective plans to interfere with our election, and how we cast our votes. But we're not going to let them. Ethan, I'm in the mood for a sting operation," Annie grinned at Ethan, as if she were suggesting they grab a couple of cheeseburgers for dinner. "How about you?"

"Love a good sting operation," Ethan nodded in agreement.

"But who's the Real Estate Ripper?" Pastor Tim asked, leaning in.

Ethan rolled his eyes, then said to Tim: "Better not to ask. If you haven't figured it out by now, just wait for Annie. She never reveals a thing until the proper moment."

"Annie, are you sure a sting operation is a good idea?" Megan said. "What if the information leaks to The Collective and they skip town before we can get him?"

"Our only choice is to trust," Annie answered wisely. "Ethan, we can count on you to arrange the necessary backup?

"I'll call the field office," Ethan said. "I know who we can trust there. We need agents in position before the polls open. Plainclothes. Unmarked vehicles." He paused. "We lay a trap. Something he has to respond to. Something that brings him out in the open, where we can see him and the Bureau can see him and the evidence can do what evidence does."

"Prim, Zara, Tim, think the three of you can help with that?"

The group murmured their agreement. Annie leaned in as a plan began to form, and the group discussed what awaited them tomorrow. She looked at the faces around her— old friends, broken friends, friends who had compromised and hidden and failed. She didn't know if it would be enough. She didn't know if the plan would work, or if the FBI would come, or if her enemy would step into the trap. She didn't know any of it. But she knew this room. She knew these people. And she knew she was trying— and that had to count for something.

The faucet dripped. Annie began to plan.

CHAPTER TWENTY-EIGHT

THE NEXT MORNING, Megan's SUV was cramped. It had been occupied by four people for too long, and the inside air had cycled through their lungs so many times it felt more like a shared exhalation. Coffees sat in the cupholders, now at room temperature, their steam long since dissipated.

Annie sat in the passenger seat with her hands on her knees, watching the polling station through tinted glass. It was election day, and Cedarsburg had been transformed by banners and balloons.

The polling station occupied the ground floor of the community center— a cinder-block building two blocks from the square. Today it wore an American flag above the entrance and a hand-lettered sign that read VOTE HERE with an arrow pointing at the double doors. The arrow was unnecessary, given that the doors were the only way in and the sign itself was visible from three blocks, but someone had drawn it anyway.

Outside the entrance, Mayor Bellows had erected a folding table draped in red, white, and blue, bearing bottles of water and individually wrapped granola bars. A banner that read GET OUT THE VOTE tried to make the table seem like a community effort rather than a bribery station to connect with voters as they entered the polling station. The Mayor stood beside the table in his white button-down and his baseball cap, shaking hands with a steady, mechanical rhythm— grip, pump, release, smile, next. His silver hair caught the morning light each time he removed his cap to greet a voter.

And there— at the entrance to the polling station, positioned between the double doors and the parking lot with the territorial stillness of a man guarding something he owned— stood Sheriff Homestadder. In uniform. A cigarette between his fingers, the smoke rising in a thin, vertical thread that the windless morning refused to disturb. He stood the way he always stood— relaxed posture, watchful eyes. His surface appearance said, *I'm here to help*, but there was a sharpness to his eyes that Annie could feel through tinted glass and eighty yards of parking lot.

Annie scanned the parking lot. She found Pastor Tim first — approaching from the south side of the community center, just as they had planned.

"Tim's on the move," Annie said, motioning out the window. Megan, Ethan, and Bill Hudson followed Annie's gaze.

"Think he can pull this off?" Megan asked.

"Can any of us?" Bill Hudson snorted.

Tim was wearing the same plain button-down shirt from last night, but now, it was wrinkled. He moved past a cluster of voters and positioned himself behind the far end of the building, near the service entrance, exactly where Annie had told him to be.

Then Zara— emerging from the opposite direction, bird-like and sharp-browed— appeared. Her thin frame cut through the line of voters with lateral, scanning attention. She had spent the night rehearsing her courage, and it showed, now, in her robotic movements. She placed herself at the Northern corner of the parking lot, and waited.

Annie rolled down her window. The morning air entered the vehicle like a change of temperature. Across the lot, near the Mayor's table, a figure in business casual separated itself from the crowd. Prim Rosington, light brown hair pulled back, jaw set, hands at her sides, moving toward Bellows. The final piece was about the move into place. Annie caught Prim's eye. She nodded. Prim nodded back.

Then Prim was at the table. Her voice carried across the lot. "Mayor Bellows." The name landed in the morning air like a summons. "I'd like to talk about what you've done to this town."

Heads turned. The voters in line swiveled toward the sound, and the Mayor's hand-shaking rhythm faltered for the first time— a hitch, a pause.

Annie turned to the back seat. Her father sat behind Ethan. His eyes met hers.

"Dad," she said. "It's your time. Today an ordinary person can make a difference."

The words sat between them the way words always sat between Hudsons— heavy, weighted with the past. Bill looked at her. He looked at the polling station through the open window. He was, at seventy-something years old, deciding to take a gamble on the idea that he could change things. Better late than never.

He opened the door. The hinges made a sound. He stepped out into the morning, and Annie watched him walk toward the polling station with the slightly stooped, unhurried gait that was his signature.

Ethan had the radio in his hand. He pressed the button, and the click was small and enormous at the same time. "Field office, this is Beckett. We're in position. Almost ready. Await my signal."

The radio crackled. A voice confirmed. The sound was bureaucratic and professional. Ethan set it on the dashboard — he knew he would need it again very soon.

Annie opened her door. The morning received her— the warmth, the light, the smell of Cedarsburg. Megan emerged from the back seat with coiled, silent efficiency. Ethan came around the front of the SUV, his injured shoulder squared now. His posture told Annie he was ready to get this over with. She didn't blame him: it had been a moment fifteen years in the making.

The three of them crossed the parking lot. Ahead, Prim's voice was rising, and the crowd was gathering. When Annie had asked Prim to create a distraction, she didn't think she'd be so good at it.

Prim's voice rose above the crowd, her words crisp and measured. "What we're witnessing in Cedarsburg is textbook institutional corruption!" she declared, one hand gesturing with academic precision. "The systematic abuse of entrusted power for private gain," She stepped closer to Bellows, whose smile had frozen in place. "And you, Mayor Bellows, are at the center of it all!" She turned to the gathering crowd. "Look around you! The economic indicators don't lie." She pointed directly at Bellows now. "This man has turned your town into his personal fiefdom while convincing you it's for your own good."

Prim jumped up on the table and started wobbling in place, doing a strange, interpretive dance. "Look at me!" She shouted. "I'm here to tell you about the corrupt system."

Annie stopped five feet from the table. She looked at the Mayor. She looked at the Sheriff, who had turned from the doorway. His cigarette had paused halfway to his lips, and his eyes — those patient, tracking, predatory eyes — had found her. He reached onto his belt and pulled out a pair of handcuffs, then moved toward Prim.

"Creating a public nuisance on election day is a problem, young lady," the Sheriff said to Prim. "If you don't get off the table I'm going to have to take you in—"

"Not before we arrest *you!*" Annie Hudson shouted. The

crowd froze. Everyone stared at her. The Sheriff took a step back, and then— he laughed.

"Arrest me?"

"It's called a citizen's arrest," Prim said, jumping off the table and moving to stand beside Annie. "

Annie turned to the crowd, desperate to maintain their rapt attention. "My name is Annie Hudson," she said. Her voice carried across the parking lot. "Fifteen years ago, my brother Joshua was murdered in this town. And a young girl named Megan Beckett was kidnapped from the same house on the same night— taken, trafficked, and lost to her family for over a decade."

She felt Megan step forward beside her. Megan, who had spent half her life invisible. She moved to where the town could see her, fully, for the first time since Bellows had ripped away her anonymity at the debate.

"Megan remembers something from that night," Annie said. "Megan?"

"The person who took me," Megan said, and her voice was steady, "smelled like mint. That's the only thing I remember."

Annie let the word settle. She watched the crowd absorb it — the small, specific detail, the kind of detail that lodged in people's minds because it was sensory and strange and didn't yet have a place in the story they thought they knew. Then she continued.

"I came back to Cedarsburg because a young woman named Brenda Welsh was found dead at the water tower. The Sheriff ruled it a suicide. It wasn't." She saw the crowd shift— The collective adjustment of bodies reacting. "Brenda had been communicating with a man named Russel Grey— an informant who had spent years gathering evidence on a shadow organization called The Collective. This organization —" Annie paused, "This organization has had its claws in Cedarsburg for years. Since the auto plant closed. Since the economy collapsed. Since this town became desperate enough to accept help from anyone offering, without asking where the help came from or what it cost."

She looked at Bellows. The Mayor stood behind his table with his hands at his sides and his baseball cap casting a shadow across his eyes.

"The Mayor knows," Annie said. "He's known since the beginning. The Collective got him elected by tampering with voting machines— the same machines being used today. In exchange, he gave them access. To the town's land. To its contracts. To its law enforcement." She let the last two words land with the weight they deserved. "Brenda Welsh found the evidence. She found the vote-switching. She documented everything. And she was killed for it. Because she didn't want your votes— all of your voices— to be silenced."

The parking lot was silent.

"We are *all* guilty in some way," Annie said, and her voice softened— not with weakness but with the particular tenderness of a woman who could see beyond mistakes. "All of us let it happen. All of us looked the other way. But someone in this crowd did more than look away." She turned. "Prim. You were at the water tower the night Brenda died. You saw who killed her. Who was it?"

Every eye found Prim. She stood three feet from Annie with her light brown hair and her business casual and her face stripped of everything she'd built. Her eyes were wet. And then her hand came up— slowly, deliberately.

She pointed past the Mayor. Past the table and the banner and the water bottles. She pointed at the man standing at the entrance to the polling station with a cigarette between his fingers and a badge on his chest.

"Sheriff Homestadder," Annie said. The name filled the parking lot. "The Real Estate Ripper. He's been killing for The Collective for years— and the Mayor has been covering for him. Fifteen years ago, when he attacked Megan, he was trying to quit smoking." She looked at the cigarette in his hand. "He was chewing nicotine gum. Mint-flavored. That's what Megan smelled."

The Sheriff didn't move. For three seconds— Annie counted, she always counted— he stood perfectly still, the cigarette burning between his fingers, his eyes fixed on Annie. His expression was cold. It was patient.

"That's a wonderful idea," the Sheriff smiled at her. "But the murderer who killed Joshua Hudson awaits trial and is currently out on bail."

A voice echoed from the edge of the crowd. It was Zara, who stepped forward. The crowd gasped.

"I didn't kill Joshua," Zara shouted. "I was in love with him, but I didn't kill him. And what Annie said is true. I know, because The Collective got to me. They helped me sell houses, land, and betray— well—" Zara looked around the crowd. "Betray all of you."

"She's not the only one," Pastor Tim Erickson called out, revealing himself from the edge of the parking lot. "The Collective is real." More murmurs echoed throughout the group. The crowd believed him. The Pastor's word was gold, in this town. And Tim knew he was about to melt it down in reverse alchemy, turning gold back into lead. He took a deep breath, felt the strength of the holy spirit in his chest, and did what he knew was right. "The Collective gave me the money to build the amphitheater," he confessed. He locked eyes with his wife, who was standing at the front of the group. She gave him a nod— encouraged him onwards. "I took money from them, facilitated by Mayor Bellows and Zara Kane. Then, I traded your secrets. I did what they asked. Small favors at first, but ones that were wrong. When Brenda turned up dead, I knew I had to say something. I'm — I'm so sorry," he said, trying not to let the tears reach his eyes.

"You killed Brenda because she knew the truth!" Annie said, pointing her finger at the Sheriff. "And you tried to kill us at the high school. You set that fire to stop us from getting Brenda's cyberlocker–"

"You don't have proof, girl," the Sheriff countered.

"We have Megan. We have Brenda's files. We have the voting machines."

The Sheriff's smile faltered. "My job is to keep people safe —" the Sheriff tried to say, but his voice was different now. The monster behind the facade was crawling its way into his eyes, and Annie knew she just had to poke hard enough to see it released.

"By killing them?" Annie asked. "The only thing I don't understand is why Joshua?" Despite her best efforts, her voice broke a little. "Why him, so long ago?"

"Because he didn't agree!" The Sheriff said, his words surprising even him. "No one says no to me. No one says to *us—*"

"That's why you joined, isn't it?" Annie said, and she was nose to nose with him now. "Because you love killing, and violence, and The Collective allows you to act with impunity! You were the Real Estate Ripper before you even joined The Collective. You went to open houses to feed your obsession—"

"They found *me,*" the Sheriff shouted, sending spit flying across the asphalt. "Because I am *special!* Because I understand how power works, and where to grab onto it—"

"They found you because you are violent, deviant, and merciless!" Annie answered, barely noticing the tears streaking down her cheeks as she thought about Joshua and how much more he deserved. "And they helped you get elected as Sheriff because they knew you'd do whatever they wanted so long as they let you kill."

The Sheriff threw his cigarette to the ground, stomping it under his boot. He put one hand on Annie's shoulder, then leaned in, whispering in her ear: "We all have our vices, don't we, Annie?"

The movement was fast— faster than a man in his late fifties should have been able to move, the speed of someone whose fitness had been maintained not for health but for violence. He wrapped his hands around Annie's head, preparing to snap her neck, and the crowd gasped— the midwestern gasp they'd been too reserved for at the debate finally arriving now, when the thing happening in front of them was not political theater but physical threat, a man in a uniform lunging at a woman in a parking lot.

The Sheriff was fast. But Ethan was faster. His hand closed on the Sheriff's arm with the force of a man who had been waiting for this— not minutes, not hours, but years. He pulled, and the Sheriff's momentum carried him off-balance, and Ethan's other hand found his face, and suddenly he was punching with no idea how many times he'd hit. But he kept hitting, and hitting, and the sound of a radio crackled in the background. Ethan looked up. The Sheriff was on the ground, and so was Ethan— dark, red blood, spotting them both— and Megan was looming over them, the radio in her hand. She held it up to her mouth and said, simply: "We're a go."

They came from everywhere. From unmarked sedans parked on side streets. From the alley behind the community center. From positions Annie hadn't known about and Ethan had arranged with a phone call at two in the morning, the federal machinery he'd spent his career serving finally deployed in service of something that mattered to him personally. It was the kind of response the two of them could have only dreamed of when they were fifteen and scared, grieving siblings they were sure they'd never see again. FBI agents in plainclothes and tactical vests flooded the parking lot, and the crowd parted for them.

They took the Sheriff in handcuffs. He went without struggling— the violence spent, the performance over, the mask removed and lying on the pavement where it could never be picked up again. Blood covered his nose, and his cheekbone was swelling purple. As they led him past Annie, he stopped. An agent's hand pressed his shoulder, urging him forward, and he resisted for exactly long enough to look at her and say, with the quiet certainty of a man who believed what he was saying: "The Collective is bigger than this town. Bigger than you. I'll be out. And when I'm out, I'll find you."

Annie met his gaze. She held it the way she held every-thing— in a mind that was cursed with the inability to erase a single thing it had seen, including this. She said nothing, but reached into her jacket pocket. She had known this moment would come, and in typical Annie fashion, she had wanted to be prepared. She removed a folded piece of paper— a note. Then, she held it in the air and opened it slowly for the Sher-iff, seeing as his hands were cuffed behind his back and he was unable to do so himself. In handwritten text, the note was just three words long, and said:

"Enjoy prison, asshole."

The Sheriff read the words, then wrestled in his handcuffs, trying to escape the agents' grasp as he yelled at Annie. She let the paper fly into the wind, and with it, she let go of some-thing else as well. Something she couldn't see, but could feel. She thought about the three-word note that had started every-thing — sent by Russel, copying the Real Estate Ripper: Try Aspen Lane. In a long-term sense, that had been a good note. But Annie liked this one much better.

She glanced at the Mayor: only one more dragon left to slay.

The Mayor was already backing away from his table. His hands were up— not the crossing-guard gesture, not the debate gesture. "I had no idea— an unfortunate revelation!— I kept this town alive," he said, and his voice cracked.

"You can prove that to a jury," Annie said. "But first—" She turned toward the polling station doors, which had opened, and through which her father was now emerging. "Let's see if the voting machines are really rigged." Bill Hudson stepped into the parking lot sunlight holding an "I voted sticker."

"Dad," Annie smiled at him as best she could. "I know this is a rude question—"

"There's no rude questions among family, Annie," Bill played along.

"— but could you please tell us all who you voted for?"

"I voted for Prim," Bill answered.

An FBI agent appeared beside Annie with a laptop open to a screen that showed, in the clean columns of a digital voting system, the record of every ballot cast that morning. The agent turned the screen toward the crowd. Bill Hudson's vote— timestamped, verified, cast for Prim Rosington— had been recorded in the system as a vote for Mayor Bellows. In fact, *all* the votes appeared as being for Mayor Bellows.

The crowd saw it. The crowd understood it. And the sound the crowd made was not a gasp or a murmur but something deeper. It was the sound of an angry mob craving their revenge.

The agents took the Mayor, and Annie thought he was lucky they didn't turn him over to the town. People spat on him as he moved, shouting obscenities in his wake. He went with less composure than the Sheriff— his baseball cap falling from his head as the agents guided him toward the waiting vehicle, his white button-down coming untucked.

FBI agents roped off the voting area with yellow tape. Others moved through the crowd taking statements, their presence both reassuring and surreal— the federal government, here, in Cedarsburg. An agent shook Ethan's hand. Another nodded at Megan with the specific, knowing respect of a professional acknowledging an informant whose cover had been deeper and longer than most people survived.

Megan was shaking. Annie saw it— the tremor in her hands, the slight vibration in her jaw, the body's delayed response to the knowledge that the man who had taken her from a house. That man had been drinking coffee in the same town where she'd been stolen. The tremor was not a weakness. It was the aftershock of a revelation that rearranged everything, every memory, every nightmare, every mint-scented ghost that had followed her through fifteen years of running.

Prim reached her first. Then Tim. Then Zara— thin, bird-like Zara. They surrounded Megan in a fragile circle, like they were children on the playground once again, and Megan had scraped her knee.

"We should have done more," Prim said. Her voice was thick. "We should have looked for you. We should have never stopped looking."

"Megan, we're sorry," Tim said. "He's gone, Megan. And you have my word— we'll make sure he stays gone."

Behind them, the sheriff's cigarette still smoldered on the pavement.

Annie looked at Ethan. Ethan looked at Megan. Megan looked at Annie. The three of them stood in the wreckage of the morning— the yellow tape, the empty podium, the abandoned water bottles, the banner that said GET OUT THE VOTE flapping in a breeze. This was what was left of their hometown. The place had been sold, and bought, and destroyed, and now— it would be rebuilt.

Bill Hudson put his arm around his daughter. "What now?" he asked.

Nobody answered, because nobody really knew. Then, Annie broke the silence in her quirky, unbreakable way:

"I guess we get some cheeseburgers." Her voice was flat as she said it, tired, and exhausted. But then, a smile played on the corner of her lips, and Ethan started laughing, and the whole group broke down in tears and chuckles, and they knew— for the first time in a long time— that one day, they would truly feel whole again.

CHAPTER TWENTY-NINE

THREE MONTHS LATER

THE DINER on Third Street had a counter window that faced the sidewalk, which bordered one of the most beautiful streets in all of Cedarsburg. In the three months since the Sheriff's arrest, Annie had come to love that window. She'd made it a habit to pick the perfect seat, from which she could watch the town rebuilding itself. The hardware store on the corner had a new awning. The bakery two doors down, which had been closed since March, had a COMING SOON sign in its window. Across the street, a woman Annie didn't recognize was sweeping the sidewalk in front of a storefront that had been vacant for years, and the broom made a sound on the concrete that reminded Annie of a heartbeat. The town was coming alive.

She sat on one of the metal stools bolted to the concrete outside the diner's pickup window, her elbows on the narrow shelf that served as a counter, her chin resting in her hand in the posture of a woman who was, for possibly the first time in her adult life, not working. Not investigating. Not filing observations in the mental catalogue she maintained of every sensory detail in every room she entered. She was just— sitting. Watching Cedarsburg on a Tuesday afternoon. Letting the sun hit her face. Feeling the particular warmth of an Indiana autumn that hadn't yet conceded to winter, the air carrying the smell of fryer oil from the diner's kitchen and the dry-leaf sweetness of trees preparing to let go of things, which was, Annie thought, a skill that trees were better at than people, though people were learning.

Ethan sat beside her. His injured shoulder, which had graduated from the protective angle to something approaching normal over the course of ten weeks of physical therapy and Annie's persistent refusal to let him skip appointments, rested against the back of the stool with the ease of a joint that had been put back together and was testing its new configuration. He wore a flannel shirt— not the suits, not the FBI-issue composure, but a flannel shirt that Bill Hudson had given him. He was also looking at the street. He was drinking a lemonade from a paper cup that the diner served in the summer and hadn't taken off the menu yet because the weather hadn't told them to.

"Number forty-seven," the woman at the window called. It wasn't their number. Annie checked the ticket in her hand— fifty-one, the ink slightly smudged because the thermal printer was old and the paper was cheap and the diner operated on the principle that food quality and receipt quality were separate budgets. She set the ticket on the counter.

"I fixed the faucet," Ethan said.

Annie looked at him.

"You fixed it," Annie repeated.

"The leaky one in your Dad's kitchen. The washer was corroded. Took eight minutes."

"Eight minutes."

"Eight minutes."

Annie considered this. The faucet in Bill Hudson's kitchen had been dripping for as long as she could remember. It had dripped through her childhood and through Joshua's death. And now it was fixed. Eight minutes. A corroded washer.

"Thank you," she said. She meant it in a way that was larger than plumbing.

Ethan smiled.

Annie looked at her left hand. The ring caught the light— a modest stone in a simple setting. Ethan knew her too well to choose anything else. Ethan had proposed three weeks ago, in the living room, at nine in the morning, without ceremony, without kneeling— he'd been standing in the kitchen doorway holding two mugs of coffee and had said, *I want to do this forever, if you'll let me.* Annie had expected the proposal, but it had still felt like a surprise. She'd said yes without hesitation. For the first time she was certain about something that couldn't be documented or proven in court but that was, she knew, the most reliable thing she'd ever held.

"Does that thing still fit?" Ethan asked, nodding at the ring.

Annie rotated the ring on her finger. It fit perfectly. It had fit perfectly since the morning he'd slid it on, standing in the kitchen doorway with coffee cooling in both hands. "It fits," she said. "Stop asking."

"I'll ask tomorrow too."

"I know you will."

They sat in a comfortable silence, letting the sounds of the town fill the empty space. A child on a bicycle shouted, and a dog barked in someone's yard, and the woman with the broom was still sweeping. Dishes and plates clanked in the diner's kitchen.

"She texted again," Ethan said. His voice shifted— not dramatically, but into the particular key that his voice found when the subject was Megan. The key of a brother.

"What did she say?" Annie asked.

"'Still here. Still working. Don't worry.'" He recited the words with the measured delivery of someone who had read them many times. "We haven't heard from her for three months and that's all I get."

"That's two words per month. She's being generous."

Ethan almost laughed. The sound came out as an exhalation through the nose, and was quickly aborted. "We both know what she's doing, Annie. The Collective is still out there. Whatever we did here— what we took down— that was one node. One town. Megan will never let it go. She knows the network is global. She has Russel's hard drive. She feels a responsibility to do something about it." He stopped. He looked at his lemonade, as if the paper cup might contain the end of the sentence he'd decided not to finish.

Annie waited. She gave him the silence knew he needed. Then:

"Are you happy?" she asked.

The question was simple. But it sat between them on the counter with the weight of everything it contained.

Ethan was quiet. He turned the lemonade cup in his hands — a rotation, slow, the paper making a soft sound against his palms. Annie watched the thought arrive in his face the way weather arrived on a plain— visible from a long way off, moving toward her.

"This is what I said I wanted," Ethan said. His voice was careful. Deliberate. "A simple life. In a town. With you. And it's—" He paused. The cup rotated again. "I've been trying to figure out how to say this for a minute—"

"Say it," Annie said.

He looked at her. The look was the one she knew— *I'm with you* and *I'm worried about you* and *what are we about to do* — except today the proportions were different.

"I don't think we can stay here and do nothing," he said. "I want to be with you," he added hurriedly. "That part is permanent, that part is the most permanent thing I've ever felt, and I will follow you anywhere and I will live anywhere and I will fix faucets in any house on any street in any town you choose. But Annie—" He set down the cup. "You showed me something. During all of this. You showed me that when ordinary people decide to sit back and do nothing— when they accept the way things are because fighting seems too hard or too dangerous or too unlikely to succeed— that's when the evil gets in."

"Go on," Annie nodded, trying very hard not to smile as the loveable idiot in front of her repeated everything she'd ever told him. God, he was stupid. And God, she loved him.

"That's when The Collective wins," Ethan said. "I thought I could just look the other way and all I wanted was a live away from the trouble and now I have it but—" He ran a hand through his hair. "I've been thinking about Megan. Out there. Alone. Chasing something that's bigger than any one person. And what about all the other people like her, who The Collective might take? And I keep thinking— what kind of man sits on a stool eating cheeseburgers while his sister fights a war?"

Annie looked at him. She looked at the ring on her finger, and the street, and the woman sweeping, and the child on the bicycle, and all the small, stubborn acts of living that Cedarsburg was performing on this Tuesday afternoon.

"I'm glad you reached that conclusion," Annie said.

Ethan blinked.

"Number fifty-one," the woman at the window called.

Annie stood. She crossed the three feet to the pickup window and collected the order— and what she collected was more than Ethan was expecting. Three paper bags, each containing a cheeseburger. Three drinks— two lemonades and a black coffee. She carried them back to the counter, balancing the items carefully.

Ethan looked at the bags. He looked at the drinks. He counted.

"Annie," he said. "Why did you get three—"

A honk from across the street. It was short and sharp— meant to get their attention. Ethan startled.

Annie looked across the street. A black SUV— tinted

windows, discreet— sat at the curb with its engine idling. The passenger window rolled down.

Megan's face appeared in the window. Her hair was different— shorter, pulled back. But her eyes were Ethan's eyes— the same steady, watching quality. And she was smiling. Because she knew her brother and she knew Annie, and she *knew* that they would come around eventually. She'd just been waiting until the reinforcements were ready.

She waved. A small wave. Hopeful.

Ethan stared. His mouth opened. His mouth closed. His eyes went from the SUV to the three bags in Annie's hands to Annie's face, and on Annie's face he found the expression she'd been holding for— if she was being honest— since she could sense that Ethan was changing his mind about the quiet life.

"You knew," Ethan said.

"I knew."

"How long have you known?"

"Megan called me a week ago. She said she had a lead on a Collective cell operating out of—" Annie paused, selecting the level of detail appropriate for a sidewalk in Cedarsburg on a Tuesday afternoon. "Somewhere overseas. She said she could use help. She said it was the last time she'd ask." Annie picked up one of the cheeseburger bags and held it out to him. "I told her I'd talk to you. But I wanted you to get there on your own. Because you needed to want this, Ethan. Not because I wanted it, or Megan wanted it, but because you knew why it mattered."

Ethan took the bag. He accepted it as if he were making a decision. He looked at the SUV. He looked at Annie. He looked at the ring on her finger, which caught the sun and threw a small point of light onto the counter.

"How did you know I'd change my mind?" he asked.

He stopped himself before she could answer. His hand came up— he was exasperated with himself for being predictable. "Of *course* you knew," he said. "This is what I get. This is my fault for falling in love with a genius detective."

Annie smiled. It was a particular smile— warm, precise. "It's true," she said. "I am a genius. I can read people like a book. Practically psychic." She picked up her own cheese-burger, unwrapped the paper, and took a bite. The cheese was melted. The bun was warm. The burger tasted like the diner on Third Street in a town that was learning to be alive again. She chewed, swallowed, and added: "But I also know because you talk in your sleep."

She winked at him. It was not a gesture she deployed often— Annie Hudson was not, by nature, a winking person — but the moment called for it.

Ethan's expression moved through several phases in rapid succession. "What do I say in my sleep?"

"You say a lot of things, Ethan. We'll discuss it in the car."

They gathered the bags and the drinks. They stood from the metal stools. Annie took one last look at Third Street— the new awning, the COMING SOON sign, the swept sidewalk, the child on the bicycle now two blocks further away. She looked at Cedarsburg and felt the thing she'd felt the morning she'd stood in the village square and decided to begin, except the feeling was different now— not the sharp, determined feeling of a woman starting an investigation, but the settled, warm feeling of a woman finishing one and beginning some-thing else. The town would be okay.

It had Prim, who had traded her congressional run for a job in social services, helping people with her own two hands everyday. It had Zara, who had turned state's witness and was now using her knowledge of every shell company and shadow buyer to help the new administration untangle the property records, parcel by parcel— one transaction at a time. It had Pastor Tim, who had torn down the scaffolding on the amphitheatre's unfinished wing and replaced it with a community garden that grew tomatoes and green beans and the particular species of stubborn, impractical hope that Cedarsburg had been starving for. And it had Bill Hudson, who was standing in his kitchen this very afternoon with a faucet that no longer dripped, who now believed that ordinary people mattered.

Annie turned away from Third Street. She picked up the third lemonade and the bag with Megan's cheeseburger and nodded at Ethan, who was already moving. They crossed the street together, the bags rustling between them, the drinks sweating in the autumn warmth.

Annie opened the rear passenger door of the SUV— the seats were clean, the dashboard bare, and a single duffel bag sat on the floor behind the driver's seat containing, Annie assumed, everything Megan Beckett currently owned, which was very little. Megan turned from the driver's seat as they climbed in, and up close Annie could see what the distance had smoothed over— the tiredness around her eyes, the new sharpness in her cheekbones, the evidence of weeks spent running toward something that kept running from her. But the smile was real. The smile was the truest thing on her face, and it was directed at Ethan, who had stopped in the open door with a cheeseburger bag in one hand and a lemonade in the other. He looked at his sister and his face showed the specific ache of a familial love that had been tested by fifteen years of absence and had held firm through everything.

"Hey," Megan said.

"Hey," Ethan said.

It was not an eloquent reunion. Annie hadn't expected one.

Ethan climbed in. He handed Megan the coffee through the gap between the front seats. Annie settled into the back seat beside Ethan. She pulled the door closed. Megan put the SUV in drive. Then she glanced at them in the rearview mirror, and her eyes were hopeful, but afraid.

"I already booked our flights," she said.

Ethan paused with his cheeseburger halfway unwrapped. The pause lasted exactly long enough for the sentence to register, for the implications to settle, for the reality of what they were doing to transition from concept to itinerary. Then his eyes narrowed— not with suspicion but with brotherly wariness.

"Tell me you didn't put me in coach," he said.

Megan didn't answer. She smiled, and took his answer as a *yes*. He was in. She pulled the SUV away from the curb.

Annie took a bite of her cheeseburger. The cheese had cooled. The bun had softened in the bag. It tasted like Cedarsburg— simple, honest, imperfect, good. She would miss these cheeseburgers, but thankfully, every town they visited had its own version. She chewed and watched through the rear window as Third Street receded behind them. She now thought of her hometown not as the place that had taken her brother, not as the place where The Collective had fed on silence and fear, but as the place where she had learned that the distance between a broken town and a mended one was nothing more than a group of people who remembered what they owed each other.

The SUV turned onto the road that led out of Cedarsburg. The same road that led in. One road, two directions.

Ethan reached across the seat and took Annie's hand. His grip was warm and certain and carried no questions. She squeezed back. Megan adjusted the rearview mirror, and for a moment all three of their faces were visible in the glass— framed together, reflected together, moving in the same direction at the same speed toward a justice none of them could see yet, but all of them believed was there.

The road stretched ahead. Indiana flattened around them into its generous, open expanse— the fields and the sky and the distance that was not emptiness but possibility. Cedarsburg disappeared behind them. The world opened in front of them.

Annie turned and focused on the road ahead. There was no reason to look over her shoulder anymore. There was nothing behind her she hadn't saved, and only a promise ahead.

Annie smiled to herself. A new case. A flight abroad. A crime ring to destroy. *International* Detective Annie Hudson. She liked the sound of that.

And just like that— her investigation began.

AUTHOR'S LETTER

Dear readers,

You've reached **the end** of the Annie Hudson Mystery series, and I want to thank you for sticking with the adventure and seeing Annie to her happy ending! As a writer, there's no better feeling than completing an entire series and sharing it with readers.

Even though Annie's adventure is over (for now!) I hope you'll stick with me by checking out some of my other mystery novels and subscribing to my mailing list. You'll find a full list of my current titles on the next page. I'd recommend starting with "Mystery at Monrovia Castle." It's a lighter adventure than our escapades with Annie, but so many of my readers hop between both and enjoy another quirky female detective.

You can always reach out to me on social media or via email at:

info@emeraldlionpressbooks.com

I love hearing from readers, and you make my day when you contact me.

I'm emotional over the end of this series, but excited to

share upcoming adventures with you in the form of new books. Let's have some cheeseburgers in honor of Annie?

Warmly, and with more ahead,

— *Valerie Brandy*

Scan the QR code below or click here to be added to the author's mailing list.

MORE FROM VALERIE BRANDY

THE REBECCA ORANGE COZY CASTLE MYSTERY SERIES

1. Mystery at Monrovia Castle
2. A Victim in the Village
3. A Royal Ruse
4. A Kidnapped Collie
5. A Perilous Proposal
6. Murder at the Masquerade
7. A Poisonous Play
8. A Christmas Crime
9. A Treacherous Train

THE PREDATOR / PREY THRILLER SERIES:

1. Trail of Obsession
2. Lies Run Deep
3. The Trap is Set
4. The Woman in the Wind

THE ANNIE HUDSON REAL ESTATE MYSTERY SERIES:

1. Murder Behind the Gates
2. Murder in the Penthouse
3. Murder on the Farm
4. Murder on the Commune
5. Murder in the Desert
6. Murder in the Hometown

Most books available in large print!